VICTORIA'S
Promise

OTHER BOOKS AND AUDIO BOOKS
BY JULIE WRIGHT

Eyes Like Mine

Cross My Heart

Hazzardous Universe

Olivia

JULIE WRIGHT
A NEWPORT LADIES BOOK CLUB NOVEL

VICTORIA'S
Promise

Covenant Communications, Inc.

Cover image *Bike at Beach* © fotofrog, iStockphotography.com.

Cover design copyright © 2014 by Covenant Communications, Inc.

Published by Covenant Communications, Inc.
American Fork, Utah

Printed in the United States of America
First Printing: January 2014

20 19 18 17 16 15 14   10 9 8 7 6 5 4 3 2 1

ISBN 978-1-62108-482-2

To Kirk Shaw
Your presence in the publishing world is missed every day.
Thank you so much for everything.

Acknowledgments

THANK YOU, JOSI, HEATHER, AND Annette, for writing a wonderful series with me. I've loved working with the three of you and cherish the memories we made and the influence these books have had for good in so many lives. Thank you for your unending friendship. To Janette Rallison, Monica Niles, Jennifer Mattson, and many, *many* other friends, thank you for letting me use your names in vain in the making of this book. Also, thank you to McKenna, Merrik, and Chandler, and my mom and dad for being champions of my writing career. And thank you to my husband, the ultimate Mr. Wright, for being the only shoulder I ever want to cry on and for supporting me in everything. I love you and those three kids we made more than anything. Finally, thank you to the readers who have supported the Newport Ladies. Victoria wouldn't exist without you.

BOOKS IN THE NEWPORT LADIES BOOK CLUB SERIES

Set #1
Olivia—Julie Wright
Daisy—Josi S. Kilpack
Paige—Annette Lyon
Athena—Heather B. Moore

Set #2
Shannon's Hope—Josi S. Kilpack
Ruby's Secret—Heather B. Moore
Victoria's Promise—Julie Wright
Ilana's Wish—Annette Lyon

For ideas on hosting your own book club, suggestions for books and recipes, or information on how you can guest-write about your book club on our blog, please visit us at http://thenewportladiesbookclub. blogspot.com.

Chapter 1

A MAN SHOULD NEVER PROPOSE to a woman in a public place. Not unless he's already talked to her about marriage and he's caught her flipping through bridal magazines while doodling hearts around his name.

And even then . . . there are no guarantees.

✂   ✂   ✂

I worked on a reality TV show called *Vows*, where a marriage proposal was a matter of contract, something the bachelor had to do whether he wanted to or not, and even *then*—with a few million dollars on the line and several nations watching—there were *still* no guarantees. Relationships were unpredictable, wretched things.

I opened my mailbox, ignoring the worn-out box tag where my name, Victoria Winters, now looked like Virta Wites. My eyes burned from staying up late the night before, *then* getting up early and spending nearly the whole day studying flash mob marriage proposals. I wanted a few new ideas that might be useful and fresh for the next season of *Vows*. It was good to be well informed on the job—especially since I was now the second assistant director.

What I'd learned from watching guy after guy get down on one knee in front of basketball fans, circus patrons, and live studio audiences was that you'd better hope your mom wasn't watching as the would-be girl of your dreams widened her eyes in horror, shook her head no, and ran like someone had called in a bomb threat.

I rubbed my eyes again, wished I'd been smart enough to have caught a small nap during the afternoon, and tugged the envelope out of my mailbox.

My heart went into some strange sort of arrhythmia after I caught sight of the return address on the envelope. Ballad Studios. News about my screenplay.

Ballad was one of the few studios that still wanted screenplay submissions in paper. Most were happy to work via e-mail, but not Ballad.

And I now held an envelope from them in my hands with a decision waiting for me on the inside.

I almost threw up on my own feet.

The sound of a car horn blaring behind me startled me enough that I almost dropped the envelope.

I tossed a quick smile at Lawrence, hoping it would keep him from laying on the horn again. I had neighbors, and some of them worked graveyards. Some had children. None of them would approve of Lawrence and his car horn.

I wanted to turn around and go back into my house to read my letter in private, but Lawrence was taking me to the Walt Disney Concert Hall to hear Holst's *The Planets*. Hiding out in my apartment and reading this letter by myself wouldn't exactly be the show of support my best friend from since forever ago had wanted when she asked me to the event. Janette had organized the concert and really wanted me there for opening night. Lawrence wasn't all that impressed with me wanting to go see the Los Angeles Philharmonic do a musical rendition of our solar system, but I hadn't really cared and told him I didn't want to do anything else for our four-month anniversary.

I had to go.

Besides, Lawrence would be insanely ticked if I missed our anniversary, which totally baffled me. Four months of casual dating was not a milestone to be celebrated. It was something to be commented on, shrugged over, not thought of again until you hit five months—*if* you hit five months.

Lawrence's hand went to the horn again, but I waved, smiled, and headed his direction before he actually made contact with it. We probably wouldn't hit five months. My dad wasn't all that fond of Lawrence. When I asked Dad why, he said something about Lawrence being the poster child for an entitled white guy and left it at that.

Dad never made racial slurs, for obvious reasons. He was also a white guy, and he was married to my Barbadian black mom. Between the two of them, one of my brothers looked like a pasty European, and one looked like a dark-chocolate candy bar. I was caught between the two, which was nice because my naturally darker skin and black eyelashes and brows meant my monthly make-up expense consisted of a tube of dollar-store lip gloss—any flavor but cherry.

Thank you, Mom and Dad, for good genetics.

I stuffed the letter in my purse and sent up a prayer that whatever the envelope contained wouldn't make me cry anything but happy tears. Sad tears were simply not allowed.

Lawrence was out of the car and opening my door before I had time to properly paste on a smile. "What's wrong, babe?" He brushed a quick kiss over my lips and motioned for me to get in so we wouldn't be late.

"Nothing."

Nothing. Nothing. Nothing. Please don't let me be a liar.

He reached over and took my hand as soon as he was back in the car and turning off my road. Our hands were a contrast and not just in color. He had baby soft hands because he had a manicure-and-pedicure habit he couldn't seem to kick. It was almost embarrassing that his hands were soft, pink things—something you'd see on a newborn—while my hands were calloused, one sporting a bandage from moving camera and light equipment on my job.

"You look amazing, you know," he said, which was *always* nice to hear.

I smiled and thanked him for the compliment. My mother taught me that pretty girls who never said thank you when they were complimented were ugly inside. She said she didn't care how pretty I was outside if my insides hid a repulsive monster. She never let my looks go to my head, but sometimes it was nice to be told I looked amazing.

"How was your day?" Lawrence asked.

"Great. Max said they were down to the final bachelor pick, so we'll start filming in the next month."

His smile turned down for a moment. "Oh. That's too bad. That means we'll never see each other."

We'd had this argument before. He'd been complaining about my job more and more as time ticked down to when I'd have to start keeping erratic working hours.

His hand hit the horn as someone cut him off.

I imagined my father raising an eyebrow at Lawrence's behavior and winced inwardly. *I know, Dad. Not what you want for me.*

I met Lawrence at a bookstore. It was part of my attraction to him. I did a lot of reading on set because no one was allowed to make any noise during a take except the talent, yet I was required to be present for every one of them. A handsome guy in a bookstore, holding a copy of *To Kill a Mockingbird* in his hands, seemed like a miraculous discovery. When he asked for my number, I nearly girl-screamed. And I *never* girl-scream. I leave that silliness to the bachelorettes mugging for reality TV.

It turned out the book had been a gift for his sister. But I hadn't known that when we'd gone on our first date, though I'd suspected by the end of the second date. By then we'd already become semicomfortable with each other. He was easy enough to talk to—which was weird, considering how little we'd known of each other. But he was safe and polite, to me anyway. He wasn't always nice to everyone else. But to me . . . he really tried hard to be a gentleman.

And I wanted a gentleman for myself. I wanted a man like my father.

Lawrence *was* a gentleman, but he *wasn't* anything like my father. He had a way of making other people feel uncomfortable. He snapped at waitresses, belittled cashiers, and treated the world with disdain in general.

And he didn't read books.

He actually laughed at me when I told him about my book club in Newport with a bunch of other women. At least, he laughed until he realized I wasn't laughing. Then he was *all* kinds of supportive. But I'd seen the scorn, and I couldn't unsee what had already been seen.

The time apart would likely be good for us. Lawrence might decide to move on to someone who didn't work sixteen-hour days for three straight months. I shot him a sideways glance as he continued to whine about my going back to work. He talked pretty much nonstop the rest of the way to the concert hall. I let him. He liked talking more than I did.

"Told you we needed to hurry," Lawrence said as he finally found parking and opened my door for me.

I laughed. "We're fine. Don't panic. Janette wants me to support her, but she didn't say we needed to be an hour early. Relax."

"I'm relaxed." He smiled and rolled his shoulders, but he didn't fool me. He was as relaxed as a hurricane hitting land.

We entered the concert hall and found our seats right up front.

Janette looked beautiful with her brown hair twisted up in an elegant knot at the side of her head. Her form-fitting black gown accentuated her vampire-pale skin. I caught her eye and waved. She waved back but returned to talking quietly with someone in a tuxedo. Knowing she was busy, I went back to chat with Lawrence.

At least, I *tried* to chat. His right leg jiggled in an almost spastic rhythm as he scanned the concert hall. I put my hand on his leg to calm him down. "Are you okay?"

But he ignored the question. He rose to his feet and mumbled, "I'll be right back."

He speed-walked toward the aisle, where he passed Janette with barely a glance. She raised an eyebrow at his lack of cordiality but shook it off and moved in my direction.

"You guys having issues?" she asked.

"Maybe he has to use the restroom. He's been kind of weird all night." I stood and hugged her. "Soooo, are you nervous?"

She laughed and kissed my cheek before she let me release her. "I thought I would be, but I'm really not. Super weird, but I'm just excited to be here. We've received permission to use dozens of NASA pictures for the visual display."

"It's great you get to do what you love for a living."

I apparently didn't hide the envy in my tone because she gave me a half smile. "You'll be there. Just give it some time."

"Time . . . right." I leaned over and pulled the envelope out of my purse. "I got a letter today from Ballad Studios."

She ripped the envelope from my hands. "No way! What does it say?" I snatched it back, and she frowned. "You haven't even opened it yet."

"I'm waiting for the right moment. I want to have a nice evening, you know, enjoying your music and science. If I open it and it's bad news . . ."

"Why are you putting that kind of talk out into the universe? Why can't you assume this letter holds your every dream come true?"

I leaned back a little on the armrest and sighed. "Because I've received so many letters like this before—well, e-mails anyway. Just because it's on paper doesn't mean it's different."

She gave me a humph and swatted my shoulder. "There you go again, putting out all that negativity. Have some hope."

"Janette . . ." The whine overtook my voice, but she was too good a friend to swat me for that too. "I'm just so tired of failing."

"You aren't failing. You're working your way through the sludge. Everybody has to pay their dues, love. You aren't the exception. But paying dues doesn't give you the right to give up. Every day you're closer to being a full-fledged screenwriter. Soon, people will be buying tickets and eating too much popcorn at a blockbuster movie Victoria Winters wrote."

"I hope so."

She hugged me again. "I know so." She looked around when she released me. "Is that boyfriend of yours lost or something?"

I glanced around as well, picking through the dresses and suits to try to find a clue as to where he might have gone. "No idea. Like I said, he's been acting weird all night."

Her hazel eyes fixed on me. "And things are going . . . okay for you two?"

I gave a wimped-out, one-armed shrug rather than an answer.

"Hmm."

"What are you hmm-ing about?"

She gave me *the look*—the one she'd been giving me since we were kids with crooked pigtails and badly painted fingernails. "You just don't seem like yourself with him. You guys don't do things *you* like to do when you're together."

I let that statement settle before pointing out the obvious. "We're here tonight. That's something I want to be doing."

"Well, sure, but was this his first choice, or did he try to talk you out of it?"

I didn't confirm her suspicions. It was bad enough that she was right, but I didn't need her to give me *the other look*—the one that gloated while remaining compassionate.

"We're fine," I assured her. "But don't worry about me losing myself to the ego of some guy. We're down to the final bachelor pick on *Vows*. We're a little behind on the production schedule, but I have to go in for the final auditions. It's back to work for me, which means no dating life."

Janette scowled. "That's not any better. You lose yourself to a guy, or you lose yourself to work. Either way *you* lose. You should open that letter. It might have a million-dollar contract in it."

"I'm okay! I'll open it when I get home. Stop worrying, *Mom*." I smiled wide for her, and then I frowned. "Wait a minute. Did my mother put you up to this conversation?"

Janette at least had the good sense to blush over getting caught. It was hard to be mad at her when her cheeks pinked up like that. Some people passed us to get to their seats, which distracted me just long enough that Janette was able to slip away with a wave and a, "I gotta get back to check on the orchestra. We'll talk later."

"Yes, we will." I shot her a look of my own—the one that said I meant business—but she just smiled and waved as though we had nothing left to discuss.

I hated that my mom and my best friend were such good friends. It was tough keeping secrets when the two women I was closest to compared notes.

Lawrence returned, looking flushed and winded.

"You okay?" I asked again as we took our seats. Was he sick? I edged a little farther from him, just in case. With the new season of filming about to start, getting sick was not an option for me.

"Fine, why?" He took my hand in his, which I reluctantly let him do, figuring I would wash my hands later if he really did have the flu or something.

Would he notice if I dug out the bottle of Purell from my purse?

As that thought crossed my mind, the lights went down and the bows fluttered over the stringed instruments. I loved the warm-up noises of an orchestra, so I pushed aside my misgivings about possibly ill boyfriends and studio contracts and settled into my seat to watch the performance.

Janette had chosen well. I loved Holst's work, and *The Planets* was my favorite. When the lights for intermission came up, I sighed deeply. *This* was what I needed, something relaxing. It was putting me in the frame of mind I needed to go home and have the courage to open my letter from Ballad Studios.

The conductor called our attention to the front before patrons could make a dash to the restrooms. He made a point of giving a special thanks to Janette Rallison for coordinating the event and to the patrons who supported the arts—naming several large benefactors—and then he said something *odd*.

He called up Lawrence Reynolds to make a special announcement.

Lawrence let go of my hand after flashing me a brief smile. He made his way to the front as my heart rate stopped altogether before skyrocketing into something that had to have resembled a heart attack. *No. Please, no.* He couldn't be doing what I thought he was doing. My mind flashed back to all of the marriage proposals gone wrong that I'd watched on YouTube the night before and all morning and afternoon. I sank lower into my seat. My face heated up; my hands gripped the armrests of my chair. My head shook *no* while my mind raced for an exit strategy.

Lawrence stood too close to the microphone, so his voice boomed out.

And then he said the words I *didn't* want to hear.

"Victoria Winters, will you marry me?"

The word *no* stuck in my throat until it felt like I'd choke on it. I didn't think my eyes could open any wider.

There was only one thing to do.

I ran like someone had called in a bomb threat. And hoped his mother wasn't watching.

Chapter 2

I WAS ON MY PHONE to the cab company before I even made it to the front entrance of the concert hall. I had the cab number on speed dial for my job and was suddenly grateful that I spent so much time playing errand girl at work for things as trivial as cab rides. I didn't cry. I was too horrified to cry. *Lawrence proposed to me.*

After four months?

Who did that after only four months?

No one fell in love and made lifetime commitments in only four months. Most people couldn't even pick a favorite ice-cream flavor in that amount of time.

The cab picked me up down the street from the concert hall. I didn't want to be caught waiting around in front in case Lawrence came looking for me. What could be said after what I had just done to him?

I had left him standing *alone* in front of a huge audience.

Guilt slapped me from all sides. I wasn't a mean person but had acted with a cruelty I hadn't ever imagined. While watching all of those YouTube videos, I had felt so horrible for the guys standing alone, left with a ring box and no bride. I thought the girls could have just said yes so they didn't publicly humiliate the guys. They could always tell them no later, in private.

But I hadn't known.

I hadn't known how awful it was to be the girl. To sit in your seat squirming and dying and wishing for the superpower of invisibility.

It had been awful.

I didn't have a choice. Staying hadn't been an option. Facing the crowd, the hundreds of nameless entities, at a time when my whole body shook with something that couldn't even be explained had been more than I could bear. If it could have been done all over again, I would have spared him the humiliation, would have shown him that kindness because now I had to face him after doing *that* to him.

I sat in the back of the cab with my head in my hands and my eyes shut. I wanted to go to my parents' home but didn't know how to tell them about something I didn't understand myself.

I went to my own home.

The phone was already ringing when my door swung open.

I yanked the key out of the lock and ignored the phone. It didn't matter who was on the other end; talking to anyone would be horrifying.

I hid under the covers of my bed instead.

The phone rang. And rang. And rang. I didn't even check caller ID but instead stayed under my blankets with my eyes closed. I had humiliated a man who I cared about but couldn't marry. He wasn't what I wanted in a husband. Or needed.

How could I assume he would always be patient and gentle with me when he treated the rest of the world with such scorn? How could I assume he would be patient and gentle with children?

But it killed me to have hurt him.

I had no idea how much time had passed but jumped when the thumping came on my front door.

"Tori? Tori! I know you're in there!"

I peeked out from under the covers. The voice belonged to Janette. Would she have Lawrence with her, or would she be alone? I finally threw back the blankets. *Be a big girl, Tori.*

I opened the door. Janette fell against me immediately, enveloping me in a huge hug. "I swear I had no idea he was going to do that," she said in a rush. "I asked the conductor what he'd been thinking when he allowed some random idiot to have access to the mic, but apparently Lawrence told him you were my friend. The conductor saw that we were talking and figured I was in on it. But I swear it wasn't me. I had no idea and would never let him do something so stupid."

I hadn't even considered how he'd managed to get access to the microphone like that. It hadn't occurred to me to ponder the details with everything else to worry about. "Don't panic, Janette. I'm not mad at you. I'm mostly mad at myself for humiliating my boyfriend in front of hundreds of people."

"Thousands, if you want to get technical. The hall seats over two thousand people. We were nearly full."

"Not helping." I groaned into her shoulder.

She pulled away and forced me to look her in the eye. "This isn't your fault. You weren't the one proposing marriage in public. He was the one who made an entire concert hall feel uncomfortable to have to witness such a scene."

"Ugh! All those people! They likely all *do* feel uncomfortable. I ruined your event!"

"I wouldn't call it ruined. You just spiced it up a bit." She tried and failed at a comforting smile.

I gasped, thinking of something else. "How many of them recorded it on their cell phones? If this shows up on YouTube and my mother sees it, I will seriously die!"

"Your mother can't figure YouTube out. She'll never see it."

I stared at Janette for a moment before shaking my head and walking farther into the house. "She knows how to click a link. Someone will definitely send her the link—probably one of my cousins. Oh, just shoot me now!" I flopped down on my couch and pulled a pillow to my chest so I could scream into it.

She sat next to me. "So what are you going to do?"

"What do you mean?" I asked, my voice muffled through the pillow.

"Are you going to try to reconcile this? How do you want it to end? I'm asking because it feels like it's my fault you ran. I didn't influence you, did I? I mean, you know he's not my favorite person, but that wouldn't mean anything if you really liked him."

She waited while I contemplated my feelings. Finally, I lowered the pillow. "No. You didn't influence me. He's a decent enough guy. I want good things for him but don't want to be one of those good things. I would've run even if you'd told me you loved him and thought we were perfect together."

She exhaled in relief. "Okay. Good. I'd respect any decision you made. No matter how stupid it might be. You know that, right?"

"I know." I nodded and took a deep, shuddering breath.

"So what are you going to do?" she asked again.

"Tell him the truth."

Dad would celebrate the news when I finally got the guts to admit all of this to them. Mom would too, but at least she'd be discreet about it.

Janette stayed with me for a while, assuring me that I hadn't ruined her event and that it wasn't my fault. She seemed a little surprised that I hadn't shed any actual tears—like she'd expected some greater show of emotion. But even when she left, I couldn't muster one drop of saline sorrow.

I almost opened my computer to prepare for the workday but remembered I was still on the YouTube page filled with botched proposals. Had mine already joined the ranks?

My mom would *not* celebrate that.

She was a conservative sort of woman. Shame broadcasted to the world made her rant in Bajan, which was a mix of English and various African languages taken from her native Barbados. When Mom spoke Bajan, all of us kids cleared out of her way. It was a sure sign she was ticked off. And nothing seemed to tick her off more than things like YouTube and reality TV.

This meant she ranted because of my job all the time, and now she had one more thing to add to her list of what was wrong in this world.

So instead of doing more research like a good little assistant director, I took my home phone off the hook, turned off my cell, and went to bed.

* * *

The conversation with Lawrence that took place after he nearly beat my door down the next morning was pretty short. He blamed my insecurities and inability to commit on my job and my book club. He said I spent way too much time navel gazing and living in the false worlds of fiction and Hollywood and that I would be better off quitting both.

I kicked him out and stopped feeling guilty for humiliating him.

And then lamented over whether or not he was right.

The fact wasn't lost on me that I *did* live in a superficial world. I saw weddings that happened because the audience expected them.

Which was why I'd joined the book club—to see how real people lived. I regretted explaining my reasoning to Lawrence, who used it as ammunition in our big fight. He accused me of using the women in my book club for nothing but research so I could write screenplays with heart. Then he laughed bitterly and said it was ironic that a heartless person was trying to write movies with heart.

I didn't miss the irony.

The truth was I had signed up for book club for a lot of reasons, research among them. Women on set were so fake, trying to get a promotion or a better part. It was hard to believe any of them said anything they really meant or believed. I wanted to know how real women felt. I couldn't use my mom or Janette for research because I was too close to them. And they'd recognize themselves in anything written about them. Joining the book group seemed like a way to make friends outside my sphere of family and fakes and find out how regular people lived so I could write something that felt authentic. But more than that, I had found myself pleasantly surprised at actually really enjoying having an intelligent conversation about literature.

A few hours after Lawrence stormed out of my apartment on a wave of righteous indignation, a coworker who had also been researching botched proposals texted me asking if the Victoria Winters at the Walt Disney Concert Hall was me. I never responded to the text but instead viewed the video footage, feeling excessive gratitude in the ineptitude of the person behind the camera, since the images were grainy and dark. No one would know for sure that it was me running away unless they recognized the name, and *anyone* could have that name.

Those were the lies I told myself as I resumed my life.

Back to my family.

Back to my work.

Back to my writing.

I opened the letter from Ballad Studios.

It was a rejection letter.

Back to my life, indeed.

* * *

It had been over a month since that night, and I was well entrenched in my work—a nice distraction from the previous humiliation.

"Tori! Do you have any idea where Max went?"

I glanced up at Darren—one of the executive producers who was not happy that auditions were already running late because Max was MIA. Darren had his hands on the hips of his khaki pants and was tapping the toe of his expensive made-in-England shoes.

"No, sir," I said, already texting Max to determine his location.

"Find him!"

"Right away, sir." I sent the text, knowing it didn't matter. He'd show up when he showed up. With as much money as *Vows* brought in for the studio, no one was going to fire Max anytime soon. The man was brilliant.

That was how things happened in the entertainment industry.

Someone tugged at my messy bun and whispered, "I heard a rumor, Tor."

I didn't bother to turn to see who'd been tugging my hair. "What exactly did you hear, Robert?" I mimicked his singsong voice.

He came into view, hefting the camera on his shoulder. "Heard you were a runaway bride."

I smirked at him. "You heard wrong. A runaway bride would imply a wedding agreement of some sort or another. I was a runaway girlfriend who refused to be the bride."

He laughed and gave me a one-armed hug. Robert was an older guy, somewhere nearing fifty, I guessed from the gray sneaking into the dark-brown hair above his ears. He had a wife and a few kids and an honesty that some people described as abrasive. But Robert was anything but abrasive. He was the first one to remember all of the birthdays on set and the last one to remember if you owed him a few bucks for your portion of the pizza run. He had a kindness to him that was hard to describe. And out of everyone on the crew, I trusted Robert the most.

"I've missed you over hiatus, kid. Glad you didn't get yourself married and end up quitting."

"Quit?" I held out my arms. "And leave all this glamour and fame? Never. And who's been spreading rumors?"

"It's Hollywood, babe. Who isn't?"

"True enough."

He pursed his lips, then asked, "Have you told your parents yet?"

A groan escaped me. "No. It's all just so horrible. And it's on YouTube. My mom will be so disappointed that I made Lawrence do the walk of shame in front of an audience. She's such a private person that this will horrify her."

"You should tell them. They'll be glad you made the right choice."

Though I was sure my parents suspected the breakup, they hadn't been truly informed. I'd been so busy with work that it had been easy to put off. But Robert was right. I'd have to tell them. Soon. Tonight, if I could swing it. Changing the subject, I tapped his camera. "Behind-the-scenes stuff for today?"

Robert nodded. Cameron had done behind-the-scenes shots last season, but his work was less than *wow*. Most of his footage was unusable and inappropriate for the viewing public—which was saying something considering the sort of public we were trying to appeal to.

Max's return text finally came in with a snippy declaration that he was already in the building and a command that I needed to find Darren so they could get the bachelors interviewed before the day was out. I rolled my eyes and gave Robert a quick kiss on the cheek. "It's good to see you too, but I better go get everyone where they need to be."

With a wave good-bye, I hurried off to actually find Max and Darren and get them to the audition room so we didn't end up with the potential bachelors cooling their heels in the waiting area, where I'd already started seating them.

I grumbled over the rumor of my personal botched proposal. Was nothing sacred? One would have thought the news to be so old it wasn't worth mentioning.

Yet, someone *was* mentioning. I'd have to play it off as no big deal. If no one could get a rise out of me, the juiciness of the gossip would dry up.

By the time I'd arrived at the audition room, both Max and Darren were already there. Sometimes those two made me crazy. The first audition had already gone inside. I expected him to be awhile since he had a pretty intense list of hoops to jump through.

And those hoops came after the insane set of previous hoops each of the potential bachelors had already jumped through to get to this point. They'd been questioned, tested, interviewed, and questioned some more. I almost felt sorry for both them *and* the bachelorettes. Almost.

Several too-good-looking-to-be-real guys were in chairs awaiting their turns, sizing each other up while they made polite conversation. I smiled at them and hurried away before they decided they needed to schmooze me in order to get the part. The only way to schmooze me was to be where you were supposed to be when you were supposed to be there.

And then I saw him.

He had the kind of sex appeal that could turn the heads of girls with shallow expectations. From just one look, I knew he'd be a great addition for the new season of *Vows*. When he walked into the final casting auditions, it was almost as if the building itself sighed over his dark hair, sculpted cheekbones, dark, perfectly shaped brows over bright intelligent eyes, and muscled shoulders emphasized by a shirt that was tight without being obscene.

He was perfect.

I laughed as Cindy, the secretary, who was handling check-in for the auditions, dropped both her jaw and her pen when he approached to announce his arrival. She didn't even notice that the pen landed point down into her doughnut when he stepped up to the desk and said, "Hi, I'm Christopher Caine. I'm here for the *Vows* audition." In spite of his olive complexion, he didn't have the Italian or Spanish accent I'd expected. He had a bit of a Southern drawl—not so much to make him seem like a hick sucking on a piece of straw between his teeth but more like a gentleman.

His accent was unexpected.

That would be a good thing to the casting director. He liked things that were unexpected. I wondered if Mr. Southern Gentility had practiced it in the mirror before callbacks today. Most of the callbacks had monologues prepared for the audition—which was not what the casting director wanted.

It ruined the point of the reality TV show to have your actors be trained and *not* real.

Which was a joke anyway. None of them were real. They played the parts they were expected to play. The hunger for fame swallowed any sense of reality they might have had before taking the first step into cast calls. Most of them acted as if they had a camera on them at all times. The people I worked with had the depth of a baby spoon.

"Of course you're here for *Vows*," Cindy said, blinking her wide blue eyes at him, her voice breathless. She didn't move to fetch her pen from the pastry or to offer him the clipboard she now held tightly to her chest as though it were a life preserver keeping her from drowning in his Southern gentleman perfection.

He grinned, obviously used to that kind of reaction when women saw him for the first time. I snorted, did an internal eye roll, and shook my head. They likely reacted that way when meeting him for the second time and the third too. He was just *that* well put together.

"I'm assuming I need to sign in?" He gave the clipboard a significant look. Cindy's face reddened as she was jolted back to her job description. She wasn't there to gawk at potential bachelors; she was there to check them in and make sure they made it to the audition room without getting lost or sidetracked at the craft services table.

She looked down at her desk, confused for a moment before she finally held up the clipboard. "Oh, right . . . I'm holding it." She laughed as if baffled by the fact that the thing was still clutched tightly in her grip. She handed it off to him, then finally pulled the pen out of the doughnut. Red jelly covered the tip. "Oh . . . um . . . I guess you don't want to use this one." She glanced around at her desk.

I stepped up and pulled my own pen from its usual place in the messy bun at the back of my head. I had the most unmanageable curls a girl could ever have to deal with. The messy bun was my best friend. "Here you go. You can use mine."

He turned his smile from engaging to outright charming when we made eye contact. Yep. He was one of *those* guys all right . . . the kind who was all pretty wrapping on the outside but likely nothing much to talk about on the inside.

"Better from a hair bun than a sticky bun, eh?" he said, accepting the pen.

I smiled at the joke, surprised he'd come up with a pun on the fly like that, and looked down at my iPad. I didn't really have time to exchange pleasantries with the talent. I'd promised to do a Starbucks run for Max while he did callback auditions.

Technically, I should have been above errand-girl status because of my new position, and technically it was my job to make sure the talent arrived where they were required, but it was Max. No one said no to Max. And he'd given me the promotion only on the condition that I'd carry out some of my former duties on set as well.

I'd been the first and last production assistant in the first two seasons of *Vows* and ended up having everyone generally like me—the director, producer, pretty much the whole crew of *Vows*—simply because I never got the Starbucks order wrong.

It took so little to please these people.

And. So. Much.

Now I was the second assistant director—which mostly meant I would get the special privilege of babysitting the talent, running *their* errands, and keeping *them* on time. I also had the special privilege of mopping up the first assistant director's messes. Pete made a lot of messes and growled loudly when he had to take responsibility for them. Since we were still in preproduction and the new production assistant was an incompetent whiner, I found myself firmly strapped back into my old job description.

At least I had the consolation of a fatter paycheck.

I went over the Starbucks order on my iPad to make sure I hadn't forgotten anybody when my pen showed up in my line of vision.

"I believe this belongs to you, ma'am."

The smoldering way he said ma'am was enough to singe off my eyebrows. I couldn't see how he wouldn't make it through this final round of auditions. Some of the others had glided in on their chariots of ego and limped out just a short while later. But not this one. He would be an exception.

"Thanks." I took the pen back and slid it into my hair.

"So . . ." He was still talking to me, which meant I had to look up and pay some amount of attention, just so I didn't come off as being rude. I needed him to like me in case he *did* end up being *the one*—the lucky bachelor finding a bride in front of a worldwide, public audience. I didn't want him to complain about my being difficult to work with later on. "Are you part of the show?"

I kept my face pasted into an expression of open friendliness, not giving into the eye roll at the question with the obvious answer. "Yes, I am."

"You one of the bachelorettes?"

I laughed outright. "Smooth. That will definitely win you butter-up points to think I could pass for one of the *girls*, but nope; I'm just the second AD."

He widened his eyes, along with his smile, to show he had no idea what that meant. His shoulders moved up in a slight shrug.

I blinked at him. If he really didn't know what a second AD was, then that meant he wasn't a professional actor, which totally threw me off because he *looked* like a professional.

"Second AD means if you get the part, we'll be seeing a lot of each other."

"Well, I look forward to seeing those pretty brown eyes on a daily basis."

I laughed again. "Look, Prince Charming, save it for the audition. And *if* you get the part, you'll be wanting to bat *your* pretty eyes at one of *the girls*, not me." I kept my tone light and friendly even while delivering my lecture. That was really the key. Give them the honest information, but do it with a smile. I had learned that lesson over the years as my parents got me to do the dishes, feed the dog, and work harder in school. They were always pushing for me to do my best and mind my p's and q's, but they were just so darn nice about it that I couldn't ever resent the constant lectures hidden within their smiles.

"So what's your name?" he asked.

"Tori Winters."

He took my hand without me offering it to him. "I'm Chris Caine. Pleased to meet you, Miss Tori. I hope I didn't offend you by saying you've got yourself a pretty set of eyes."

"Not at all, Chris. Good luck with your audition."

"Thank you." He glanced around. "Do you know where I . . ." He shrugged again.

I gave a pointed look at Cindy, who was checking in someone else while also fielding a phone call. She'd been so jaw-dropped over this guy she'd failed to give him directions to the room they were auditioning in. "Looks like Cindy's busy." I sighed and checked my watch. "I'll take you there. Follow me." I would have just given the instructions myself, but that wasn't exactly a skill of mine. I could always take someone to something, could show them where the extension cord they were looking for was located, or show them where the honey wagon had been parked, but I could never explain the directions well enough for a person to find those things without me.

"I'm a little nervous about all this," Chris said as we walked.

"You'll do fine. Just be honest, be yourself. That's what they want—your honest self, not any made-up persona you might slip up on later, but something that is naturally, unarguably you." I wondered if he'd take my advice and drop the Southern-charm thing, but as he continued talking, the Southern actually kicked up a notch.

Go figure. He had to be a genuine Southerner.

Or maybe he was afraid he needed to wrap the Southern persona a little tighter around himself so he didn't lose it.

"Where'd they find you?" I asked, pushing through a set of glass doors.

He actually blushed a little. Now *that* was cute. A man who could blush was a valuable thing. "I was shopping in my hometown of Dahlonega. Some woman handed me a business card."

"Why the blush? Were you shopping for something embarrassing?"

He cocked his head to the side and smirked at me. "And if I was, you think I'd tell you?"

"Touché, my friend. Here we are." I pointed toward the heavy wooden door.

"Thanks." He put out his hand.

I took it in my own and gave it a single shake before releasing him to his fate.

"Any parting words of advice?" he called out after a moment of staring at the door. I'd almost made it back to the stairs.

"It's reality TV. Be real."

He nodded, gave a short salute, then stopped, giving me a serious look. "Do you really think I have pretty eyes?"

He smiled and turned away before I could answer in any appropriate way. I smirked as he wiped his hands on his jeans before turning the knob on the door. His nervousness made him that much more appealing. He was likely acting out some farm-boy persona before ever showing up at Cindy's table. It would probably pay off because even *I* thought it was cute. And after three seasons of working on *Vows*, I didn't think anything was cute anymore.

Not that he shouldn't really be nervous. Behind that door sat his competition. Eight producers sat behind the door beyond that. And if they didn't see the green aura of dollar signs hovering over Chris's head, they would be cold and a smidge cruel as they showed him out.

I shook my head and returned my focus to the place it needed to be—my job.

* * *

Many hours later, when the sun had made a full tour of the sky over our offices, the bachelors had mostly been axed. We were down to two.

Exotic Southern Hospitality.

And Blonde Surfer California Hottie.

I tried not to think about the fact that Chris Caine had made it to the final two choices for bachelor. The two contestants for the part had last been seen clothed in high-quality suits the studio had made them spend their own money on. Seeing Mr. Caine in a jet-black suit with a black-and-silver tie sent the entire monarch migration fluttering through my stomach.

No suit had ever looked as fine on any man as that one did on *that* man.

Every time I tried to close my eyes to shake my head clear of what he looked like as he nervously crossed the hall, the picture of him only became that much clearer.

He *would* be the bachelor.

I knew this because, though the other guy had been walking across the hall as well, I had no recollection of seeing him.

Chris Caine.

Bachelor.

I hadn't known how much I'd hoped he wouldn't make it, how much I'd hoped he'd be left still available after this day until the moment our eyes met and he smiled. There was no chance he wouldn't be the last man standing.

Which meant he wasn't allowed to smile at me like that—in that way that made my legs turn to water and my breath catch in my throat.

All of those smiles would now be reserved for the bachelorettes.

And I suddenly hated all of them, every last undeserving one of them.

"You okay, Tor?"

"Fine." I glanced up to see the red light of Robert's camera on me and blinked in surprise. My hand went to block the camera from filming me any further than it had. "Get that thing off of me. This show is about the glamorous, not the plain."

He shifted the camera from off his shoulder and laughed. "As if there's anything plain about you. So how has your day been?"

"Busy. Call sheets are done though." I handed him his, ignoring his compliment to my lack of plainness.

He stuffed the call sheet into his pocket without checking the call time. "You should look at that," I said, pointing. "It's early."

"I never look at tomorrow until the day I'm in is over. That way I can hope for a late call time." He narrowed his eyes at me. "Well, at least I could have until you messed it all up by telling me it was early."

I shrugged. "Sorry, I guess, in a round-about, not-sorry kind of way."

He blew a raspberry and nodded his head toward the room the two last bachelors had disappeared into. "So . . . anything interesting there?"

I shrugged again. "We'll have to see."

We moved toward the craft services table. Lunch felt like it had been a million years ago. My stomach rumbled with need. Robert fixed himself a sandwich. I loved how he did everything one-handed without even thinking about it. The camera was an extension of him, not just metaphorically, but in reality.

I took one of the hot chocolate packets and made myself a cup, making sure to add extra vanilla creamer. I held it in my hands and let the warmth seep into me. I hated being cold, and the production company kept the building at a chilly sixty-nine degrees.

"Got plans tonight?" Robert asked me.

"Yeah, book club."

He snorted. "You're in a book club?"

I gave him my drop-dead glare. "Is there a problem with that?"

He talked around the bite of sandwich in his mouth and leaned against the table. "I just always think of those things as being for old ladies. You're practically a teenager. What would induce you to join something for geriatrics?"

I rolled my eyes. "It isn't for geriatrics. Most of the women in the group are in their midthirties to midforties."

"Which is still outside your age group."

"You're annoying. I like books. I don't know if you noticed, but I do a lot of reading." I tapped my iPad for emphasis.

He swallowed and took another bite. "Thought you were playing Angry Birds on that thing."

"I do that too sometimes. Actually . . . I joined the book club because the only normal women in my life are my best friend and my mom. It's good research."

"For your writing?" he asked.

"You caught me." I smiled and took a sip of my hot chocolate. Everything in my life was for my writing. Which was what freaked me out about tonight's book-club meeting. We'd been assigned *The Help*.

I loved the book. But hated how much like Skeeter I was. Skeeter was a relationship failure. No romantic interests beyond a guy who was a creep—a guy a little too much like Lawrence had been. Friends with women she was only kind of using for a writing project but with whom she had no personal investment—like my book-club friends were to me. Skeeter gave up almost all interpersonal relationships in favor of her career.

Was I like that?

I hated the question because deep down, I really thought I might be. The only thing different between my life and Skeeter's was that I had a good relationship with my parents. Though I hadn't told them about my breakup with Lawrence yet and hadn't seen them or visited for over a month. What did that say about me?

I resolved to tell them the truth right after book club. I'd drive straight over. Mom and Dad deserved to know those details in my life.

Glad to have made a decision that solidified my difference with Skeeter, I took another sip of my hot chocolate. I jumped when a door banged open against the wall and Blonde Surfer California Hottie stormed out of the audition room. "This is rigged! This whole thing is totally rigged!" he shouted as he ripped off his black suit coat, screaming about the fact that he'd had to buy his own suit, and stomped our direction.

Robert's arm swung up, and the red camera light was on.

I grinned at that. Robert was good at what he did.

I wouldn't have cared about the tantrum. He wasn't the first potential bachelor to throw a complete fit over not being chosen. I wouldn't have cared except that Exotic Southern Hospitality came along right after, trying to apologize and calm the surfer guy down. "I wasn't trying to trip you up. I promise," Chris Caine was saying as he hurried after the angry surfer. "I was just asking a question about where you grew up. I wasn't saying you were lying about it." Chris's Southern accent was noticeably thicker, as if he were deeply agitated. Max and Darren trailed behind, each looking amused and unconcerned that another would-be bachelor was ranting through our halls.

They weren't concerned because they'd already decided.

Chris and the surfer had almost reached where Robert and I stood by the craft services table when the surfer whirled around, throwing his suit coat to the side so he could confront Chris directly.

The suit coat fabric whipped into me, knocking against my hands.

My hands that were holding a full cup of hot chocolate.

The brown liquid shot from the heavy cardboard cup, splashing my hair, my face, my neck, my chest, and my hands.

Steaming hot liquid.

And it hurt.

A lot.

I shrieked with the burn, calling all attention from everyone to me . . . well, from everyone except the surfer, who seemed pretty determined in his focus. Chris ducked a punch from the surfer and hurried to my aid, pulling wads of napkins off the table to try to towel me off. I batted Chris's hands away and used the surfer's jacket to mop the searing liquid from my skin. "It's burning!" I yelled.

Chris yanked a water bottle out of the cooler, ripped off the top, and began dousing me with it. The cold relief was an equal shock to the burn, making me shriek again before grabbing the bottle away from him at the same time the surfer finally figured out how to land a punch.

Right across Chris's jaw.

Chris went down.

I jumped back to avoid going down with him. My fingers rounded into a fist, and I was pulling back to swing at the surfer, but Robert caught my hand. "Lawsuit, sweetie. Bad idea," he whispered. Robert did all this while the red light of the camera remained focused on the scene around us.

The surfer seemed to awaken to whatever good sense he may have possessed with the word *lawsuit*. He yanked his chocolate-soiled suit coat from my hands and stormed off.

Chris maneuvered back to his feet. He held his jaw and made a sound that was something between outrage, surprise, and pain. "He hit me! That no good, dirty rotten, son of—" He looked at me and apparently thought better of finishing the insult he'd been brewing. "I can't believe he hit me!"

Max and Darren and the rest of the auditioning panel no longer looked amused now that their main choice for bachelor had been marred in a fight with an idiot. They crowded around him, checking his chin and face to make sure there wouldn't be bruising.

No one checked on me.

At least almost no one.

Chris shoved his way through the production execs and put his fingers softly under my chin as he moved my head to the side so he could look at my neck. "I'm so sorry you were burned." His eyes looked sorry, all downcast and pitiful. "Do you need anything? An ice pack? Should we take you in and get those burns checked?"

I backed away enough that he couldn't touch me. The burn from the hot chocolate felt like nothing compared to the searing burn of his touch.

It was the gentle touch of true concern.

My face heated up, and I looked away. "It's fine. I'm okay. I'm fine." I nodded as if that proved my words to be true somehow. I tried to laugh as I continued to back up. "The chocolate probably makes it look worse than it is. I should go . . . wash up." I nodded more and turned to hurry away.

Christopher Caine.

With those intense eyes and a burning touch. With that genuine compassion in his heart.

Chris Caine.

Bachelor.

And totally off-limits.

Chapter 3

I REACHED INTO THE BACKSEAT of my car as I drove, slamming on the brakes as some idiot in a truck tried to cut me off. My fingers sifted through the various fabrics: the velvet from the black club top, the silk from the yellow sundress, the pleather from that vest thing Janette gave me as a joke but that actually ended up being pretty cute, the varying polyesters from random shirts I loved because they looked nice and never wrinkled, the flannel from the button-downs, the fleece from the jackets for when the weather turned on me during exterior shots, and finally the cotton-poly white blouse I'd been searching for. I noted the gas gauge was close to empty and flitted off the freeway to fill up the car and change shirts.

Going to the book-club meeting doused in a nearly full cup of chocolate seemed like a dumb thing to do. The ladies would ask questions that had no answers. I should have changed at the production office but was so embarrassed and so *mad* that Chris could be so amazing and be so totally off-limits that all I could think to do was get out of there as soon as possible.

The gas station had a restroom accessible only from the outside. I had to ask the cashier for the key—hooked to a foot-long block of wood that said "Women" on it. I swallowed hard and tried to make as little contact with the wooden key ring as possible since the whole thing looked like it had been dragged through a sewage pit.

"Should have gone to a fast-food place, Tori-girl . . ." I said out loud as I eyed the black-smudged sink, yellow-stained toilet, and floor that looked as if it hadn't seen a mop since the place was built in 1962. I changed quickly, hating the cold shock of fabric on my skin in the little room that had no heater. Southern California was known for warmth, but while still in February, *warm* was definitely not the right adjective to describe the state at that exact moment.

"Don't think about it, Tori. Don't think about why the toilet is stained that color, and do *not* think about the smell." Of course, I *was* thinking about it, or I wouldn't have needed the self-pep talk that didn't work. My neck and chest had red spotting from the burns, but there wasn't much that could be done about that. I'd already cleaned the chocolate from my skin and most of it from my hair.

Instead of paper towels or an air dryer, this bathroom provided an overused towel dispenser with a cloth that hadn't been removed or washed *ever*. I admonished myself to not think about the hundreds of diseases crawling over that piece of cloth hanging from the metal dispenser.

I was out of that bathroom faster than Monica from the make-up department could finish a french manicure when Max was screaming for the talent to take their places.

Changing into a white blouse in a bathroom that was every health-code violation known to man had not been my best idea, but the shirt made it through unscathed. As long as I stayed away from guys with looks and tempers, the shirt just might actually remain spotless.

I pulled up to Ruby's house at the same time as someone else. As she got out of her car, I recognized her as Athena—the career girl with the great hair. She had some new red highlights that added a hip edge to her businesswoman exterior. And she was wearing pink. I only looked like that when Janice, the set hairdresser, took pity on me for wrap parties and for a couple of really special dates where I'd wanted to impress. I hadn't had any of those since before Lawrence.

"Hey there, Athena!" I grabbed my iPad, where my copy of *The Help* was stored, and shut my car door.

She smiled when she saw me and waited for me to catch up to her so we could walk up together.

"Hey!" She didn't use my name, and I wondered if it was because she didn't remember. Not that I would've blamed her. Most people had difficulty recalling names. That had never been a problem for me. My memory was the gift that allowed me to get the Starbucks order right every single time.

"How's your magazine doing?" I asked her.

"Great! Got a new employee and finally feel like I have a life."

"Well, that's wonderful, except . . . I was sort of hoping you'd be my wingman when Ruby goes off on the whole workaholic problem in our little group."

Athena laughed. She had a great laugh. "Sorry about that. And now that I'm in a relationship, you can bet she'll set her sights on you."

"She'll have to get in line behind my mother. Though I wouldn't put it past my mother to be handing out cue cards to the people I know, telling me to get a job that works human hours."

"Human hours are so overrated." Athena pushed the doorbell, and we stepped back, waiting for Ruby to answer. We didn't have to wait long.

"How is that man of yours?" Ruby asked as she pulled Athena into a hug.

"Grey?" Athena said into Ruby's shoulder. She gave me a poke in the side as she returned Ruby's hug, whether a cue to keep quiet about her admitting to her relationship or as a little joke to tell me I was next on the hit list of love.

"Of course I mean Grey." Ruby let Athena go.

"He's . . . really great," Athena answered with a laugh that I felt certain was directed at me.

They talked for a moment longer, and then I stepped up to claim my hug. Ruby was so like my own mom, always loving on people and making them feel important and welcome. A lot like my grandma too, whom I never got to see because she remained stubbornly on the island rather than coming to visit us ever. "So when are you going to tell us about your boyfriends, Tori?" Ruby asked.

I nearly exploded with laughter as Athena shrugged her innocence at me. "You'll be the first to know," I promised. "Your home smells like heaven. Where's the kitchen?" I inhaled deeply.

Really. Heaven.

"If you're hungry right now, I can bring out some hors d'oeuvres."

"Oh, don't trouble yourself." I waved my hands to show I didn't really need anything at that exact moment. "I'm saving myself for whatever it is you're baking." I inhaled again. Definitely worth saving for. Craft services was great, but nothing could beat the smell of baked goods at home.

Ruby smiled and directed us to the living room. She hadn't shut the front door yet because another car was pulling up in front of the house. But I didn't hover in the foyer to see who it was. My feet were killing me from all of the running around I'd done, and the idea of sitting sounded as heavenly as the baked goods in the kitchen smelled.

I followed Athena to one of the chairs and sat next to her. She asked about my day, and I turned my head and tugged on one of my curls so she could see the chocolate-crusted remnants of a day in my life. We had a good laugh over it, and I told her about the new promotion and how I'd had to work as a complete servant to the whims of pretty much *everyone* on the set. She asked what my new promotion entailed, and I explained the duties of the second AD.

Athena furrowed her brow. "Wow. That is a load of responsibility. So is this like a stepping stone to eventually be a director?"

That question came a lot when I met new people. The truth was *no*. I had no desire to direct films. I had no desire to produce films—not like that. I wanted to *write* them. I wanted to write the words that actors would breathe life into that would make audiences around the world weep and laugh and *feel*.

For me, everything began with the words.

I explained that to Athena, and she nodded like she understood. I rubbed my hands together and leaned back in my chair. "I got started as an extra. I just figured it would help to be on sets and learn a little about the business and meeting the people who ran the business. And once I realized that crew ate better than extras, I moved straight up to stand-in. Then a production assistant job opened up, and I'd made a lot of friends, and one of them recommended me. One thing led to another. Now, here I am, climbing the hierarchy of Hollywood but kind of on the wrong ladder."

"You're still writing though, right?"

"Absolutely." I gave two short nods.

"And making contacts with people who make decisions about screenplays?" I saw the wheels in Athena's head turning. She was a business woman and knew what games to play and how to play them to her advantage. I could learn a lot from her. I nodded again. "Then you're where you need to be. All ladders lead up, right?"

"Exactly." I considered her words a moment before giving her my best sly grin. "So, this Grey guy . . . He's doing really great, huh?" I poked her knee much the same way she'd poked at me a moment before.

She laughed. "Oh, here it comes. Are you going to interrogate me too?"

I scooted her direction on my chair. "I just want all the beans, girl. Start spilling. Is the *great* he's doing the reason you have a new employee?"

"You know . . . not really. I mean, yes, but no. Does that make sense?"

"No." I smiled to show that my blunt response was a friendly one.

She smiled too. "He just reminded me that there is more to me than a job, you know what I mean?"

I blinked, feeling my smile slip a little. Her words sneaked their way into my heart and planted the fear that there *wasn't* much more to *me* than a job. I nodded slowly. "I know what you mean."

Somewhere in our conversation, others had shown up. I felt a little startled to see them all there. I must have been more tired than I'd thought. Not paying attention to a room filling up and being oblivious to conversations around me was proof that my game was off.

Livvy and Ilana were already seated; Livvy looked happier than she did last time I'd seen her, and her new haircut looked fabulous on her. She looked like she'd never be able to wipe that little Mona Lisa smile of contentment from her face, which meant she must have had a pretty good month . . . or at least a pretty good day. Ilana's arm was slung in an arm brace, and she winced as she readjusted herself. I wondered what had happened to her but decided to wait before asking. She might volunteer the information. Ilana leaned over to me. "I know we've met before, but what was your name again? I'm Ilana."

"I'm Victoria, but people usually call me Tori," I said with a nod, letting her off the hook for not remembering my name. Some people became uncomfortable when they realized I remembered them when they couldn't remember me. It was nice that Ilana was trying to reach out and get to know me. I took a deep breath and smiled wider for her in an attempt to let her know I appreciated her efforts. That's what I'd come to book club for, right? To form real relationships with real women?

I didn't let my smile dip when I thought about Skeeter and her relationships. I did not want to end up like the character in our book of the month. I wanted to genuinely be friends with these women.

"Nice to see you again, Tori." She glanced at the other women. "Livvy and Athena, right?"

"Right," they both agreed.

Livvy smiled broadly at me and exclaimed that it was very nice to see me again. The nice thing about her was that I believed her when she said it.

Livvy asked about Ilana's arm, which was good since I'd wanted to know as well. Years of working with people had taught me that most questions were answered if I was just patient enough to let people talk.

Ilana promised to tell the story when everyone was here since she wanted to avoid repetition, but she mentioned it was an on-the-job injury.

"Remind me what do you again?" Livvy asked.

"I'm an event manager at a convention center," Ilana said.

Ruby's niece Shannon and some girl not much younger than me were sitting on the opposite side of the room from Livvy and Ilana. Shannon wore her Walgreen's uniform, which I took to mean she'd just come from work too. If I'd had a glass, I would have raised a toast to the working women. They may have just shown up straight from work, but at least they showed up. Ilana asked the girl her name.

"I'm Keisha, Shannon's stepdaughter."

Shannon looked comfortable and happy to have her stepdaughter with her, so it must not have been a Cinderella-stepdaughter sort of relationship. Keisha eyed the arm sling and finally blurted, "What happened to your arm?"

Ilana looked from her arm to Keisha and Shannon. "Stupid accident at work," she said. "My elbow's broken."

"Ow." Keisha wrinkled her nose in sympathy. "Does it hurt bad?"

"Not so long as I keep on top of the pain with medication. They're talking about surgery, possibly, so I go in again this week to get it checked out."

"That totally sucks," Keisha said.

I would have said the same thing if I had been an active participant in the conversation instead of just an eavesdropper. Broken bones were the worst. I'd had plenty of bones casted throughout my life.

Ruby and Paige entered the living room together. "I guess we're all here." Ruby clapped her hands together, getting everyone's attention.

"Is Daisy still on bed rest?" Athena asked.

Ruby's smile shrank a little. "She is. I offered to have us go to her place like we did last month, but she said she'd moved and her new place was too small." Ruby shot a look at Paige. "I didn't want to pry by asking too many questions."

Paige picked up where Ruby seemed to be floundering. "She got her own place a couple of weeks ago, close to where her first ex-husband and daughter live. She's still on partial bed rest, but the baby's doing well."

Wow. That was great news. I'd liked Daisy when I'd met her. I hadn't been as regular to the meetings because of work, but even going the one time before had been enough for me to feel like I belonged. It was the only reason I'd come back in spite of being exhausted and wanting to wash the crusted-over hot chocolate from my hair. Daisy's life had been in some pretty dramatic turmoil before. "Did her life turn a 180 or what?" I said out loud. "But she's okay?" I wanted to confirm that. The baby doing okay and the mom doing okay were not the same thing.

Paige confirmed that Daisy was fine.

"Well," Ruby said. "Daisy chose the book, but since she isn't here, I guess I'll lead the discussion. What did everyone think?"

Ruby looked directly at me, and it took me a moment to realize why. I was the lone black woman in the room, and we were discussing *The Help*, which was about black maids in the South during segregation.

I then realized pretty much *everyone* was looking to me to start the conversation, like they were worried they might say something wrong and offend me, which, unless they told me they hated my shirt after all the effort

I'd gone into changing it, they weren't likely to do. I couldn't imagine any of them being the sort of person capable of blind prejudice. Not that you ever really knew that about a person. Lots of seemingly good people were capable of awful things.

A couple of them weren't just waiting for my response, but they stared at me as if they planned on basing all of their opinions on whatever I might say. Athena must have sensed my discomfort and began the discussion.

We talked a little more about opinions on the characters, and then we came to the discussion on the ending. "I wasn't a huge fan of the ending," I said. "Maybe I watch too many movies, but I wanted a happier ending for these characters. The writer did such a good job at making these women my friends that I wanted my friends to have happiness. Celia is still basically friendless and can't have children; Minny's husband is threatening to kill her, so she has to move out of her home and raise her children alone, and we can suppose without her husband's financial help; and Aibileen is fired and not only doesn't know how she'll make ends meet, but she's also lost Mae Mobley—and worse still, Mae Mobley's lost the only person who genuinely loved her. Makes me wonder what her childhood will be like. And Skeeter?"

Would I be like her? A career woman who was eternally hopeless at meaningful relationships? My thoughts on Skeeter felt too personal. Sharing them would be like laying my own soul out on Ruby's coffee table. But I forged ahead. "Skeeter is friendless, boyfriendless, and her mother is dying at the end. Yes, she's got her dream job, but she has no real relationships. The friendship she's managed to make with these maids is one she can't really keep long distance—even trying to keep it puts the women in danger. She's alone. I found myself worried about her for a long time after I closed the book." *And worrying about myself too* . . . But I didn't say that out loud.

They all spoke of the demeaning way the maids were treated, of the significance of these uppity white women worrying about sharing a toilet seat with the same woman who cooked their meals and cared for their children. They had a lot to say, and they were all fired up over the cause of justice for the maids.

"Have you ever felt persecuted?" Ruby asked me after the discussion had died into something less intense.

Well, that was certainly direct. I liked Ruby for that. She really wanted to know, and she was genuinely worried about my answer, as if she planned on hoisting up her sleeves and personally beating up anyone who might have wronged me in my life. There was a long list of people who'd wronged me but not for the reasons she was thinking. "For me personally, I haven't experienced racial prejudice in the US. Maybe because I'm in the entertainment industry, it just hasn't been an issue for me. I find it much harder to be a woman than to be black."

They all nodded. It wasn't the answer they'd expected, but I could tell I'd struck a common chord with them. Some of them had obviously had hard experiences with their own versions of persecution.

"You've experienced prejudice for being a woman?" Ruby asked.

"Oh yes," I said. "There's still a lot of opportunity for me within my industry, but most of the top spots are filled with men, and most of the decisions on who fills the open positions are made by men. And a lot of women fall victim to unprofessional ways of furthering their career, if you know what I mean." I didn't mention that a lot of men fell victim to those same unprofessional means. There were both cruel men and women at the top. It was the way of things.

"Though I haven't ever really experienced persecution, I have run into a lot of well-meaning, misinformed people over the years. My parents are a mixed couple—half white, half black. My dad calls their marriage Oreo perfection, and Mom smiles every time he says it and kisses him. They're a little goofy, but they really are perfection together."

I rolled my eyes because I could mentally see the two of them practically making out in front of me. Some parents really needed to figure out what the lock on their bedroom door was for. "Anyway," I continued, "when we went on outings all together, no one noticed us much, but when Dad took me out on his own, people always asked where he'd adopted me from. That was a hard thing. The first time I heard it, I went home in a tantrum because I thought the lady in the park knew something I didn't. It took them hours of begging me to come out of my room to explain to me that I was *not* adopted. So it wasn't prejudice, but it was a misconception that needled me until I was old enough to shrug it away. My dad is white. I'm still his natural daughter. The end. I've since learned that I can't always be running around taking offense people don't necessarily mean. Better to smile and assume they're nice but stupid people and not let it bother me."

"It wasn't until junior high that I really understood what racism meant," Athena said. "There was a group of kids in my school who decided to make me their target."

She talked about the jokes and name calling she'd endured because of her Greek heritage.

"I had similar experiences." Ilana pointed to her nose, which fit her face fine but was long enough to give away her Jewish descent. "I suppose if I'd grown up in New York or something, it would have been different, but I grew up here in California, in an area with very few Jews." She told us of a time when her friend's mother had disallowed her friend to play with her anymore due to her religion. "We went from having regular sleepovers to never making eye contact. She even took different hallways at school so she wouldn't run into me." She tapped her copy of *The Help.* "Prejudice against black people has come a long way since the sixties. And in a lot of ways, prejudice against Jews is much better than it was during World War II—but there's a long way to go in both areas."

They talked for several minutes more about prejudices and how strange it was that even now such things existed, then Ruby perked up and looked at Shannon. "Shannon, what did you think?"

She looked perplexed to be called out by name. "Uh, I liked it." She frowned slightly as if annoyed with herself for only having that to say. I certainly hoped she had more to say since I'd about talked myself hoarse. "It's been a long time since I've read a novel; I don't like much fiction. I really liked this one though."

Wow. She must have completely loved her aunt to show up at a book-club meeting when she didn't even like fiction. And obviously, she had a demanding job because she'd come straight from work, and from the couple of times I'd seen her, she always looked tired. I liked that she was willing to support Ruby that way, even if it made her uncomfortable. Family was important. Anyone else who thought so was okay in my book.

It was cute that her stepdaughter had either read the book or watched the movie because she added several comments to the discussion.

"I'd say it's about time for dessert. I'll be right back." Ruby stood and moved toward the kitchen, and Livvy and Paige started to stand up—likely to help her—but Ruby said, "It will only take a second. You stay and visit." Shannon got up anyway and hurried after Ruby. It was nice of her to help. We all made polite conversation, and Athena made another comment about Grey, which made me smile.

Not all relationships were staged for a viewing audience. Some people had the real thing.

Ruby came back a moment later, making me laugh almost as hard as I had when I'd read about the Terrible Awful in the book. "Speaking of chocolate pie, would anyone like a slice?"

Groans and gagging noises followed the question. I had to admit it, even with how great the house smelled and how hungry I really was, there was *no way* I was eating that pie. I'd stop at my favorite pastry shop with the cute Hispanic guy working the counter on my way home.

Shannon showed up right after, carrying a tray with several dessert plates holding what turned out to be red velvet bread pudding and ice cream. And my taste buds opened up to the idea of eating at Ruby's house all over again.

"So that's the amazing thing we've been smelling," Ilana said—echoing my own thoughts.

Yes, it was. Heaven on a plate. Shannon handed a cup of water to everyone, then went back into the kitchen.

I wiped out the first helping and served myself a second as Paige asked, "Will our next meeting be March 5?"

Ruby looked up from her own plate. "Yes. Does that still work for most of us?"

Worked for me.

"So whose turn is it to pick a book?" Ilana asked.

Ruby gave Shannon a pointed look. "Why don't you choose one, Shannon?"

Clever Ruby. Shannon had looked uncomfortable since admitting she didn't like fiction. Poor girl almost looked like she might be sick.

"Oh, that's okay." Shannon waved her spoon around. "I'm not nearly as well read as you guys are."

"Oh, baloney," Ruby said, not about to give in. "You have a PhD; surely you're as well read as anyone here. Just choose a book for us to read, something you'd like to share with us."

"Really?" Shannon said, and if she'd looked a little sick before, now she looked panicked. "I don't know. I don't read much fiction."

Athena shrugged. "It doesn't have to be fiction. Do you read nonfiction?"

"Mostly only for work." Shannon dropped her gaze to her book. "Well, there is one that might be interesting."

She suggested a book called *The Immortal Life of Henrietta Lacks*.

I'd never heard of it; not surprising since most of my reading consisted of scripts. Paige spoke up. "I read a review about it. I tried to check it out at the library once, but it had a few holds on it—that was almost a year ago though. I heard it was really well done."

That was interesting. People actually read nonfiction enough to have holds on it?

Shannon seemed encouraged by having at least one person who knew what she was talking about. "It *was* really well done. It's about a woman who had cervical cancer. The doctors biopsied the tumor and discovered that her cells reproduced continually, which opened the floodgates of medical research. Her cells are why we have a vaccine for polio and why we've made such advances in cancer research. Fascinating history."

"You're such a nerd, Shannon." Keisha laughed at her stepmom but not in a mean way. They seemed pretty chummy together. It was kind of adorable.

I laughed along with her. "We love nerds. My dad's a nerd. Huge one. He's a biomathematician. He hates that I work in the useless field of entertainment but loves me too much to say anything too horrible about it."

"I think it sounds great," Athena said from beside me. "What was the title again? I want to order it from Amazon before I forget."

Shannon clammed up again, but Paige stepped in. "*The Immortal Life of Henrietta Lacks.* The author had a weird name though. I can't remember what it was."

"Skloot," Shannon said, not looking up at any of us. "Rebecca Skloot— S-K-L-O-O-T."

"I'd have never remembered that," Paige said.

Who could have blamed her?

Ruby promised to e-mail us the details since everyone professed an inability to remember the title or the author's name. I'd already tapped the name into my iPad—not that I worried I wouldn't remember but because it was what I did. Good notes meant guaranteeing I wouldn't forget. Shannon disappeared into the kitchen as soon as she could get away. I wondered if we'd put her on the spot by making her pick a book for us like that.

Exhaustion sank into my bones, and my bed started to seem like a more glamorous dream by the minute. I hurried to eat a third helping and excused myself for the night. Paige stood as well, and Ruby escorted us to the door, making sure to give us each a hearty hug good-bye.

I really liked Ruby. I'd pretty much decided to make her a bit character in my next screenplay. She'd be a perfect character, warm and comfortable, a kind of save-the-day woman . . . Maybe a mystery . . .

I passed the time plotting out the details as I drove home. I had a tendency to run my finger through the loops in my curls when I was thinking, and this time I hit a snag of crusted hot chocolate, which also made me hit a snag in my plotting.

Curse that stupid actor with his tantrums and inability to apologize. And curse that real guy with his Southern-boy sweet talk. I considered all the ways I could have handled the situation—like punching the surfer in the gut for needing anger management classes—though that would have made me look like the one who needed the classes. And I should have told Chris that gently touching my chin like that and making my legs turn to water wasn't going to get him the part. I should have explained that the only way he was going to get any part was for him to stay as far away from me as possible.

Which was impossible.

He was now my job. It would be my knuckles rapping on his bedroom door to hurry him back to set. It would be my voice calling to update him on call times and location details. I would drive him places, run his errands, and know his shoe size and what brand of underwear he preferred.

I really should have told him to stay away from me.

But instead of telling him anything, I'd been my typical self: smiled, insisted that I was fine, and waved away help.

Not that I had needed help. I could take care of myself.

And just as I confirmed this thought to myself, my cell phone rang. I tucked the Bluetooth in my ear and pressed the answer button.

My mom's voice came through the device. She'd been in the States most of her adult life, but the Barbadian accent still lingered in her words—little whispers of my mother's past life making themselves known—refusing to allow her to forget where she'd come from. "Hey, my baby. You have tomorrow off. Come over and let me take care of you. I don't see you enough when you're working."

I agreed to go over right then, since that had been my plan originally, so *she* could take care of me. There wasn't anything wrong with that. She was *Mom*. It was perfectly natural to let my mom baby me every now and again. It wasn't perfectly natural to let some smooth, fake-Southern actor try to worm his way into a part by pretending to worry about me.

Only I didn't think he was faking.

And I didn't think he was pretending to be worried.

True compassion.

Had I ever witnessed that in any man besides my own dad?

I was glad to be going to my parents' house. Not only did I owe them an explanation about the breakup with Lawrence, but it would help take my mind off things I had no business thinking about. Things like the gentle worry in Chris Caine's eyes.

And since I'd been steadily employed for the last three years and was no longer dating a guy Dad didn't like anyway, I'd probably only get a lecture from my mom on keeping private business private. She was not going to like that I'd dumped Lawrence in front of a thousand people.

I walked in without knocking when I finally arrived at my parents'. "Mom? Dad? I'm home!"

"In here, baby." The voice calling from the TV room was my mother's. The TV was on, but even without having gone in yet, I knew she wasn't watching it. She would be curled up next to my dad with a book in her hand while he watched the screen.

That was what they called quality time together.

I smiled and leaned into the doorframe. They were arranged on the couch exactly the way I'd pictured them.

Some things in life were constants.

My parents were one of those things.

Mom looked up from her book—a worn paperback romance with some woman dressed like she was on her way out to a regency tea on the cover. She frowned and put the book down. "What's wrong?"

I jostled my way in between them, and then, while surrounded by my parents' love, I finally confessed the whole marriage proposal and subsequent breakup.

Dad's grin practically split his face in two by the time I was done. "That's wonderful! Best news ever."

I rolled my eyes at his overenjoyment of my moment of humiliation.

"This little choice of yours proves you really are my smart girl." He knuckled my head even though I was way past too old for such a thing.

"No. She's *my* smart girl this time," Mom said.

Dad smirked and shot me a look that said no way was Mom winning smart girl rights on this particular issue. "How do you figure?" he asked. "Since I'm the one who told her to dump the guy from the start."

Mom gave a tiny smile, the kind that was almost secretive, the kind that made you lean in closer, hoping she'd share her secret. "I let her make up her own mind, knowing she was clever enough to make the right choice without my interference. That means I get to claim ownership of her intelligence on this one."

Dad's smirk fell into a fake scowl. "And your mother wins again. You'd think after all these years, I'd know enough not to argue with her."

Mom blinked her eyes in a slow, lazy acknowledgment that he really should know better but that she was nice enough not to say so. She didn't give me any grief over making private things public. A lecture on that might come later, but at least it wouldn't happen tonight.

I explained the chaos of my day, showing them my hair as exhibit A for all the reasons men were evil. Mom tsked and went to make coconut sugar cakes for me like she did when I was little.

I sighed in contentment. Being doused in a cup of my own drink meant I'd earned this time with these people who actually loved me. I had totally earned my weekend off from anything that had to do with work *or* men.

Chapter 4

I ARRIVED AT THE PLACE Robert called the Love Shack but that the studio called the mansion. Max liked the pun of the word *mansion* having the word *man* in it.

The mansion sported four hot tubs outside. Who on the planet needed four hot tubs for one house?

People in the business of finding love—or some strange semblance of love anyway.

The first set was still close to home, where there was still sun and surf to be had but also where plane tickets for the unlucky bachelorettes to be flown home would be cheaper. The exotic locations would come later when the choice was between three or four girls, not the thirty that would soon chatter and flirt throughout the mansion. On the mansion grounds were several bungalows. That's where the crew slept. *Slept* because any moment we were awake, we were at the mansion doing our job.

The show was supposed to be reality TV. But some things were loosely scripted. We told them where to be and what time to be there. They woke up when we said and went to bed when we said. They ate meals, took showers, and felt like a swim or a moonlit stroll in the sand all when Max wrote it on the call sheets I delivered to their rooms the night before.

None of the talent would be arriving until the next day. A few of the crew wandered in and out of rooms, making sure the cameras were all in their proper places and in proper working order. It was my job to make sure the rooms were ready for the bachelor and his bachelorettes. Flowers had to be set. Favorite foods and brands of water and soft drinks had to be placed in the kitchen fridges.

The world assumed the bachelorettes were living a life of luxury in the mansion. The world imagined it to be nothing but sipping smoothies and lying out in the sun. The truth was that the studio provided very little in the way of luxuries for the bachelorettes. The studio made the girls do their own hair and make-up. There were no professional masseuses hiding around the corner for when the camera lights went off, no wardrobe call, no manicures. It was a very shallow imprisonment the girls would live in for the next couple months. They provided all of their own stuff—dresses, swimsuits, make-up, *everything*.

But there would be a private beach. There was a pool and the four hot tubs. And there would be food—a lot of food. That was one place where the studio never skimped. All of the players would be well fed. It made up for the fact that they all had to turn in their phones and had no TV, Internet, or any other kind of access to the outside world.

Well . . . sort of made up for it.

The cameras on them all the time—their chance to have the spotlight so that perhaps they could find fame under that light—*that* was what really made up for it.

It was interesting how much freedom people would give up for a moment of fame. Oh, sure, they all claimed they were looking for love, but everyone knew they were hoping to get discovered and to land real acting jobs.

And it was hard to be critical of that fact when the shallow antics of all the people involved provided me with a decent paycheck. I profited from their frivolity. Did that make me frivolous too?

Maybe. I was determined not to think about it too much because I simply didn't want to know the answer to that question.

After shelving the mansion's library with books of my choosing, I was in Chris's room making sure it was well stocked with towels and toiletries, since, while the studio did very little for the bachelorettes, the bachelor was totally cared for.

Robert found me when I was nearly done. The red eye of his camera fixed on me.

I rolled my eyes at him. "Isn't that thing supposed to be on the elegance of the room rather than the bedraggled outfit of the second AD?"

He grinned. "You're what gives this room elegance, sweetheart. Anyone who says differently is blind and stupid." But the camera moved off me to sweep over the room. It caught all of the finer details of the bed mounded with more pillows than any one head would ever need, the outer room that sported a sitting area, and the minibar season one's bachelor had used far too liberally. He'd been a brooding sort of drunk, which had made everyone, especially the bachelorettes, uncomfortable. We didn't stock anything in the minibar anymore. As the show would go on and bachelorettes dropped to the wayside, they would fill the bar with drinks that would allow rendezvous opportunities with guests the bachelor seemed interested in.

It was a closed-bedroom show. No actual intimate relations were allowed beyond kissing. With all of the cameras tucked into every available space, no one dared to push that rule too far. It wasn't like they weren't always being monitored. There was no hope of not getting caught with all of those cameras trained on you every second of the day.

The cameras were why it shouldn't have surprised me that I was caught breaking one of the rules set up for me specifically.

The minibar was supposed to be absolutely empty. Max wanted the bachelor to use the kitchen if he needed a late-night snack in the hopes that he'd catch the bachelor meeting some lucky bachelorette also looking for sustenance in the middle of the night.

Max was sneaky like that.

As a rule, I always kept the rules, but I had read Chris's files. I knew his likes and dislikes probably better than he did after all the studying I'd done. It was my job. I knew he worked for a farm, though he hadn't given any financial information. The idea of *Vows* was that the girl and boy would commit to each other regardless of finances. But if the bachelor chose to actually marry one of the girls . . . he'd be awarded the gift of half a million dollars, so it was pretty much a moot point.

Most of the guys who tried out were living below poverty level. I couldn't leave the kitchenette empty after reading his profile and discovering that he loved Bit-O-Honey candies and Fudgsicles.

They were unique and honestly endearing details. What grown man admitted to loving a Fudgsicle? The same kind who made sticky bun jokes and worried about me when I was burned.

He had just been punched in the jaw, and he had worried about me. I couldn't forget the tender look in his eyes as he gently tilted my chin to examine the burns. It was a gesture of kindness I had really needed. The candy and frozen fudge bars were meant as a small thank you for his concern over the hot-chocolate fiasco.

And it wasn't exactly actual rule breaking. It wasn't like I'd filled the freezer with frozen pizzas and provided a microwave. The treats were a small thing—a courtesy, a debt owed and repaid.

My internal thoughts hit the brakes on my personal justifications when Robert opened the freezer door and zoomed in on the box of frozen contraband.

Then he swung the camera back my direction. "Any good explanations for that, Tor?"

"What?" I tried to sound innocent, even though I could feel the heat rising in my face.

The eyebrow not hidden behind Robert's camera went up. "This sort of thing needs to go downstairs."

"And it will," I said. "I was coming up here to get something, and I had that in my hand. I didn't want it to melt while I worked."

"So why is it placed in the center of the freezer facing out like it was being stocked on a store shelf? And why is there a jar of the bachelor's favorite candy on the counter set up like an ad for Bit-O-Honey?"

I scowled and shook my head. "I was just finishing setting the room. Those *will* be going downstairs when *I* go downstairs. Who died and made you the food police?"

"Just making sure everything's ready. Pete told me to come check on you. You've been a little . . . *off* since we chose the bachelor."

I stared at him, my jaw hanging slack. Pete was the first AD and my direct boss. He'd never sent anyone to check on me before. "I have not been *off* at all! What is that even supposed to mean?"

"This guy's prettier than any of the previous bachelors. Just worried you were getting like the others."

"Of course I'm not. And what others?"

Robert laughed. "Every other girl on set. I swear that guy can't walk into a room without every girl sighing like they're all fourteen years old again. Pathetic." He gave my arm a squeeze as he adjusted the camera off his shoulder, which meant he had likely turned it off since our conversation had moved into something more personal. "Just don't want you getting pathetic on me. No fraternizing with the talent. We've got contracts. I'd hate to see you wrapped into a lawsuit."

I blinked and stammered, blinked and tried again. Was I that transparent? Had my feelings shone out like a beacon when Chris had touched my chin?

And yet I wasn't anything like the other girls on set who'd done nothing but ogle Chris's pictures since he was announced. I hadn't ogled once—hadn't honestly allowed myself to even look at his pictures for fear I might never look away.

But the fact remained that Chris was the first bachelor I referred to by his actual name rather than just calling him *the bachelor*.

I crossed over to where Robert stood and shut the freezer door. "The ice cream is going to melt if you leave it open like that. Is there a reason you're giving me this unnecessary reminder about contracts?" Surely a few little treats were discreet enough to not cause alarm.

Robert leaned against the counter. "He keeps asking about you. Max wants to know why."

"He is *not* asking about me." I kept my tone light, making sure it revealed nothing about what those words did to me. My insides melted into my knees somewhere. I wanted to girl-scream and grin until my lips fell off. *Chris Caine had asked about me!*

"He has been. He wants to know where you live, what kinds of foods you like, how long you've been working for the studio, whether or not you ever considered being on the show as one of the girls, whether or not you're in a relationship with anyone. He's asking all the stuff that green-lights his interest in you. He's supposed to be asking those questions. But he is *not* supposed to be asking them about *you*. Max is furious because you aren't one of the girls. You are not allowed to fraternize with the bachelor."

I lifted my arms in the air to emphasize my frustration. "I haven't been! I've only seen him the one time!"

I didn't mention that I saw him every time I closed my eyes. I didn't mention that thoughts of Chris never left my head. I didn't mention that I would have asked all of those same questions about him if I hadn't had his file to review, where the answers were given to me.

And because Robert never missed anything, I didn't have to say any of that for him to know it was all true.

He took the Fudgsicles out of the freezer and picked up the jar of Bit-O-Honeys. "Just be careful, Tori. You're good at what you do. And I know you're scratching your way into the writing side of the business. I don't want to see you throw any of that away just because some guy with a pretty face smiles at you."

He left the room with my small gift to Chris in tow. I wondered if the treats would end up in the kitchen so they became community property for all of the bachelorettes.

And then I hoped they would because the girls were notorious for trying to keep their figures perfect. A little temptation would be good for them. I decided then and there I'd be stuffing the downstairs freezer with ice cream and filling the pantry with cookies and chips.

"I am careful," I muttered. But Robert was right. Careful meant more than just not crossing a line. Careful meant staying as far away from the line as possible.

How had a guy I'd met only once reduced me to this?

"Not worth it, Tori-girl. Keep your head on straight." I took a deep breath and got back to my job—determined to stay as far away from the line as my job would let me. Chris . . . *No, not Chris. The bachelor* . . . would be meeting the girls first thing in the morning. I would do my job to make sure the meeting went exactly as it should. I would not fill the freezer with ice cream. Well . . . it was possible I wouldn't.

* * *

The bachelorettes were more like very pretty monkeys. Not a lot of intelligence but just enough to get them into trouble. The first day of filming went deliciously awful.

They were already making fake girl alliances—frenemies at its finest. There was eyelash batting at Chris—no! *The bachelor*. I had to remember to call him the bachelor. And there were a lot of smiles at the other bachelorettes—smiles with poison in them. I took two ibuprofen for my headache and refrained from throwing the pill bottle at Becky, the bachelorette with the snakiest grin. Chris had better watch out for that one. She'd have her claws and jaws sunk into him tight if he wasn't careful.

Please don't let him choose Becky, I thought over and over as the day progressed. It was March, and the weather was still cool enough to be prohibitive to scantily clad females, but Max had prepared for that with the provision of many outdoor patio heaters and blazing outdoor gas fireplaces—adding both romance and warmth to the girls with spaghetti straps for shoulder covers.

I wore jeans and a thick tunic sweater. Since the heaters were all placed where the cameras were pointed and none of those cameras were pointed at me, I didn't get to enjoy their warmth.

It bugged me that we were filming the first cocktail party outside at night. They could have played football inside that huge house. Why be outside in the cold?

Because Max knew his business. He knew how to create atmosphere.

The dark sky and fires blazing in the outdoor braziers definitely created atmosphere, even as I clenched my teeth to keep them from chattering where the boom mics could pick up the noise. All that fake giggling from the girls started sounding like braying after the first ten minutes.

Except one of them wasn't giggling. Her smiles were nervous, tentative, careful. She looked like the stereotypical new girl gripping a lunch tray, staring over the sea of students, wondering where she might fit in or, at the very least, where she might sit down to eat without being sent away. Only instead of a lunch tray, this girl's fingers had a white-knuckle grip on a black evening bag. Instead of students, she was staring at her competition.

Her name was Gemma Mays.

Her file indicated she liked 80s soft rock—all those sappy love songs with the synthesizer accompaniment. She was a sucker for dogs, dimples, and cotton candy. She was the sort of person I'd have taken by the hand and led to my table to be my friend if she had been the new girl in my school lunchroom. But as it was, I would remain on the sidelines, and she would have to make her own way through the next couple of months.

But that didn't make watching her any less painful.

It was tough to watch both the awkward, shy girl and the brazen girl who'd come in wearing the least amount of cloth over her body. Becky zeroed in on her target from the moment he walked out onto the patio. "Can I get you a drink, Chris?" was her first question.

His reply was something I'd expected from reading his files. "A Sun Drop would be great, thanks."

But Becky didn't know how to process that information. "A Sun Drop?" She blinked her long, mascara-smothered eyelashes and tried to frown, which was almost impossible since her french twist was so tight at the back of her head it was shocking she was able to use any facial muscles at all.

"Yeah, Sun Drop . . . It's like the Southern version of a Mountain Dew, though Mountain Dew isn't nearly as good."

She smiled wider, as if he'd made a joke rather than stated a preference. "Wouldn't you rather have something a little more . . . lively?"

The bachelor also smiled, revealing a slight dimple in his left cheek. "Not when I'm surrounded by thirty beautiful women. For now, I'd like to keep my head clear."

Her smile remained bright and sparkly, but anyone watching could tell Chris's response had surprised her. She'd possibly been hoping to get him a little drunk. If she could muddle his mind, she might be able to fool him into thinking she was brilliant and witty. But she dutifully scuttled over to the drink bar and found the can of Sun Drop in the ice bucket.

It was hard not to swell with a bit of pride that the right drink existed in that bucket.

I'd put it there myself.

It had been a lot of extra trouble to find the actual drink. Anywhere I asked after it, I was referred to Mountain Dew. The catering guys had given up and purchased the competing brand. When I saw that, I made it my special mission to get the bachelor his preferred beverage.

I reasoned I would have done the same for any of the bachelors on the previous episodes.

I watched as Becky returned with a glass half filled with ice in one hand and a can of Sun Drop in the other. But Becky's smile dropped for a fraction of an instant, so fast no one who hadn't been watching closely would have noticed it.

I hoped Robert had caught the infraction on camera. I wanted viewers to see Becky for the icy little snake she was.

I turned to see what had made Becky's sunny little smile take a dip behind that cloud of fury.

Gemma.

Becky had noticed Gemma.

And the bachelor had noticed Gemma.

Which meant Becky would be out for blood.

I almost felt sorry for Gemma, except some evil little part of me kept repeating Robert's words from the previous day.

He's been asking about you, Robert had said.

I narrowed my eyes at all the girls smiling and talking and trying to get the bachelor's attention. *The bachelor you're all flirting with* . . . I wanted to say out loud to them, *well, he's been asking about me.* No matter how many ways I tried to view the girls differently, they just kept looking like *my* competition.

Becky handed the soft drink to the bachelor with a silky, "Here you go, darling." The word *darling* was wrapped in ownership. Becky had decided she liked the guy and made her move in staking her claim.

As soon as the bachelor had accepted the gift—*my gift*, I thought with a flash of irritation—Becky had held her hand out to Gemma.

Gemma looked confused as she took the offered hand and gave it a slight shake. "I'm Rebecca Hastings. What's your name, hon?"

"Gemma Mays," Gemma said carefully. I'd almost expected Gemma to have some kind of Southern accent as well, considering her sweet look and her name, which felt Southern for no logical reason other than it just did. But she was from Michigan, and her accent was remarkably clean.

"Gemma . . ." Becky mused. "What an interesting name."

My attention was drawn away when the first AD called me over the headset to attend to my actual duties. I wasn't there to gawk at the events unfolding for the cameras. I was there to work. And the first AD, Pete, was my master.

I sneaked out around the house to where Pete had summoned me. Or, at least, I *tried* to sneak. Chris met my eye and smiled at me.

It was a smile of recognition, of greeting, of gratitude to see me again.

It was a smile of all that and so much more.

I smiled back.

I couldn't help it. My mouth muscles tugged up before I knew what they were doing. And then my hand went up as if to wave, but then reality crashed over me in the form of Pete's voice in my headset asking why I wasn't already where he'd asked me to go.

My hand dropped to my side, and I shook my head no. Whether I meant to tell Chris no, he wasn't supposed to smile at me or to tell myself no, I couldn't smile at him, I wasn't certain.

Pete had me running all kinds of errands for the rest of the night. Getting things for Max, figuring out where a certain bachelorette had run off to when she was supposed to be on camera.

I knocked on her bedroom door at the same time I turned the handle and let myself in. "Alison?" I said and blinked at what I saw.

A tear-streaked woman on a cell phone.

"Where did you get that?" I demanded to know at the same time I crossed the room and snatched the phone from her hand. "She'll call you back in twelve weeks!" I said into the phone and snapped it closed before shaking it in front of her face. "Where did you get this? Who did I just hang up on?"

How had she ever smuggled a phone into the mansion?

Max would have her strung up by her toenails if he thought she'd been sent in as some kind of spy who planned on releasing spoilers to the public before episodes could be aired.

It turned out she was talking to her boyfriend, Nathan. She missed him. She realized that she loved him. She didn't ever imagine things would get this far with the *Vows* auditions. She hadn't meant to break the rules. Please don't tell on her. Please tell them she was just sick or something.

I was grinding my teeth by the time she finished blubbering and apologizing and pleading. I made no promises and hustled her to where she was supposed to be. Max glared at Pete, who in turn glared at me. I glared at everybody out of principle alone.

Not much had changed since I'd left the patio earlier that evening. The girls were a blur of legs and heels. My headache thumped a little harder behind my eyes, and I wondered if stress could give me a brain aneurism.

I was readying the call sheets to hand out to the crew and talent as soon as they cut for the night when I noticed the anomaly.

Gemma.

She'd curled up on one of the plush patio couches and had gone to sleep.

Two of the other bachelorettes were standing close together mocking their sleeping competition. It surprised me that women who were being gossipy and snide did it behind their hands like they were still five years old.

Lame.

They made it impossible to focus on getting the call sheets organized and marked so I didn't miss anyone on the list.

But more than the girls was the bachelor himself. He was an incredible distraction to me. A half smile slid into place as he looked down at Gemma. The fire in the nearby brazier added a romantic glow to his face. The firelight reflected the kindness shining in his eyes. He looked so handsome, so . . .

I blinked and tore my eyes away for a moment. I wasn't allowed to entertain those kinds of thoughts.

I couldn't be like the others.

Already, the females on the crew were starting to wear make-up and brush their hair. And it was only the first day of filming. I couldn't allow myself to fall into that silliness.

I heard a gasp from the patio and turned back to look in time to see Chris drop a kiss on Gemma's sleeping forehead.

The cameras were rolling. The other bachelorettes were fuming. Becky was probably digging gouges into her palms from the way her fake dagger fingernails were tucked tight into her fists. The audience would love it.

For no reason that made sense to me at all, I felt just like Becky at the moment. A little pain erupted in my chest. I closed my eyes, not wanting to see anything else.

* * *

I'd handed out the call sheets to everyone before the PA delivered sides to me. I now needed to hand those out too, which meant I had to go to rooms.

But I so did not want to go to Chris's room, not after he'd kissed a forehead on the first night of filming. I hated how sweet it had looked, hated how I'd felt as a result. None of it made any sense, and going to his room was the last thing I wanted to do. At least I didn't have to actually see him. I could knock, drop the sides in front of his door, and leave before he answered.

I ran into Robert after I'd delivered every single side but the bachelor's.

"Early call time," I said. "What are you still doing out so late?"

He sighed. "I told you not to tell me when call times are early. I don't ever look until I'm setting my alarm. And I'm interviewing some of the crew on their feelings about love."

I snorted at that, which led Robert to grin wickedly.

He swung the camera up onto his shoulder and pointed it in my direction. The red light flipped on. "So, Tor, tell us what you really think of love."

I smirked into the camera. "You do *not* want the jaded opinion of a single woman who's worked on *Vows* for three seasons."

"Actually, I want your opinion exactly *because* you've worked on *Vows* for three seasons and stubbornly remain single in spite of that rather blustery proposal by . . . what was that guy's name again? Harry? Larry?" The camera made it so I could only see half of Robert's grin. I hated it when he baited me like that.

"Lawrence. His name was Lawrence." I finally turned full-on to the camera. Robert loved little side interviews. Who knew what he did with them since I never saw any of them again. Even when the first season came out on DVD, there weren't bloopers or behind-the-scenes bonus features. But I felt angsty enough to let him carry on his interview and angsty enough to give him my full-on rant as to why love was an absurd pipe dream.

"Tell us about why you not only turned Lawrence down but turned him down in front of an entire concert hall." The red light from the camera stared at me. In a way, that red light was like the all-seeing eye of Robert—an extension of him that reached into people and made them say things and do things they wouldn't normally say and do simply because the glow of red swept their direction.

"I turned him down in front of an entire concert hall because he asked me in front of an entire concert hall."

Robert chuckled but in his way that happened only as a sound. His shoulders and body didn't move when he held the camera. He stayed steady—no bounce or sway to him in spite of the actual humor in his laugh. "Ouch," he said.

"Yeah. Ouch."

"Why not just say yes?" he asked.

I rolled my eyes. "You want me to go on camera with the faults of an ex-boyfriend? The early call time news must have cracked your reasoning because I am not that stupid."

"Not his faults. Don't say anything that'll get us all sued, but I'm genuinely curious why you turned down the offer of marriage from a guy who seemed pretty nice."

I waited precious moments, knowing we were just wasting time—time I didn't have and couldn't afford to spend. Nothing was worse than putting time on a credit card. On the set of *Vows*, the interest rate was just too high. "Look around, Robert. We see all the glitter and roses and candlelight of marriage proposals, but we're the ones dressing the set. We placed the roses, lit the candles, poured the wine. Believing in marriage after working on *Vows* would be like believing in fairies just because you went to Disneyland and met some girl in a wig and a short green dress who signs her name as Tinker Bell in those autograph books."

"So you didn't want to marry him because you don't believe in marriage?"

I shifted my weight, my muscles itching to move with the action of the things that had to be done before Max or Pete or a member of the cast or a member of craft services crackled in my ear piece demanding my attention before I could call it quits for the night. I needed to get to bed so I could get some sleep before call time the next morning. "I didn't want to marry him because I *do* believe in marriage. He just wanted to play house. Marriage is more than rings and dresses and tuxedos. It's more than the idea of playing house. It's genuine friendship, being there to mop up the tears even if you're the one who caused them. It's commitment and time and—" I shrugged. "Let's be honest . . . I'm already married."

"What? You? Married? Without telling me?" His eye not covered by the camera looked past me at something down the hall, but when I started to look behind me, he called my attention back to him. "Come on. Share the details, Tor."

I smiled wide for the red light. "I'm married to the job." I tapped the clipboard resting in the crook of my arm. "I'm already committed to the love of my life."

Robert laughed outright at that. "So you don't plan on getting married? You don't want me to get the set dressers in here to light a candle and place a few rose petals at your feet?"

"No, thanks. Marriage is for the 'other' people." I did air quotes around *other*. "Nothing is going to come between me and my illustrious career goal as a scriptwriter." I did the cheese smile and gave a nod.

The red light went off.

He hefted the camera up and off his shoulder. When I moved to turn back to the hall to Chris's room, Robert dropped an arm over my shoulder, almost like he was refusing to allow me to return to my duties. I was tired and starting to feel annoyed but knew Robert was just being chummy and hadn't done anything to earn my irritation. He hadn't kissed a girl's forehead right in front of me after making me think he liked me. "We should do a different kind of show—the anti-*Vow*. We could call it *Cynics*." He gave my shoulder a quick squeeze.

"Yeah, but then you couldn't work with me because you're a mushy romantic."

"Shh! Don't you go telling my wife that. She'll start expecting me to do a little set dressing at home. I can't afford flowers every day."

I looked to where the bouquets of roses sat in their water pots, waiting to be placed in the arms of the lovely bachelorettes. "No one can. Not these kinds of flowers anyway. But I've heard Mrs. Conder is a daisy sort of girl anyway. I've also heard that she gets fresh daisies every Saturday morning."

He lifted a shoulder in a shrug. "A good woman deserves flowers every once in a while."

"Yeah, well, you're a rarity. Once in a while to most guys means every three or so years. Definitely not every week."

He made some noncommittal noise that led me to believe he was embarrassed to have his soft-man side brought up.

I waved at him, taking advantage of his embarrassment so I could leave, then turned around to continue toward Chris's room.

I set the sides on the ground in front of the door and was about to knock, but the door flew open before my knuckles could fall against the wood.

Chris Caine stood before me. He didn't have his suit coat, and his tie had been undone so it hung in two black lines over his shirt. He looked at me with those eyes and that half smile . . .

But he'd also looked at Gemma the same way. I would not allow my knees to get all watery for a guy who was so obviously flaky when it came to who he half smiled for.

"Tori." He'd moved close enough to me that I felt him say my name in the warm breath that washed against my cheek. "I was hoping to be able to talk to you more before we began filming. I wanted to call you, but no one would give me your number and—"

I hurried to pick up the sides from the floor and thrust them into his hands. My own words rang in my head. *Nothing is going to come between me and my illustrious career goal as a scriptwriter.* I had a contract to the studio that I would not fraternize with the bachelor. This meant he couldn't be asking for my phone number, and did he really not remember that he'd just been all smoochy—sort of—with someone else just an hour prior?

"Here are your sides," I interrupted him. "They have your basic directions for filming tomorrow. Things the director would like to hear you say to certain girls, things they'd like you to do. Call time's super early, so you better get some beauty sleep—not that I'm saying you need . . ."

"Tori, I just want to talk to you for a minute." He glanced down the hall. "Can you come in for a second so we aren't out in the hall?"

He was inviting me into his room? Alone? Now? When I felt attracted to him and annoyed for feeling attracted and heartbroken over not ever getting the chance all those other undeserving girls were getting? I fumbled for a moment but then looked at my empty clipboard. "There are a lot of deliveries to make before I can get some sleep. So I can't really talk right now. I'll see you in the morning, bright and early!" I gave a fake smile and frowned as soon as I turned away from him.

"Tori . . ." he called from behind me.

I couldn't let myself turn around. "See you tomorrow!" I waved a hand behind me and kept walking.

I hoped Robert hadn't been lurking anywhere nearby with that camera of his as I escaped the mansion and fled to the safety of my own little bungalow on the grounds a short distance away.

When I closed my eyes, all I saw was that half smile.

I cursed in my mom's native Bajan and forced the image of Chris out of my mind by opening up my new book-club book on my iPad: *The Immortal Life of Henrietta Lacks.*

Maybe reading would take my mind off the one thing I could not allow myself to think about.

Of course, I did think of him.

Even as my mind filled with information about a woman who was long dead and the cells that changed the face of medicine, I thought of him.

Chapter 5

I woke up with a cold. The new schedule and staying up late to read the *Immortal Life of Henrietta Lacks* were the reasons I blamed. My stuffed head and sinuses made the dull headache from the day before a raging migraine. I probably had a sinus infection since even my teeth ached if I took a step too hard or tried to run anywhere.

Like I had time for a cold. It was one of those days where I would have loved to call in sick but instead kept a box of tissue with me and went through my duties as required.

Pete was exceptionally on edge. It felt like his voice was a constant annoying buzz in my headset all day. I didn't need someone telling me what to do all the time. I was a smart girl. I usually anticipated the needs of everyone on set and was already on my way to a solution long before Pete's voice interrupted me to tell me to fix something. Some evil part of me hoped Pete would get fired and I could be the first AD, and then I'd only have . . .

Well, I'd still have Max and Darren and half the production studio bossing me around.

"You might as well keep your stupid job, Pete," I grumbled softly to myself as I stared at the catering cart menu to get some lunch.

"Pete did a stupid job at what?"

I nearly dropped my tray in surprise and turned a glare in Chris's direction. "What are you doing sneaking up on people like that?" I demanded to know.

He held up his tray. "I didn't sneak. I just got in line."

I grunted and moved forward, realizing there wasn't anyone in front of me.

"So what did Pete do wrong?"

"Shh!" I cast a hurried glance around. "Are you trying to get me in trouble? You do not have to repeat everything you hear. And aren't you supposed to be dining with the girls?"

"Sorry, it's just that no one else is around, and I wanted to have a minute to talk to you and—"

I put up a finger to silence Chris. Pete was squawking in my headset again. "What?" I asked Pete. Chris looked like he was about to answer, thinking I was talking to him. I gave him a look that shut him up again.

"One of the girls is covered in hives?" I asked Pete.

Chris nodded knowingly. "Max wanted to film it, but she won't come out of her room. They filmed me trying to talk her out, but she's one stubborn woman. She doesn't want the world to see her out of sorts. Max refuses to leave her door until he gets his shot. They finally sent me down here for lunch."

Chris said all of this over Pete's instructions. I scowled at Chris again. "Sorry, Pete. Can you say that again? I couldn't hear you." I plugged the ear not covered in the headset with my hand to make sure Chris Caine understood he needed to stay quiet. He finally caught on and fell silent.

"Yes, I'll be right up," I said, then tossed one last sad look at the catering cart.

"I'll save you something, Tori," the caterer said.

I put my tray back and gave a curt nod to the bachelor before rushing upstairs in the girls' wing to see what I could do to help.

"She's apparently allergic to one of the chemicals in the hot tub," the medic said once I reached them and gained access to the room. Though Max had never been let in with his camera, the medic and I were allowed in because the bachelorette wanted us to fix the problem as soon as possible.

To be fair, she really did look like a splotchy, puffy, pink frog. I could see why she didn't want to leave her room, but she'd also signed on for reality TV. What was the point if she never let the TV viewers see *this* reality?

Max was furious and told me he'd get me something nice if I managed to talk her out of her room.

"Did you know you had allergies before now, hon?" I asked, making sure to keep my tone as soothing as possible.

She shook her head miserably. "My parents had saltwater pools."

I nodded. A chlorinated pool would have a totally different pH balance than a saltwater pool. The medic continued his exam while I kept her talking. "Saltwater, huh? Where did you grow up?"

I already knew. Her name was Terri Walker. She was from Houston, Texas. She hated guys who made fart jokes, and she wanted a guy who would look after her like her daddy did. If the bachelor chose Terri, I was going to stick sharpened pencils in my eyes.

She told me about her home in her private gated community and then went back to lamenting the lumpy skin covering her body. She'd just die if her friends back home saw her in this condition. How was she ever going to be a real actress if all the public saw was her looking like a freak? And didn't we know that saltwater pools were better for people with delicate skin?

I managed to hang on to my smile while she ranted and spewed and cried.

Sometimes my job felt more like babysitting.

"I completely understand your pain," I said. "But think of how amazingly strong you'd look if you went walking out that bedroom door like it was no big deal. People would think of you as a confident, intelligent woman if you can hold your head high and shrug this off like it's nothing."

Her shoulders straightened as she considered my words. I had to give her credit for that. My thoughts at least gave her pause. But she went back to ranting, and we ping-ponged between me giving positive-attitude pep talks and her blaming the studio for doing this to her on purpose.

Which we hadn't, though Max would have arranged it if he'd thought he could have gotten away with it. The fact that it happened naturally would be a bonus to Max. Even with her locking herself in her room, he had the footage necessary to make some riveting drama. Of course, if she stayed hidden in her room, she would look like the shallow, vapid, drama queen she really was.

"But they'll all think I'm a hideous beast if people see me like this."

I'm already there, I thought. Instead I said, "But directors care more about what you're made of on the inside. If you let this little thing beat you, you'll prove you aren't strong enough to really handle Hollywood."

"If you run out and get this cream, she should be healed up pretty quickly." The medic handed me a sheet of paper.

"That settles things," Terri said. "If you get the cream, I'll come out."

"Then I'll hurry." I smiled wide for her, really wanting to roll my eyes instead, and left the room armed with the paper.

It was almost noon. I hadn't had breakfast and, thanks to Terri and her *delicate skin*, I wouldn't be getting lunch either. My sinuses felt worse than ever. How was I supposed to get healthy if I was skipping meals?

I left the mansion grounds, looked up the nearest pharmacy, and fed the coordinates to Tom—the name I'd given my GPS.

It was nice to get away from the mansion for a minute. It was nice to see real people doing real things. It was nice to *not* see Chris everywhere

I turned. The break from the set felt vital to my ability to breathe, and I silently thanked Terri for her delicate skin.

Armed with my paper detailing exactly what I needed, my phone with the medic's number already on screen in case I had questions, and my purse, I went to the two closest pharmacies. Neither store had the cream. Though the break from the set was nice, I knew Pete would feed me to the producer's Chihuahuas if I didn't get back with the right product so the show could go on.

I spied a Walgreens on the corner and made a quick turn into the driveway. I grabbed my purse and the paper and entered the store.

And nearly ran straight into a familiar face. It took a moment for me to realign my thinking from people I knew from work to people I knew socially. I could tell she was doing the same.

"Shannon, right?" Shannon from book club.

"Yes," she said. "And you're Tori?"

It was nice to see she'd remembered my name with no prompting from me. Not many people could do that.

"Great to see you," I said, looking around at the place where we'd run into each other. "I didn't know you worked at this Walgreens." I thought she worked somewhere closer to where Ruby lived.

She shrugged. "I just fill in now and then. Do you live around here?"

"Kinda," I said. "The house we're using for the show I'm working on is a few miles away." This was likely information I shouldn't be sharing, but Shannon didn't seem like the fan-girl type. She probably never watched reality TV. Besides, it wasn't like I'd handed out the exact address to the mansion. I held out the paper the medic had given me. "But I was sent to find a special cream for sensitive skin. One of the girls on the set has developed a reaction to something in the hot tub. The onsite nurse told me what to get, but I've already made two stops, and neither store had it."

"Let me help you look." She let the door she'd been holding open fall shut as she reached for my paper. She practically led me right to it, which made me sigh in relief. I'd never have found it on my own, and I now strongly suspected the other two stores *had* stocked it. They just had ignorant staff who didn't know where to look for it when I'd asked for help.

"I can't believe you knew where something so obscure was located." I held the tube of cream in wonder. "Thank you."

Shannon shrugged again.

"It's a lot of schooling to be a pharmacist, isn't it?"

Her eyes widened as she nodded emphatically. "Oh yes! Definitely that!" She walked back to the front of the store with me.

"You have two children?" I asked, remembering her stepdaughter.

"Yes, Landon and Keisha."

"Is it hard? Being a mom with all the responsibilities of your job?" It was something I'd always wondered. I worked crazy hours. I often wondered how women with careers made everything fit together. I could barely find time to water my plants.

"I find that people make time for the things that matter most to them." She smiled the kind of smile that said her kids were one of those things that mattered most.

We'd come to the registers, and I got in line behind an old woman who was trying to be sneaky about reading one of the tabloids on soap opera stars.

"Thank you so, so, so much, Shannon. It's been a crazy day. I couldn't go back empty-handed, and I was starting to worry I'd never find this. Every minute delayed is a minute Pete will be saying things that aren't nice with my name attached to them. You have no idea how much I appreciate your help."

"Not a problem. It's what I do." Her tone indicated she really hadn't thought of me as an inconvenience. She'd been glad to help. I appreciated that fact almost more than I appreciated the help in the first place. I also appreciated that she was like me. She remembered names and faces with the same ease.

Lawrence had called the book club stupid. Robert had told me I had nothing in common with women who were so much older. But in that moment, I decided that both men were entirely wrong. Commonalities among friends had nothing to do with age. Friendship had nothing to do with age.

Shannon held up the banana she'd been holding. "Well, I'm on break, so I better get to it."

I grinned, feeling sheepish for not noticing the food in her hands before. "Sorry I interrupted it."

"Not a problem." She waved away my apology and, with it, my worry that I'd been an inconvenience.

I put my hand on her arm as she started to turn away. "I started that book you recommended," I said, wanting to let Shannon know her book choice had made an impact on me. We talked about the book for a short

moment, and Shannon assured me the entire book was as interesting as
the beginning.

"Good," I said. "I'm really glad you chose it; I feel smarter already for
having read just that first part."

She laughed and waved good-bye, and we went to our separate cars. I
hurried to get back to the mansion before I started getting ranty texts from
Pete, Max, and half the crew.

Seeing Shannon had reminded me that I really needed to finish reading
the book for book club, which was on Saturday. There were only four more
days until Saturday, and since that day was entirely morning shots of a big
brunch scene where Max hoped one of the girls would start a catfight that
involved flinging eggs Benedict at each other, we'd be done filming by late
afternoon. Which meant I could drive up for book club, then stop by my
house to sleep in my own bed, bring in my mail, and water my plants.

I found I really wanted to be at book club to support Shannon's book.
She was nice and funny, and I liked her. The least I could do was show up
having actually read the book she'd picked out.

Back at the mansion, the bachelorette with the rash had finally come
out of her room. Max was happy, which meant Pete was happy, which
meant no one seemed to care that it took me so long to obtain the cream
Terri slathered over her body as soon as she yanked it from my hands.

I felt Chris's eyes on me while the rest of the cast and crew fussed over
smoothing cream over Terri's hives. His eyes stayed on me as I hurried off
determined to find something to do in a place his eyes could not follow.
Later that night, I dropped his sides and call sheet off in his room when
he was still filming. I couldn't risk him trying to talk to me alone again.
I couldn't risk it because I wanted to talk alone with him. I left the sides
and call sheet on his pillow, noting that he'd made his bed. None of the
mansion's occupants were granted maid service in their actual rooms.
Chris would have had to make his own bed. Which was a detail I couldn't
stop thinking about after I went away.

I spent all my spare moments the next two days avoiding Chris and
reading the book for discussion at book club. It helped take my mind
off of my aching head and my sniffly nose and the scratchy tightening in
my throat. Reading had become a way to hide in little corners where I
remained relatively safe from Chris's notice.

He tried to get me alone to talk to me every time he saw me when the
cameras weren't filming. I sometimes felt his eyes on me even when the
cameras *were* rolling and hoped no one else noticed.

I had to be curt and abrupt when dealing with him because he obviously didn't understand he'd signed a contract. He obviously didn't understand that *I* had signed a contract and that by continually trying to be personal with me, he put us both in big jeopardy. He was going to mess up my career goals if he didn't get his head on straight. And I didn't trust my cold-muddled head to be around him. Plus, I didn't want him to see me with my nose all chafed and swollen from constant wiping and blowing.

Finding little alcoves and cubbies where no one ever went in the mansion had really helped. I couldn't leave the building until we'd wrapped for the day, but when there was a half hour or so that no one needed me, it was nice to snuggle into a private place and get my reading done and blow my nose without an audience. I hated being sick around other people.

A wide window seat hidden by a thick set of draperies was something I very much doubted anyone else in the mansion even knew existed.

It was the perfect place to hole up during the lunch break—especially with the warm sun shining through and heating the space between the glass and the drapes. My body had been shivering with the chills all morning. I leaned my back against the glass and tucked my legs underneath me. It was absolutely perfect.

At least it was until the bachelor found me.

"You doing okay?"

The warm Southern accent was an arrow dipped in Icy-Hot straight to my heart. It really bugged me that Chris's voice melted me and froze me all at once. How had he found me here? I tried to hide my wad of used tissues behind my back.

"Did you need something?" I asked with a look that clearly indicated I had no desire to be bothered. Of course, with my stuffed nose, the word *something* came out more like *subthig*.

"I was wondering if you needed anything." He pulled out an apple. "They say an apple a day keeps the doctor away." He smiled wide—that charming, melt-a-girl-into-a-puddle-of-sighs smile. I couldn't let him see how that smile affected me.

I kept my tone frigid enough that he should have dropped the smile and scampered away with his tail between his legs. "Would it keep *you* away if I throw it at your head?"

"Nope. But, then, I'm not a doctor." He placed the apple next to me. Then, without asking, he scooted onto the window seat next to me, arranging the drapes so we were hidden from anyone else's prying eyes. "Did I do something to you? I don't understand why you're completely nice to everyone else but you treat me like I have a disease or something. I'm sorry if I did something wrong. Tell me what it was so I can fix it."

I blinked in surprise at this direct course of action he'd taken. The fact that we were now snuggled into a single window seat and that if anyone found us there we'd both be in some pretty intense trouble made me want to lash out even more. He couldn't be here—not with me. He could have done it with any one of the bachelorettes in the mansion but *not* with me. How did he not see that?

"You haven't done anything wrong," I said finally. "I'm sorry if I came across as rude to you. I just . . . want to stay focused on my job."

"And your job disallows friendships?"

"My job disallows fraternizing." I gave him a meaningful look, hoping he'd finally get it and go away, leaving me alone to wish things were different.

Because I wanted to talk to him.

I wanted him to smile at me and *for* me and *because* of me.

I wanted to get to know him better.

"A friendly conversation is hardly fraternizing," he said.

But he was wrong. If he knew what was going on in my head during the friendly conversation so far, he'd know he was wrong.

"Well, with my drippy, swollen nose and my watery eyes, I'm not really much up to friendly conversation either."

"I think you look kinda cute with a cold."

I ignored that—or tried to—by turning my attention back to my iPad.

He took the hint and changed the subject by tapping the edge of the iPad cover. "I assume you're reading a book since there isn't Internet anywhere on the property." He moved closer so he could read the screen, close enough our legs were touching. He peered over my shoulder. "Ah. *The Immortal Life of Henrietta Lacks*. Are you enjoying it?"

"Have you read it?"

"Nope. That's why I'm asking you if you're enjoying it. Maybe I'll want to read it later."

"Do you read?" I asked. His file had indicated that he was very well read, but I'd assumed he'd put that on his application because it made him look good. Most of the applicants did. What they meant to say was that they'd seen the movies based on the books. Not that I was opposed to moviegoers. As someone who aspired to be a screenwriter, I was very much in favor of moviegoers. I just hated it when people weren't honest about themselves. The books in the library were there to create an opportunity for the bachelors and bachelorettes who lied about being well read to be caught in their lies.

Sometimes I wasn't a very nice person.

Chris furrowed his brow. "Are you assuming I'm illiterate because of my accent? You do know a person can be Southern and smart. Most of us are." His leg moved so it wasn't touching mine any longer, and he looked like he might scoot on back out of the window seat.

Now that he was there, the last thing I wanted was for him to leave again. "Sorry. I'm not trying to be rude. Of course you can read. You'd never have made it through the audition process without an abundance of education. Those applications sometimes feel like they require a lawyer to translate them."

He relaxed a little—enough to stay but not enough to make his leg touch mine again. "Sorry if I seemed touchy. People make assumptions about me all the time because of the accent. Nothing bothers me more than people assuming I haven't gone beyond the second grade just because of a little drawl. It's wrong for people to make assumptions about others they haven't taken the time to get to know."

"I agree." And I immediately felt ashamed. I'd made assumptions about the entire cast of *Vows* without bothering to know any of them beyond their files. "Yes, it's a really good book. I'm actually surprised to be enjoying it so much, since it's not anything like my typical read."

"What's it about?" His leg came closer, the energy warming between us, but we were still separated by a small space.

"A black woman in the sixties who ended up dying of cervical cancer, but her cells lived on in cultures and became one of the most important tools in modern medicine."

The Immortal Life of Henrietta Lacks had managed to hook me. It gave me the fury and indignation the other ladies in the book club had expected to see when I'd discussed *The Help* with them. For reasons I couldn't understand, the injustices to Henrietta, her children, and many other black people who'd had medical tests done on them without their consent, or even their knowledge, struck me much harder than that of the plight of the maids. The idea of using poverty-stricken black people as lab rats made me sick. How could humans do that to humans? Who cared what color anyone was? How could a person watch another person cry, be in pain, *die*, and not want to do something to help?

"So what important tools?" Chris asked, pulling me out of my thoughts.

"Advancements in infertility treatments, cancer treatments, vaccinations—all kinds of things."

"Cool. So if this isn't your typical book, why are you reading it?"

I hesitated. Telling Lawrence about my book club hadn't turned out so well. I didn't want to be made fun of again, but Chris wasn't a potential dating option. He did say we were only having a friendly conversation. "My book club. I belong to a book club, where we meet and discuss books we've read." At least that's what I tried to say. It was hard to make it sound as smart and savvy as I felt my book club to be when my plugged nose made me sound like a stuffy two-year-old.

He tilted his head in a way that showed interest, not mockery. "Really? Is this with friends from college or something?"

"Nope, not for school. It's just for fun. And I'm the youngest in the group. The oldest is in her sixties."

Here was his chance to be like Robert and tell me I should be hanging out with women my own age.

"That actually would make the group more interesting. You get a wider variety of opinions and experiences that way. I was in a book group with some of my college buddies, where we wrote papers on the books we read and then met to discuss our findings. It was a little nerdy, since we hadn't been assigned to do the papers or even read the books, but I learned a lot from the experience. Being that we were all the same age, though, we had a lot of similar opinions. Age variety would have made a difference."

I'm sure the surprise was written all over my face.

He grinned. "You *did* think I was some ignorant hick, didn't you?"

"No, but I hadn't realized you'd gone to college." I didn't remember reading anything about his education. Perhaps I had skimmed over it since I'd already made up my mind that he was a farmhand. "Where did you go?"

"University of Georgia."

"I thought you worked on a farm."

"I do work a farm. I love that more than anything. The early morning sun coming up and kissing the tops of the plants—it's heaven. We grow peanuts. It's my favorite joke."

I gave him a look that said I didn't see a joke anywhere.

His grin widened. "You know . . . I work for peanuts . . ."

I laughed, finally seeing the humor. His knee bumped mine as we shared that laugh together, and he left his leg resting against mine.

I stopped laughing, my breath catching in my throat as I looked up at him. He licked his bottom lip and leaned in. All I had to do was lean as well—give him the cue that I liked him, that I was interested. All I had to do was . . .

"I have to go!" I jumped up from the window seat straight into the curtains, getting tangled enough that I stumbled. Several of the used tissues went flying and now littered the floor around the window.

Chris caught my arm to keep me from falling. And when I turned again to assure him I was stable and not falling anywhere, I was caught in some strange sort of embrace. Only now we were exposed to the open air of the room. There were no curtains to hide behind. Now we were out where anyone could see us.

"You don't have to go," he said.

"I do." I looked away and nodded with vigor, which made my stuffy head hurt even more. I'd need to see if the medic had any cold medicine that didn't make a person drowsy. The cold had put me off guard enough. I couldn't let some drowsy medication make me a bigger idiot than I already was.

If someone saw us together?

What had I been thinking, allowing him to stay in a little window seat with me like that? I'd be fired immediately. He'd be sent back to the farm. I'd be a blacklisted Hollywood scandal.

I had to keep him at arm's length. I pushed my hand against his chest, giving us the literal space I was trying to keep firmly in my mind.

"Really, Chris . . ." I closed my eyes. Did he hear the way I said his name? Did he hear my attraction to him? "I need this job. And if someone saw us together right now, they would assume that—"

"That what?" he interrupted, taking hold of the hand that I'd been using to push him away. "That we're talking? We're not doing anything wrong, Tori."

I loved the way he said my name almost more than I loved saying his. "We are." I insisted. "I have a very specific job to do. And hanging out with the cast is not part of that. I have to go." I sneezed in the middle of my grand exit and groaned at the pain of the harsh tissue against my nose, rubbing the skin raw.

Then I remembered that tissues still littered the ground. I grumbled and bent over to pick them all up and stuff them into my pocket.

Chris was on his knees picking up the ones that had been caught under the curtain. I cringed as he handed them to me, mortified that he'd touched my used tissue. He really must be a farm hand if something like that didn't gross him out.

"Chris, I like you. I'm just not allowed to hang out with you." There. Honesty would triumph.

"Tori, I like you too. But I didn't sign anything that said I couldn't talk to who I wanted to talk to. However, if it makes you uncomfortable, I'll give you your space."

I nodded. Hating that he said it out loud, even while, at the same time, it was what I wanted. Wasn't it? I nodded again, not trusting myself to speak, and turned away, hating that I sneezed twice more before leaving the room.

I heard a small "Bless you" following the sneezes and hated that it was cute that he'd done that.

He kept his word for the rest of the day. He didn't once try to engage me in any kind of conversation, though I still felt his gaze on me and had to really focus to keep my gaze from falling and lingering on him. I'd decided we'd made some real progress.

At least I'd thought so until I got back to my bungalow and found a box of lotion tissues with a note taped to the top. I held it up to the porch light above my bungalow door.

> *Tori,*
> *I really don't want you to be uncomfortable.*
> *Hope these tissues make the cold a little easier.*
> *Take some vitamin C.*
> *You've got an adorable sneeze.*
> *~ C*

I gasped and hurried to stuff the note into my back jeans pocket, then tossed a quick glance around to be certain no one saw. No one was anywhere near me, and it was a dark night. No one would have had any idea what the little box meant, but I felt the need to hurry and hide it regardless.

My heart hammered as I unlocked my door and shoved my way through it, rushing to close and lock it behind me.

I placed the box of tissue on the table as if it were a centerpiece—a lovely bouquet of flowers. The box had a floral print. Delicate pink roses. I wondered if that was on purpose. Was this his way of sending me flowers in secret?

Paper flowers . . . They were better than any real ones I'd ever been given, at least that's what the flutter in my stomach was telling me.

And tissues laced with lotion? I'd never once had a boyfriend do anything so thoughtful.

"Chris isn't your boyfriend, idiot Tori," I said out loud to myself. "He's the bachelor."

But that didn't stop me from smiling as I took one of those soft, lotion-laced tissues and used it to wipe my nose. In a weird sort of way, it was like getting a soothing one-armed hug from someone who cared, from someone who wanted me to be comfortable.

Chapter 6

THE NEXT MORNING, WITH CHRIS's note taped safely at the back of my clipboard so I could look at it whenever I wanted without getting caught, even Pete—grumbling about stuff he'd failed to do but that he planned on giving me the blame for—didn't bother me.

My head felt lucid, and the body chills were gone. I'd taken the vitamin C like Chris had suggested. It must have been working.

Even Becky, with her diva attitude as she stomped down most of the other bachelorettes, didn't bother me. I learned a lot about Chris by watching him interact with the girls. He didn't like being served all the time but actually enjoyed being the one to do the serving. He didn't like gossip or backhanded behavior. He liked singing off-key while he worked on anything and loved to have the girls join in—even when they sounded worse than he did. He liked dogs. He was afraid of spiders; from the sounds of it, he was more afraid than I was, which meant it was good that he and I could never be together. Every relationship needed a spider killer. I needed a guy who could fill that role since I'd already decided the spider killer would *never* be me.

We broke for lunch. Most of the meals for the cast were filmed, so we were working while they ate, but when we weren't filming during a meal break, we all ate together—one big, happy family of cast and crew.

I made sure to stay in a very public place in case Chris decided to come find me again. He did find me and sat almost directly across from me at the table.

I gave him a pointed look, to which he made a motion to the table. Every other seat had been taken.

How could he be blamed for that?

He didn't talk to me at all. He talked to Robert, who sat right next to me, and Gary, who sat on the other side. He talked to Pete and to several of the bachelorettes who were scattered in the nearby vicinity. He asked them if making movies was what they'd wanted to do when they were growing up and how they'd fallen into their current roles on set and if they planned on going further up the silver-screen ladder.

He didn't talk to me at all until he'd exhausted conversation with the others. Only then did he finally address me. "What about you, Victoria?"

"Call her Tori," Robert said, bumping my shoulder with his. "No one calls her Victoria."

Chris smiled, pleased at having been given permission to use my nickname so casually. "Okay, Tori. You've been pretty quiet during lunch. How about you? Any thoughts of moving up to director in your future?"

"Not really." I felt squirmy inside, like a bug being too closely inspected by a kid with a magnifying glass—wondering when the kid would shift the glass so the sun sizzled it to the ground.

"Our Tori is a writer." Robert announced this proudly, as if I was moving on to great things.

"A writer? Really?" Chris steepled his fingers under his chin. I tried not to notice how elegant he looked when he did that.

I nodded and stuffed a forkful of portabella mushrooms into my mouth so I wouldn't have to talk.

"What sorts of things do you write, Tori?" Chris asked, resting those steepled fingers against his cheek.

My name seriously never sounded so good coming from anyone else's lips. I chewed faster, realizing everyone was looking at me, waiting for an answer. Several of the people on crew had no idea I wrote and were suddenly interested in me in a way they hadn't been before.

"Screenplays." The one-word answer should have been enough of an answer, but then Gary—one of the grips next to me—asked what genre. And Ben across from me wanted to know plot summaries of stuff I'd already written.

We spent the last of the lunchtime with me explaining plots to a couple of mysteries, a few romances, and one drama.

Even the bachelorettes were listening, probably hoping one of the parts would be perfect for them.

I couldn't help but let my guard down. I got more excited and animated as I explained the characters and why they did what they did and how it would all end.

None listened with more interest than Chris.

As I explained the plots, he managed to pick the theme and tone of each screenplay. He was right on with every one of them—even with having precious little information given. He asked intelligent questions about settings, plot points, and characterization.

It was glaringly obvious that he had, indeed, spent a lot of time writing papers dissecting others' writing.

He also gave suggestions for ways to improve plots—ways to hide the killer from the audience for a little while longer, ways to keep the hero and the heroine apart for a little longer, ways to make the writing stronger, ways I hadn't ever considered on my own.

And I knew that as soon as I was alone in my bungalow, I'd get out my computer and make the changes he'd suggested.

He smiled like he also knew I'd be making those changes. I couldn't help it. I returned his soft smile.

Touché, Bachelor, I thought. *Touché.* He got up and cleared his tray, seemingly happy to have been able to make me talk in an unguarded manner.

"I wasn't aware you wrote screenplays," Max said, pulling me from my thoughts as I watched Chris leave the room. "You should send them to the studio. Darren might be interested in purchasing them from you."

Tears of shock and elation welled up in my eyes. "Really? You think he might?" I'd never sent them to my own studio because I wasn't sure what the reaction would be. They didn't really green-light movies. They were a TV studio doing TV series. But they had done a few made-for-TV movies . . .

Max was still talking through the static of shock in my head. "I was listening to your layout of the summaries. A few of those have quite a bit of potential. Send them over to me. I'll talk to Darren about them personally.

"Really, sir?"

"Of course, really. You're a loyal part of our team. We'll want to support your creative endeavors in the same manner you support ours." He gave me a look, one I didn't dare interpret, one that felt like he was calling me out somehow for betraying the production studio. Did he know? Did he know I had some strange kind of schoolgirl crush on their bachelor that I couldn't manage to get over?

Whether he knew or not, I felt the warning of his words. He was giving my writing career a chance because he appreciated my loyalty. He wouldn't be willing to give me that chance if my loyalty failed him. I understood. I'd be more careful.

* * *

I stayed true to myself for several days—avoiding Chris whenever possible. He made it hard because he always managed to delay me for an extra moment when we did find ourselves with a moment to talk. He made sure he used the moments. Part of me wanted to think it was because he had a secret attraction to me the way I had to him.

But watching him helped me see that he was like that with everyone.

And it didn't matter because Max had personally hand delivered my screenplays to Darren. He'd told me so the day after he'd done it. He waved away my gratitude and told me not to thank him just yet. He also told me Darren was seriously busy and might be several weeks or even months in making a decision.

The next day I left the mansion to pick up a few things for Pete, for Chris, and for a handful of the bachelorettes. When I returned, I delivered all the necessary goods to the necessary people, and I ended with Chris, delivering his tuxedo for the night's candle ceremony.

I knocked on his door, feeling the flutters of seeing him, making eye contact with him. His voice came from deep within, which meant he was in his actual bedroom and not the small sitting room at the front. "Come in!" he called.

"I just have your tuxedo!" I yelled back through the door. "I can just leave it here, and you can—"

"No, bring it in, please. I don't want it to wrinkle," he called back to me, interrupting my decision to not have to make eye contact at all.

"Just leave it in the coat closet in the sitting room and then get out of there," I whispered to myself before opening the door.

I made a beeline for the closet, but Chris appeared in the doorframe to his bedroom. I stumbled at seeing him but looked at the ground and kept heading for the closet. I swung the door open wide to hide Chris from my view and hung up the tuxedo.

Taking a deep breath for strength, I closed the door and turned to face the only exit to the hallway.

"I don't think I can go through with this tonight, Tori," he said before I could make it past him.

That made me stop. Other bachelors had said similar things. It was my personal job to keep them on task. This was something that couldn't be left for another person to do. This was my job. If I somehow failed at my job, it would reflect badly on Pete, and Pete would make sure I paid for it. Then Max would find out I'd failed at something, and then he might not be as enthusiastic to take my screenplays directly to Darren in the future.

I had to handle it. The candle ceremony was important because it was the big banquet of food almost too beautiful to eat and the ceremony after when the bachelor lit the candles of the girls who had made it through the first week.

Three of the girls would not have their candles lit. Three of the girls would be going home.

I hoped Becky was one of the three. Becky *and* Alison.

Becky because she was a complete monster of a female. And Alison because she loved her boyfriend back home. I had the cell phone I'd taken from her to prove it. The idiot guy texted her every day several times . . . the exact same message: *I love you. Come home and marry me.*

I kept the phone in my bungalow, hidden underneath my clothes hamper so no one would find it. I knew she wanted to go home. It was written all over her pretend smiles and eyes that seemed to wander off—looking to a distance no one else could see.

It was bad enough to have one of the bachelorettes want out, but the bachelor had no outs. I slowly turned and allowed myself to meet Chris's eye. "Why would you say that?"

"I have to pick three girls today. I have to pick three people and tell them they aren't good enough to make me happy. How do you do that? How do you tell someone they aren't what you want at all?"

"Don't light their candle." My simple answer didn't impress him.

"Could you be that heartless?" he asked.

"We're all a little heartless sometimes. But then I've never agreed to be a bachelor before, which is a new level of rejection. I get rejected enough with my writing that the sheer empathy I have for those being rejected would never allow me to be the one to go skeet shooting with their dreams." I yelled, "Pull!" and mimed shooting an imaginary skeet with a shotgun.

Chris put his hand on mine and gently lowered my arm. "Exactly. I don't think I'm up to this." He moved away from me and began pacing. "I think I might throw up. Can you tell them I'm sick?"

"Absolutely not." I walked back over and opened the closet. "Don't think of it as skeet shooting. Sorry about that example. That was cold." I pointed at the tuxedo and smiled. "Don't think of it as giving three rejections. Think of it as giving twenty-seven acceptances."

He crossed the room and tugged the door carefully out of my hand and shut it behind me, effectively pinning me between him and the door.

"What if I don't want to accept any of the twenty-seven?"

"You signed a contract," I whispered.

"So you keep reminding me."

"You've only had a week. You don't know that you don't want any of them after only a week."

"You're wrong. I know a lot of things after only a week." He stepped away, pacing again. "I'm just not really cut out for this."

"Then why did you go through the audition process?"

He frowned and paced more energetically. "It's complicated."

I sighed and sat on the couch in the sitting area so I could at least watch him pace in comfort. "What's the real problem here?" I asked.

"I don't have three girls picked out."

"I can give you a hint on one but only because it's in the best interest of the show."

He halted midpace. "Okay. Who?"

"You've got to promise you won't tell anyone I told you any of this. You could get her into a lot of trouble with the studio. She could be sued for breach of contract. I could be sued for breach of contract because I didn't go all Nazi on her and turn her in the moment I found out."

"I promise everything you say to me will stay with me."

I looked him long and hard in the eyes before finally nodding and agreeing to trust him. Not that I didn't trust him already, because instinct told me he was trustworthy, but more than that, I wanted an excuse to look at his eyes for a minute.

Then I told him about Alison, with her cell phone and marriage proposal waiting for her at home. She'd only have to wait two weeks until the episode aired on TV and then she could be with her boyfriend again.

He laughed. "That explains a lot."

"What?"

"She's been giving me the strangest answers to questions, things that make her sound totally yonkers." His Southern accent made the word *yonkers* sound cute.

His smile faded, and his brow furrowed again. "What about the other two, Tori. What do I do about the other two?"

"Think about things you don't really like, and then think about the girls who've displayed those characteristics. You know who you would never ask out again for a second date. Make sure those girls are the ones on the list. You're smart, Chris. You'll make the right choices, but . . ." I stood. "I better go. I need to make sure the girls are all ready for the night."

"Thanks, Tori. I know you're busy. But I appreciate that you took time for me."

"I'm happy to spend time with you." And when our eyes met, I thought of what Max had said about me being loyal to the studio and hurried to modify the statement. "It's my job, after all."

"Right. Your job." He nodded.

I tried, and failed, to smile. And then I left, wondering why I'd had to take a good moment and sour it.

"Because it *is* your job," I muttered to myself. I suddenly hated my job.

The day had gone pretty well until I stopped by Gemma's room to make sure she was on schedule. I'd checked everyone else, and everyone had almost completed perfecting their hair, wardrobe, and makeup before the big night.

Even Alison, who wanted nothing more to do with the show, was already dressed and ready to go to the ceremony.

Gemma, on the other hand . . . Well, Gemma wasn't ready for anything. She was still in her regular clothes from the day.

I stared at her, blinking, unable to comprehend what she was trying to pull with not getting ready when her call sheet clearly stated the time for dinner. "What's going on here? You've got to be ready in less than forty-five minutes."

Gemma's lip quivered. "I don't want to go to the candle ceremony."

"Are you kidding? You don't get to miss this; it's part of the schedule—part of your contract. Why don't you want to go?" *What is with everyone and their issues today?* I wondered.

Her lip quivered harder, and her eyes swam in tears. "It's not like I'm here thinking love is going to find me or anything stupid like that. Don't know that I even want to find love yet. I was just hoping to make it to the end and win the cash prize to help pay for school and to help my mom out a little. I thought I had a chance to be the last girl standing, but these other girls . . . they know what they're doing. You know my candle will be the one unlit tonight. I'm the only one who fell asleep at the cocktail party. I don't even know how to paint my nails or do my hair like the other girls do." She groaned and fell back on her bed, grabbing an armload of pillows to bury her head under. "I'm ridiculous."

She *had* been the only one to fall asleep. She had also been the only one to have Chris pay that special attention of settling his suit coat over her shoulders, slipping off her shoes for her, and dropping a gentle kiss on her forehead.

No one else got a forehead kiss.

The entire scene had been tender, sweet, achingly private in a way viewers loved. My own heart felt a little cracked after having watched it. Every time my mind went to the crack to feel around those jagged edges of my heart and wonder why they were there, I had to make myself refocus. We had signed contracts that said it couldn't hurt our feelings when he kissed the forehead of a sleeping bachelorette.

It did hurt my feelings.

But it wasn't supposed to.

The worst part of it was how much I really liked Gemma. She was sweet in a very real way. Sweet enough for a boy raised with excellent Southern manners.

The very act of his chivalry and her innocence would make her a favorite in the ratings.

I didn't know what it would make her in the eyes of Christopher Caine. But like it or not, she had to go to the candle ceremony. Even if I was the one not liking it.

I glanced at her hair. She had tried curling it, but she'd done the curls too tight and looked like the victim of a bad perm.

Against my better judgment, I swept the brush off her dressing table. "Here. Let me help."

Her eyes went wide as she stared at my reflection in the mirror. "Seriously? You'll help me?"

"A girl should look her best for her first candle ceremony. I'm absolutely certain." I smiled at her reflection and went to work softening the curls around her face so they made a gentle frame and pulling enough of her hair back to be elegant yet leaving enough draping over her neck and shoulders to be flirtatious.

I went the extra mile and applied her make-up and nail polish as well.

I hated myself when she was finished and I stood staring at the results of my labors in the mirror.

She looked beautiful. Even a total idiot would drop his jaw over the Gemma seated in front of me now.

Chris wasn't an idiot.

Why was I doing this to myself? Why was I helping her get the guy who never left my thoughts? The guy who'd made it clear he liked me as much as I liked him?

Because the contract says it's your job, Tori.

And it did.

And I always did the work I'd agreed to do.

Gemma stared at herself, turning her head right and left so she could see from all angles. I gave her a hand mirror so she could see the back of her hair as well.

"Wow," she finally said. "Where were you when I went to prom? You wouldn't believe the pictures I have of that night proving I am totally incompetent when it comes to my own hair."

"Well, tonight the pictures will show that you're beautiful," I said. "And you didn't need me to show that. You were beautiful in your own way before I got here." I smiled at her in the mirror.

Instead of smiling back, she jumped to her feet, spun around, and gave me a hug. "You really don't know how grateful I am for this, Tori."

I returned her hug, conflicted with liking her and glad to be able to help . . . and being jealous of the opportunity she had in front of her.

"You deserve a nice night," I said.

And she did.

I left her and took my place opposite Pete so we could work both ends of the room outside the camera line.

During dinner, I delivered the call sheets and sides and ran a few errands around the mansion under Pete's direction. Relief flooded me in not having to witness the first half of the night, to not have to see the flirting, the maneuvering, the fakeness of it all.

But I finished in time for the candle ceremony, and then Pete required my assistance in organizing the circle of girls around the fire fountain, which was a stone pedestal that had a propane-fed flame flickering from the top. The bachelor used that flame to light his candle, which he would then use to light the candles of the girls who would stay.

I set them in the order prescribed in the chart Pete had given me and made sure the ends of the wicks on the candles were clear of wax so they lit quickly and without any issue. We'd had problems in the past with candles not lighting.

Gemma's was the first candle lit. She was radiant in the glow of that one little flame. I took in a sharp breath as I watched the exchange of glances between them as he lit her candle. He looked confident and strong in his decision to light her candle. She looked accepting and happy.

I wanted to turn away, to not be a witness to that moment, but I couldn't help it.

And what bugged me more than anything—even more than doing her hair and make-up for her—was that they looked right together.

Alison did not get her candle lit. She was crying as the other girls hugged her and wished her well, but she shot a glance of gratitude at me. I shrugged. She needed to go home—not that she actually got to go home just yet. She still had two weeks where she had to stay holed up in a nice hotel of the studio's choosing so no one knew she was sent home before that episode aired.

She would have more luxury in those two weeks than she'd had in the one at the mansion. It was how things worked on *Vows*.

The other two girls were, ironically, the girls who had made fun of Gemma when she'd gone to sleep.

It was at the moment when everyone started figuring out that Gemma was chosen first to stay and the two who had been mean to her were the first to go that the other girls knew exactly who their competition was.

I almost felt sorry for Gemma and the future she'd have to endure for the next couple of months. There would be those who would shun her completely—pretend she wasn't there—those who would scorn her and be cruel in ways Chris would never discover, but the worst would be those who would be her friends.

No one needed friends like that.

Becky was all smiles when she hugged Gemma. Becky wasn't eliminated. Becky was one of those friends Gemma would not realize she didn't want until it was too late.

* * *

Pete's voice came through the headset as the final hugs were given and final tears shed for the girls relieved to be staying and those sad to be leaving. Pete needed me to pick up the new sides with last-minute changes for the next day's shooting schedule, and then he needed me to drop them off at four particular locations: Gemma's, Becky's, Terri's, and Chris's rooms. I'd have to go there again, which shouldn't have surprised me since the sides were always a work in progress, except now, Chris would be there.

And there was nothing I could do about it.

Chapter 7

He whipped the door open before I could knock.

How did he always seem to know when I'd come to his door?

I handed him his new sides before he could say anything and turned away with a quick, "See you Sunday night."

He caught my arm. "Sunday night? Are you leaving?"

"Just for a day. I'll be around for the brunch shot, but I'm leaving right after. It's my weekend. I have book club."

"Right. HeLa."

I gave him a quizzical look. Had I mentioned the word *HeLa* before when we'd talked about Henrietta Lacks?

"Have you read all the books in the mansion's library already?" he asked.

"Oh, right. That's how you . . . The mansion library . . . yes. I've read every book shelved in the library."

"Really?" he asked. Somehow he had led me back to his door. Somehow, we were now conversing casually, and I felt no compulsion to leave. He leaned into the right side of the doorframe.

I leaned into the left side. "Yes, really."

"That's a lot of books." His soft smile spread to his eyes.

"No. It's nothing compared to a lot of people I know."

He blinked long and lazy as if we had all night to sit in his doorway talking, as if it didn't matter if anyone saw us together. "Next time you want to start something new, put in an extra copy at the library so I can read it with you. We can have our own book club."

The compliment of him wanting to do things I was doing warmed me. "You don't have to read a book just because I am."

He swept his fingers through his hair, messing up the perfect molding the set hairdresser had given him. "True. But I can still do something because

I want to. You obviously have good taste. I enjoyed *The Immortal Life of Henrietta Lacks*."

"Enjoyed? You finished it already?"

He nodded with his slow, lazy smile.

"How? I'm not even done yet."

"I'm having a hard time sleeping here."

"Really?"

"Yeah." He scrunched up his face. "The pillows are all wrong."

I didn't know why that statement disappointed me. Had I wanted him to say he couldn't sleep because he'd been thinking about me? It would only be fair since sleep had eluded me while thinking about him.

"Anyway, I wanted to thank you for all you did today."

I waved the compliment away. "It wasn't anything."

He turned so his back was against the doorframe, and he laced his fingers together behind his head. "It was so much more than you think. She told me everything you did for her. And I wanted to thank you for helping her out like that. It means a lot to both of us."

I blinked, my heart rate speeding up. *She? Her? Both of us?* "What means a lot?" I asked, trying to process all those words that didn't fit in my head. Hadn't he been talking about when I had talked to him about who to pick out for elimination?

"You helping Gemma like that. She looked beautiful. You have some mad fairy godmother skills. Cinderella would have paled next to Gemma. She told me how you found her crying and picked up the brush and wielded it like a wand. She said you were kinder to her than she remembered anyone being in a long, long time. She told me all about what had happened to her at her junior prom in high school, how those girls in the bathroom had cut her to pieces and made her feel small and stupid for even trying, how her date had left her by the punch fountain while he went and flirted with one of the same girls from the bathroom. She was really terrified to come to the candle ceremony tonight. You made all the difference. Thank you."

My lips wouldn't move, not without trembling. I nodded numbly.

"You look tired, Tori. I'm sorry for keeping you up later. Just because I have trouble sleeping doesn't mean I should make everyone else stay up with me. Thanks for the sides." He held up the papers and moved into his doorway. "Good night, fairy godmother." He flashed me a smile that I couldn't be sure I returned or not, and then he shut his door, leaving me in the hallway, hyperventilating.

The walk to my bungalow was a blur.

"I shouldn't have helped her," I said out loud to the lock on my door as I swiped the key card through for the third time. It flashed red again. After the fourth time, it finally glowed green. I shoved through the door and slammed it closed behind me. "She should have had to stand on her own two feet like everyone else." I threw my clipboard and my bag to the table with a clatter, not caring that my iPad was in the bag.

I grabbed the clipboard and tore away the top sheets protecting the note I'd taped to the back. I read it again.

Tori,
I really don't want you to be uncomfortable.
Hope these tissues make the cold a little easier.
Take some vitamin C.
You've got an adorable sneeze.
~ C

I noticed for the first time that he'd prescribed me to take vitamin C for my cold and then signed off as C. Did he consider himself a vitamin to the world of women? Was he just some player like Henrietta Lack's husband?

I harbored a belief that Henrietta wouldn't have had cervical cancer if her husband would have stayed faithful to her. Her children would have grown up with a loving mom who took care of them if their dad hadn't been bringing home sexually transmitted diseases to his wife.

Stupid man.

My dad had once told me that all boys were stupid and I should throw rocks at them. This was right as I was starting to date. My mom was quick to step in and tell him to stop filling my head with such things and that just because he didn't want me to be around boys until I had graduated college and had a doctorate didn't mean he had to make *me* not want to be around them.

I had laughed at Dad trying to keep me safe back then. Now I wished I had taken his advice. How had my heart become so invested in this guy I hardly knew? How come it hurt for me to see him finally doing what he was supposed to be doing?

He was supposed to be flirting and falling for the bachelorettes. That was what I kept telling him he needed to do. I should have been happy. Gemma really was a nice person. Chris really was a nice guy. Shouldn't it make me happy to see two nice people get a spark on a show where sparks seemed so unlikely?

It should have made me happy.

But it didn't.

I ripped the note out of the clipboard, crumpled it up, and threw it to the trash can. Except I missed and hit it against the rim, where it bounded into the doorway. I didn't care. I left the little white wad on the floor, changed into my pjs, and climbed into bed with my iPad.

"Show me up by reading my book and finishing before me?" I grumbled as I tugged the covers up to my armpits, fluffed the pillows behind me—secretly glad that his were uncomfortable—and read until I finished the book.

* * *

The next morning, I had a hard time smiling at anyone. Even though Gemma and Chris made me crazy, I still took no joy in watching Becky maneuver. She was slithering her coils all around them, and I wondered how long it would be before she pulled those coils in tight so they both suffocated in her grip.

The brunch went off with the food fight Max had orchestrated. Gemma had been splattered by a jellied roll, but instead of being affronted by it, she jumped in with gusto and started flinging the whipped topping for the crepes at any target standing still long enough. She was laughing like a ten-year-old as one of the other girls tried to stuff banana slices up Gemma's nose and ended up smearing it all through her hair. Max had planned the foods well. Creamy, soft substances made excellent ammunition in a food fight.

When Max called, "Cut!" with that gleeful laugh of knowing he'd created great footage, Chris grinned at me and winked a strawberry-jellied eye at me. I tossed a wan smile back and hurried to gather my stuff. I was wrapped for the day and wanted to simply be anywhere but on the mansion property.

I headed straight to my bungalow, trying to erase all thoughts of Gemma and Chris flirting and laughing.

"Hey, what's the hurry?" I turned to see Robert with his camera on his shoulder.

"I have things to do tonight, and with traffic, it's possible I won't get there on time. What's up? Does Pete need something?"

My headset was still on so he could reach me without sending a messenger, but sometimes Pete became so frantic on the job that the reasonable, efficient response escaped him.

"No. Pete's got a date tonight. He was the first one out the door when we wrapped for the day."

I couldn't hide the surprise. "Really? A date? Huh. I didn't know Pete had it in him."

"Be nice," Robert said, but his grin indicated he agreed with me.

"So what's up?"

"Just seeing if you're okay. You seemed upset back there while we were filming. Something going on?" He shifted his weight, hitching the camera higher on his shoulder. There was no red light indicating he was filming, so he had come to me out of personal concern.

I shrugged. "Just feeling a little underwowed with *Vows* right now. I need a break. And I'm antsy to be home for the weekend. I have book club tonight."

"You mean old ladies club?"

I cut him a glare. "Chris thinks it's a good idea to be attending a book club with a variety of people so we can have a broader perspective during our discussions."

"Chris? You mean, the bachelor?"

I sucked in a breath. "Right. The bachelor."

"You're on a first-name basis with the talent, huh?"

I rolled my eyes and glanced behind me to the safety of my bungalow just twenty feet away. "You're on a first-name basis with the talent too, so stop acting like a conspiracy theorist."

"I heard what you did for Gemma. It was a really nice thing to do. And I know it cost you something emotionally. I just wanted to say that you're my hero for being the good guy all the time."

I nodded my acceptance of his compliment. It *had* cost me emotionally. It shouldn't have. But it had.

Robert grinned. "And who knows, babe. You might be on the verge of your big break. I heard Max talking on the phone to Darren—about your scripts. Keep your eye on the goal. You're going to be a rock star screenwriter soon."

"Yeah. Rock star. Thanks, Robert. It's a good reminder."

He winked and turned back up the stone path to his own bungalow.

I threw my stuff in a duffle and hefted it out to my car, thinking about what he'd said. Everyone must know by now that I'd helped Gemma. But did everyone know it had come at a personal price? I hoped not. I had to be more aloof—less easy to read. Good things were on the horizon for me if I could keep my eyes on the goal like Robert had said.

I thought about the goal the whole way to book club. I thought about the obstacles too. There were a lot of obstacles. I was my own worst obstacle. If I wanted to get an acceptance letter for my work, I needed to wade through the rejections. It was the way of the business. Everyone had dues to pay.

Chris was another obstacle.

But with Gemma firmly in the picture, he wasn't *my* obstacle anymore. So why was it that he still *felt* like my obstacle?

* * *

I'd been right about traffic. It was a mess, and I only arrived just in time. Ilana showed up at the same time, and I smiled wide at seeing her.

"Hey there, Ilana!" I said.

"Hey." She still had her arm in a sling, but she looked a little better.

Ruby gave me a hug after opening the door. Then she hugged Ilana. She was more careful with Ilana's hug and cooed over hoping Ilana was feeling better. Ruby seemed a little distracted, so I didn't bother her with small talk. "I'll save you a seat, Ruby," I said with a smile.

She waved in acknowledgment.

Olivia was already seated, so we sat close to her and caught up on our lives for a minute. Olivia wanted to know about *Vows*, when it came on, what station, that sort of thing. So I gave some basic information, feeling a little strained by doing so. I always worried when discussing the show that I would slip up and say something that wasn't allowed.

Olivia talked about a weekend getaway her husband had surprised her with.

Ilana just listened, acting a little tired. I hoped she was okay.

Shannon showed up with her stepdaughter in tow.

Paige came in a few minutes behind that, which accounted for everyone but Daisy. Once we were all settled, Ruby was finally able to settle too. She sat next to me on the couch, where I had kept my word and saved her a spot.

Ruby got the party going. She let us know that Daisy would be absent again due to being on bed rest. I wondered if Daisy had dropped out of the group altogether because of all the new adjustments in her life and just didn't know it yet—or didn't want to admit it to Ruby. It happened. People had a tendency to fall in and out of things depending on their needs and stages. I fell in and out of things all the time. Anyone who saw my boyfriend history would agree with that.

"Anyway, now that Shannon is here, let's get started." Ruby gave Shannon a big smile. "Why don't you lead us off, dear?"

She flushed as if embarrassed to be called out. I flashed her a grin. She'd chosen a great book. And I was grateful to have been able to read it.

She smiled back at me and began speaking. "I thought I'd ask if anyone had any questions about the medical events that took place."

I had a ton of questions. "I think I was lost half of the time," I said, having no problem admitting it. I *was* lost through a lot of the medical information. "My brain can compute production schedules but not so much how the different parts of cells work. It's amazing—and terrifying—to try to comprehend how anything that small could be so destructive."

"And *constructive*," Paige said in reference to the medical discoveries made because of those cells.

Athena agreed, commenting on how all of the factors had to be present in order for the perfect storm of immortal cells to take root and grow. She was absolutely right. The world in which we all lived would be dramatically different if HeLa hadn't happened.

Shannon was nodding and agreeing and looking comfortable with the discussion for the first time since she'd started coming. I was glad we'd chosen a nonfiction she could enjoy.

"It was interesting to read about the doubts that medical professionals had about the main doctor"—I looked at my book. I'd taken the copy I'd placed in the library back out since Chris had already read it and some part of me wanted to keep that between us. I didn't want him mentioning it to one of the girls and having them read it to try to impress him—"Gey. He was revolutionizing medicine, and yet so many people discounted him."

"And this certainly isn't the only example of doctors who dealt with that type of thing." Shannon leaned forward. "William Harvey was a doctor in the seventeenth century who first introduced the concept of blood circulating through the body, and the medical world considered it a ridiculous theory. Josiah Nott introduced the possibility that mosquitoes were responsible for transferring diseases like malaria and yellow fever. He was completely discounted for fifty years before his ideas were given any credence, which was one of the single largest discoveries regarding pathology and has affected billions of people. Medicine is such a transitional field, with things changing and new ideas being acknowledged all the time. Henrietta's story is one more example of the need for an open mind and skilled ability to test and prove theory."

I agreed completely, thinking of my own mom's trials in having children. There were a few people in the medical community who had been open enough to let miracles happen so I could be born. I looked at my book again. "I also found it interesting that despite the eventual tragedy for Henrietta, she went to the right doctor at the right time. I don't know that any other hospital could have done what Johns Hopkins did back in the 1950s."

Shannon agreed, which was nice to have someone as smart as her agree with me. "Even with all the mistakes along the way and the breakdown of ethics, Henrietta left behind an incredible legacy that has changed the world."

Legacy felt like the wrong word. A legacy was something that someone intended to bequeath to the generations that followed. "But an unwilling legacy," I said.

Ruby interrupted my thoughts by saying, "I think this is one of the most important books of our century. Really. It's amazing how Henrietta's contribution has led to saving millions of lives and treating even more people. Her story should be required reading in every high school."

Even Keisha agreed that she would have read it if it had been available. Then she excused herself for a moment.

Ilana nodded her agreement. "The development of modern medicine was a rocky road, but it had so many breakthroughs along the way." She glanced down at her arm sling. "I mean, with my arm, what they've been able to fix is remarkable when you think about it. Although, now they explain things a little more before surgery." She frowned. "It made me sick to think of how they didn't inform the women about the side effects of those surgeries. Henrietta had a real shock when she found out she'd been made infertile."

I spoke up because, really, Henrietta hadn't had a choice in her therapy. The cancer would have killed her if she hadn't done it. "But getting rid of her cancer was more important than having another baby."

"But they *didn't* get rid of her cancer," Ilana's voice quaked as though she was really mad, which seemed a bit like an over-the-top reaction.

"Still, I couldn't believe Henrietta said that she wouldn't have done the surgery if she'd known she wouldn't be able to have any more children," I said. "I mean, Henrietta was a little bit crazy to even think that. Her life was more important than having more babies. She already had five. And she couldn't have had a baby if she'd died from cancer, so either way, she wasn't having more children."

Ilana looked miffed. I wondered if I'd offended her somehow. But I couldn't see why or how.

"Women have to make hard choices sometimes," Ruby said, sounding like a woman who knew.

I thought about what Chris had said about different ages offering different perspectives. He was right about that.

Ruby patted her book. "It broke my heart when Henrietta's daughter talked to the author in that first phone call." She searched her book until she found the passage. "Here, Deborah says, 'You know what I really want? I want to know, what did my mother smell like? For all my life, I just don't know anything, not even the little common little things, like, what color did she like? Did she like to dance? Did she breastfeed me? Lord, I'd like to know that.'"

I thought of my own mother. She smelled like vanilla—the scent she always bought for her hand lotions, which she used all of the time. Her favorite color was green because she liked to see things grow. She had enough houseplants to qualify my childhood home as a jungle. My mother loved to dance. But my dad was a complete klutz. She had nursed me. I had all those answers about my mom and so many more because I knew her. She was still accessible anytime I wanted her. I took that for granted and decided to visit her more. "How old was Deborah when her mother died?" I asked.

Shannon furrowed her brow. "She was the baby of the family, but I don't know how old she was when she lost her mother. Henrietta was only thirty-one when she died, I think."

Athena supplied the information from her phone. "Deborah was born in 1949, two years before her mother died."

"No wonder Deborah didn't remember her," Ilana said.

Olivia and Athena were more emotional than the rest of us, which made sense since they'd both lost their mothers. Yes. I definitely needed to call my mom more often and visit more often too. I had no excuses for being negligent on that. A busy life didn't mean a stupid life. I did not want to end up like Skeeter from *The Help* with nothing but my career to show for my time on this planet.

Keisha came into the room, probably back from the bathroom, and announced, "Deborah sounded like a hillbilly."

I almost laughed. I thought about what Chris said about judging people because of an accent, but then, what did I care what Chris said about anything?

Shannon didn't get after Keisha for being crass about another person's education but explained the situation so maybe Keisha could understand where Deborah was coming from.

Athena was still spouting facts from her phone. "Deborah passed away in 2009. She never even saw the book in print."

She must have Googled the book.

"At least she knew about it, and she probably read a draft," I said, trying to feel hopeful about it. Poor Deborah had so much go wrong in her life. I wondered how she would have felt holding a finished, published book in her hands—a real object that declared her victorious over something. "It would have been nice for her to see the book come out and to know about its success though."

Olivia looked thoughtful and then asked about Henrietta's husband—the no-good cheater who basically killed his wife as far as I was concerned. "I wonder what would have happened if she'd lived. Would they have stayed together, do you think?" she asked.

"I bet they would have," Athena said with a shrug. "Times were different back then, and Henrietta knew Day was unfaithful all along. I think it was much more common in that generation for women to turn a blind eye to infidelity."

Times were definitely different back then. Black people used as lab rats and women not feeling like they had the power to demand their husbands be faithful. I shuddered. Being both black and female, the past seemed like a horrifying place to have lived.

"I agree," Paige whispered.

Paige had been through a brutal divorce with a creep who couldn't stay away from other women. The past of women staying in those kinds of marriages must have filled her with the same kind of dread that being a black woman in those times did me. Her face reddened as all attention turned to her. "Remember how he took her to the hospital every day so she could be treated for pain? And when not having her children nearby upset her too much, he kept the kids right outside, under her window, so she could at least see them? I thought that was very sweet. Maybe he just didn't know another way to live."

It was a point of view I hadn't expected to see or understand. It was looking at someone's whole and not just pieces of them. It was an interesting alternative perspective. And though it tickled a little wave of guilt in the back of my head, I memorized that perspective so I could use it in future writing. Looking at the monster from a different point of view was a good way to dig deeper into characterization.

Shannon agreed. "I wondered that too. How many of our choices are actually based on the choices our parents made? Not that it's their fault or that Day wasn't accountable, but he didn't abandon Henrietta when she got so sick, and that says something. Their lives were a bit dysfunctional, but Henrietta seemed to be an overall happy person."

"Because she chose to be that way," I said. "Henrietta had really harsh trials to deal with—she lived in a time where she wasn't yet seen as an equal human with the white people around her; that was her reality every day of her life. And yet her sister Sadie said she was the life of the party, that she loved people, and that everyone wanted to be around her. I think she was a very strong, optimistic person. Maybe it's not so surprising that a woman like that would leave such a mark on the world—even if it took fifty years for the world to know it. Maybe the cells she left behind were the only way the world would notice this black woman from the South who was so easily discounted by the times."

Then Shannon said something that made more sense to me than anything else. "She lived her life with such a great attitude and left that legacy for her children while at the same time creating opportunity for the world. She worked hard, and she loved her family. Even though they didn't know the impact she had on medicine, they knew the impact she had on them."

That was what I wanted. To work hard and love my family. I wanted the career but wanted relationships too. I wanted to leave a legacy. One screenplay that would stand the test of time. But more than that, I wanted to have a husband and children someday who would remember me and talk about me long after my death. Not even that they would remember *me* exactly but that they would remember being loved and that they, in turn, would love.

Olivia smiled. "She changed the world. How many people can say that?"

"Mothers can." Paige grinned at Olivia. "Mothers have that kind of impact on the lives of their children. All of society starts with a child's mother."

That was exactly what I was thinking. Mothers. My own mother and all she meant to me, even when she was cussing at me in her native Bajan. And the mother I wanted to be someday.

"I'm really glad you chose this book, Shannon," I said, having gained in my learning through reading outside of my comfort zone. The discussion had widened that learning into something else. I wanted to make sure Shannon knew I was grateful.

Olivia looked to Ruby. "I wonder what HeLa will do in the future. I mean, it's done so many great things already; I wonder where it will go from here."

We discussed possibilities for a while. I was such a fan of science fiction that some of my ideas were probably a little out there for everyone else, but they humored me.

It was getting late enough and I'd not been sleeping well, so I was biting back a yawn when Athena said, "So, Ruby, do you have any trips planned?"

Ruby looked surprised, which could only mean she *had* been planning a trip and hadn't planned on anyone knowing. "Well, actually, yes, I do have a trip planned. I'll be going to Greece on a two-week tour with a group of people I met at the senior center."

"You are?" Shannon blinked in surprise. "When are you going?"

"We leave March 10."

"How lovely!" I said. "I've heard that Greece is *gorgeous*." I had always wanted to go to Greece. It was on my list of places to see before I died.

"There's nothing like the Greek isles," Athena said. "Anytime my mother heard someone say Disneyland was the happiest place on earth, she would lean over and tell me that was only because they'd never been to Greece."

Everybody laughed. I would take either option myself. I hadn't had a real day of entertainment for so long that to get away and do a Disneyland trip would be as good as anything.

"Do you have a Kindle?" Ilana asked Ruby as the conversation moved ahead without me. "They're great for travel; you can take thousands of books with you for less than a pound."

"Oh dear, I don't want thousands," Ruby said. "Just one would be good, maybe two. I worry those things—are they called e-readers?—are hard to use."

"Or you could invest in an iPad," I said. "It's more like a small computer. Then you can e-mail us updates and pictures and not worry about trying to find a computer. I have mine in the car if you'd like me to get it and show you how it works. It's very user-friendly."

"Oh, I'd absolutely love an iPad," Paige said. "My boys would go crazy over it."

"The Kindle is pretty easy to learn. I could show you how to work it," Ilana said, holding up her Kindle.

I got up to make room on the couch. "Ilana, why don't you take my place, and you can show Ruby the Kindle?"

Shannon must have figured this was a good time to have dessert because she and Olivia left for the kitchen.

Ruby looked up from where Ilana was teaching her about the Kindle and said, "Tori, you can choose our next book."

I blinked, a little surprised to be asked, especially when the others weren't even back from the kitchen yet. I thought about what kinds of books Shannon might like since she didn't really like fiction and thought about what kind of book I personally needed in my life. And then I knew exactly what I needed. With Max offering to look at several scripts and with the distraction I'd allowed a man—who was not even a possibility for me—to become, I needed a refresher course on how to follow my own path. "I have the perfect book," I said. "*The War of Art*, by Steven Pressfield."

Shannon and Olivia brought in the dessert just as I announced the new book. "I read it a couple of years ago," I said. "But I'm due for another reading." Boy, was I ever. I needed to remember how to fight for my art. It had been a long time since I'd felt any fight in me.

"It's that good?" Ruby asked.

"It's that important," I said. And at that moment, it struck me that it really was that important. "It's about following your dreams and not letting anything stop you."

I looked over at Shannon. "And it's another nonfiction book."

Shannon acted interested, and I hoped she'd get something out of *The War of Art* the same way I'd gotten so much out of *The Immortal Life of Henrietta Lacks*.

"*The War of Art* it is," Ruby said.

I suddenly felt nervous about my selection. "It's kind of a self-help book," I said, trying to explain it a little better. "It's a good way to reevaluate priorities."

"Well, it's settled, then. And I'll have a full report of Greece at our April meeting," Ruby said, which pretty much wrapped up the meeting.

I ordered two copies of the book as soon as I arrived at my own apartment. Two, because one needed to go to the library at the mansion. Chris probably wouldn't even notice. He'd never read it even if he did notice it was new.

He had someone else to try to impress now. In just one week, I felt like I'd been through an entire romance and breakup. This came on the heels of my being appalled that Lawrence would dare propose to me after only four months. The absurdity and immaturity of the situation did not escape me. I also downloaded the e-book of *The War of Art*, deciding I didn't want to wait for the hardcopy, and began reading.

And thought about *him* the whole time.

Chapter 8

I FELL ASLEEP READING AND couldn't remember anything I'd read since I'd really been thinking about Chris. Thinking about what he might have been doing at that exact moment. Wondering if he was talking to Gemma, or worse, Becky, or maybe one of the others—Rachel or Sara or Becca.

To take my mind off things and to be true to my previous night's resolutions, I packed my stuff and went to visit my mom and dad.

Mom was decluttering Dad's office, so naturally, Dad was in the kitchen replumbing the sink. Every time Mom invaded his space, Dad took the chance to invade hers.

Watching the two of them cuss and fume about each other while they worked on the individual projects would have been hilarious if I wasn't in the midst of my own romantic confusion. The way they grumbled about each other even while they served each other sparked with something that felt familiar. I'd grown up with it my whole life. She'd pick up his socks and complain because he'd left them on the floor. He'd see that the gas light was on in her car and go fill it up for her while growling about her inability to see the light was on for herself and how she was going to get herself stranded one of these days.

She never got stranded because he always noticed when her car was on empty. He never bothered putting his socks in the hamper because she always picked them up.

And those acts of service fueled their relationship in a way that could only be described as passion. Albeit strange, passion nonetheless.

The passion felt familiar, not only because I'd lived with it my whole life, but because on some new and smaller scale, that was what being around Chris felt like to me.

I cleaned the office with Mom and helped with several other projects I'd been promising to do but had been too busy to make the time for. After reading *The Immortal Life of Henrietta Lacks*, I didn't want to ever be too busy for my own mom again.

I asked her questions about how she felt when she met Dad, about how she knew he was the right one when he asked her to marry him, about how hard it was to be a black woman married to a white man in a time where that wasn't as widely accepted.

Finally, after laying out the entire romance between Dad and her—giving me details I'd never known before—she straightened from where she'd been repotting her herbs and put her muddy, gloved hands on her hips. "And where are these questions coming from now?" Her Barbadian accent had thickened a little with the strain of exhaustion from all the work we'd done. "You found someone, hmm?"

I frowned. I had started asking the questions because of Henrietta and the fact that her daughter would never be able to ask her mother those kinds of questions. But somewhere along the way, it had become a quest to determine how I knew if I'd found the right person or not.

I blew out a long breath. "I don't know. How do you know when you've found someone?"

"People find people every day, but it's a rare thing to be finding someone *worth* finding. Take your Lawrence. You found him. He found you."

"But was he worth finding?"

She smiled knowingly. I loved that smile. Henrietta's daughter never got to see her mother smile. "You knew he wasn't worth finding from the start. You kept thinking you'd grow into something, but you didn't because that something's got to be there in the beginning, from the first moment. From almost the first look. You feel a connection, a pull, a familiarity to the one who is worth finding. When you find the man worth finding, you'll know, 'cause it'll feel like coming home. Trust me, bebe. So tell me about this man you've found."

I sighed. I couldn't. Even though she was my own mom. I'd signed a contract that protected the interests of the studio. Chris's identity had to remain firmly in my head only. "It doesn't matter," I said finally. "He's already spoken for."

Mom blinked in shock, cursed in Bajan, yanked her gloves off her hands, and pointed her long, thin finger in my face. "You better not be messing with any married man! No daughter of mine is tangling herself in that kind of stupidity. Cat luck ain' dog luck. No man straying to other women is worth having, and no woman willing to tamper in another woman's marriage is worth talking about. Those lines don't be getting crossed, you hear me,

Victoria Winters?" She snapped her fingers twice in my face and pointed again, her mouth a dark line of fury.

I smiled. "He isn't married, Mom." I hugged her, but she was still furious enough over what she thought might have been happening that her arms stayed stiff at her sides.

"He better not be," she grumbled.

I laughed. "He isn't. I promise." *Not yet, anyway*, I thought.

"Then what be the problem?" She must have been really agitated to let her grammar slip like that.

"Nothing. Nothing at all. It really doesn't matter." I looked at her—really looked at her. Her black hair had gray curls straying out from her messy bun, the one I'd taught her to do to keep her curls under control. Her dark brown skin had some sag under the eyes and under the chin. Black sun freckles had appeared over her high cheekbones, a place that had once been a rich, smooth surface. My mom was getting old. How had I not noticed it before?

"I love you, Mom. I don't think I tell you that enough."

She smiled her little smile. "Not maybe so much as a mom would like to be hearing, but I know it, bebe. You prove it every day in the life you live, the breaths you take. And I love you too."

She gave me a real hug this time, not the stiff-armed thing she'd done a moment before. "And when you find you the man you're looking for, you'll know. Don't worry. It'll happen when it's the right time."

"I'm not worried about that. I just wanted to know more about you and Dad." I picked up the sack of potting soil and turned away, hoping she'd stop fussing over me having a love life.

But I didn't stop thinking about it. Her words replayed over and over in my head. *That something's got to be there in the beginning, from the first moment. From almost the first look. You feel a connection, a pull, a familiarity to the one who is worth finding. When you find the man worth finding, you'll know, 'cause it'll feel like coming home.*

I was too much of a realist to believe in love at first sight. But there had been something in that first look with Chris. Something that felt alarmingly like coming home.

* * *

I got a message from Ruby that her new iPad had arrived and she was wondering if I'd come help her set it up. Since I was still in town and not technically due back to work until morning, I kissed my mom and dad good-bye so I could help her out. Mom took my cheeks in her hands, and her dark eyes scoured every inch of my face as if searching for something there. "Stay away from the married man," she said. "But don't be so quick to give up on a single man just because you see phantom trouble that isn't there." She nodded, kissed both my cheeks, and nodded again.

I smiled. "Love you, Mom."

"What's this about a married man?" Dad asked.

But Mom shushed him with, "We'll talk about it later."

I drove to Ruby's feeling better about life. Reading the story of Henrietta Lacks had been good for me. It had allowed me to spend most of a day with my mom that otherwise might not have existed. I was grateful for that renewed look at my own life. Ruby was responsible for all of that because she had started the book club. Helping her with her iPad felt like a bonus because I owed her so much for the help she'd inadvertently given me.

"Hey, Ruby!" I said as soon as she answered the door. "Show me the new toy!" I loved technology and loved that Ruby was daring enough to try something new, even though a lot of people her age refused to look at it without arm-twisting. When we'd suggested she upgrade to something beyond a paperback, Ruby had hesitated for all of two minutes, and before we knew it, she'd ordered an iPad for herself. No arm-twisting required.

"Come in. Come in! I have to be honest, I am really excited about this. Almost more excited for this than I am the trip to Greece."

I laughed. "I think I'd take the trip since I already have the toy."

Ruby brought me into her kitchen, where the package was still bundled tight in its box.

I laughed some more. "What? You didn't even open it?"

She ducked her head in a way that made her look abashed—a look I'd never seen on my confident friend. "I was waiting for you."

She actually looked nervous about the whole thing, as if there was a bomb in that box instead of a way to make life a little easier. I took a step and swept the box from the table, slipped my finger into the plastic wrapping, and tore it off.

Once the whole thing was open, Ruby immediately went to the manual while I immediately went to the device. I set up her account, showed her how to change her passwords once I was gone so she didn't have to worry about me having access to that information, and downloaded a few apps I knew she'd want—a few games, Pages so she could type out letters or documents with relative ease, and Kindle. I made sure she had music, which was fun, since her taste in music was so different from what I'd expected. Then I got down to the nitty-gritty, scooted my chair closer to hers, and showed her how to use the apps I'd downloaded.

"You're distracted today," Ruby observed. "Something in life bothering you?"

"Love." I shut my eyes briefly and coughed, hoping to somehow cover up that one word. *Did I say that out loud? Smooth, Tori. Real smooth.* "Just work, mostly."

"Oh, how is that going? You started filming recently, didn't you?" She must not have heard my slip, or she would have jumped all over it.

"Yep. We're moving forward. It actually looks like another banner season for *Vows*." I checked my watch. "The first episode starts in fifteen minutes. How about we do this crash course on learning how to navigate the apps and then watch the first episode together."

She was all for it. I doubted Ruby was very much of a reality TV girl. I doubted she was an any-kind-of-TV girl, but I loved that she found interest in the things that interested me. She made a good friend that way.

Before long, she had a complete grasp of the Kindle app and had downloaded a sizeable number of books for herself, could send and receive e-mails, and could take pictures and send them in e-mails to people. She oohed and aahed over the Stargazer app that allowed her to position the iPad any direction so it would show her the stars and map out the constellations for her. She fell absolutely in love with that one. She acted as though she'd been handed the universe.

She did all of this before the theme music to *Vows* started playing.

I explained to her how the show worked while characters were being introduced, but she sat straight up in her chair and stopped listening to me when they introduced the bachelor, Christopher Caine.

"You work with him?" Her voice held a reverential sort of awe. Ruby had been captivated the same as every girl on set—the same as me. And I knew at that exact moment the entire nation was breathing out a collective sigh for the man on their screen. The man who brought me an apple when I was sick, who read books I was reading just so we had something to talk about, who had smiled down on Gemma as he lit her candle.

"Yep," I said, trying to sound like it was no big deal. "That's my bachelor." I had meant to say, "That's our bachelor," meaning the studio's. I had no idea how the word *my* had slipped out. But Ruby hadn't noticed.

She didn't turn away from the screen until it broke for a commercial and Chris couldn't be gawked at any further. "I suddenly wish I worked in the film industry."

I laughed at that, not really feeling the humor because I suddenly wished I *didn't*. "You have no idea, Ruby darling."

I stayed through the whole episode, working with Ruby on her iPad during the commercials and watching the show when it came on again. I was glad for the company while watching Chris's smile up close because if I'd been alone, I would have been too tempted to pause the TV and stare and stare and stare. That sort of thing would not have been healthy for me.

"That Becky sure is a cat, isn't she?" Ruby asked.

I smiled. Robert had caught all the little nuances that really showed Becky's dark side. He'd filmed from all the right angles, putting Becky and Gemma on very clear opposite sides from each other.

Other girls I hadn't noticed so much on set really popped on the screen. They had charisma and personality I hadn't seen in real life. The camera truly worked like a magician's wand sometimes, pulling out the unseen from midair, hiding the things it didn't want out in daylight.

And Robert was a grand magician.

I hated having to go back to the movie magic, hated knowing how it all would have to end on *Vows*. There would be a happily-ever-after ending for someone, but it wouldn't be for me.

Chapter 9

UPS DELIVERED THE BOOKS TO the studio the next morning with the bin full of other mail and necessities. I placed one of the new books in the library while the entire cast was up filming another hot-tub party scene. Very little bothered me more than the hot-tub parties. It was a lame way to get to know a person. How could you really find anything out about a person who was sipping drinks with umbrellas and wearing a couple pieces of string as clothing?

There was nothing real about that environment.

I ground my teeth together and straightened the books on the shelf so the new one sat in line with all the others. Chris wouldn't read it, I kept telling myself. He wouldn't even know it was there. But I shot it a long last look before leaving with my own copy so I had something to do during takes.

Robert met me at "cheese thirty"—the caterer's idea of a snack break. Every day at three thirty we could count on a tray filled with cheeses, fruits, and meats to be delivered to the crew. I loved that the studio brought in only the best of caterers because I really loved cheese thirty.

Robert had actually put his camera down on an electrician's cart and was next to me at the table smearing brie cheese over water crackers. "Any word from the head honchos on your scripts yet?" he asked.

I shook my head instead of verbally answering because I was busy stuffing my mouth. I chewed fast and swallowed, dodging a glance around in case anyone else was within hearing range. "Not a word," I said. "I'm feeling really nervous about the whole thing."

"Is that why you bought the new book?" Robert picked the book up from where I'd laid it on the table. "*The War of Art*. I read that back in film school."

"Yeah?" I asked. "What'd you think?"

"It had some good ideas. Some totally stupid ones. Ultimately, there was a lot of takeaway in that book. It helped me remember I wasn't the only artist in my family. My wife had dreams of her own, and I had a tendency to quash her dreams because mine felt like they needed to come first, and I wanted her supporting me. It never occurred to me before reading that book that I should be supporting her."

"That's an interesting perspective. Of course, since I'm not married, I didn't get that memo at all."

"You're already done with it? You've got a bookmark that's barely made its way through a third of the book."

"I've read it before . . . a creative-writing book report."

"And you're reading it again on purpose? You are such a strange kid."

"I just feel stuck in this business and needed a little pep talk on how to stay motivated." I nodded and stuffed another cracker into my mouth. When I chewed it enough to talk without being gross, I said, "I actually prepped a bunch of screenplays today during lunch and e-mailed them off. I even printed one out and snail mailed it. I'm only into this thing three chapters this time, and I'm already motivated."

Robert made a noncommittal noise as he munched on several slices of smoked Gouda. He always tried to make it to cheese thirty early so he could get to the smoked Gouda before Pete did. On occasion, when I knew Robert couldn't possibly make it in time, I took the Gouda off the tray and saved it in a lunch bag for him to have later. Pete annoyed me enough that it gave me an evil thrill of pleasure to be able to annoy him on occasion.

"I've made a decision," I announced.

"Oh yeah? What's that?"

"Nothing and no one is going to stand in the way of my art. I'm going to be a real screenwriter. I'm going to have *my* name flash over the screen when it says *written by*."

"And nothing's going to stand in your way?"

"Nothing." I gave one sharp nod.

"And no one?"

"Nope."

"Not even a pretty boy with a Southern accent?"

My nod wasn't nearly as sharp. But I nodded just the same.

"Good!" Robert clapped his big hands together, making me nearly jump out of my skin. I hated it when he did that. "Because just between you and me, I think that Chris Caine is a faker. I'm betting he went to years of acting classes to learn his Southern accent."

"You're only saying that because you think it's what I want to hear."

"I'm only repeating what you've said about all bachelors." He shrugged, pursed his lips, and bobbed his head while scanning the table for something else. He was about to reach for the grapes, but when one of the grips made a move for them, he stood aside and let the kid take them. Robert was the sort of guy who could never wrong anyone—except Pete, but that was more of a game than a deliberate attempt to hurt Pete. If he thought Pete would be heartbroken over the cheese, Robert would likely give that up too.

"So you've declared war for your art?" Robert asked as I wiped the crumbs from my sweatshirt.

"Yep. The missiles are loaded and headed to enemy territory."

"Atta girl. It's good to not have to worry about you anymore. And I'm keeping my toes and eyes crossed for good news from Max and Darren."

"Not your fingers?" I asked.

He grinned. "My fingers are busy working the camera."

"Oh, well, I guess I can forgive you this time."

Pete's voice fuzzed in my headset. I rolled my eyes and waved good-bye to Robert.

There was work to be done.

* * *

The next week felt like seven days in a medieval torture chamber. Chris seemed to be honoring my wishes to let me be comfortable and just do my job. He was honoring those wishes so much that he barely spoke to me. But I still felt him watching me, and *The War of Art* was missing from the library shelf.

It had gone missing the first day, but as fast as he read, it should have been returned within at least one day. With him, it was likely he could have had it back in an hour. But it remained steadfastly absent from the mansion library.

Which made me wonder. What was he doing with it? Had he actually read it, or was he too busy wiping lipstick off his cheeks to have time for reading?

I took a deep breath. *Tori, you're not being fair.* I kissed cheeks all the time. A kissed cheek didn't mean anything but friendship—especially in Hollywood. Most of the time, a kiss on the lips didn't mean anything but friendship. Besides, it was his job to have girls smearing their lipstick all over his face.

He was the bachelor, and he wasn't *my* bachelor, no matter what I'd said to Ruby while watching the first episode.

Ruby had sent a couple of e-mails detailing how great her trip was. "At least one of us is having a good time," I said out loud to my iPad as I hit send on a return e-mail to her. I'd given some brief and noncondemning information about the show. I mostly told her about Robert and the funny things he managed to catch on film and about the scripts I'd sent out to studios and agents. Ruby made a good correspondent. Gratitude filled me for the small distraction she gave me.

Because the week really was awful. It was awful to not have Chris talk to me. I *wanted* him to talk to me. I wanted to know what he thought of *The War of Art.* I wanted to know what he thought about the weather or politics or space travel. *Anything,* as long as it meant we were having a conversation.

Delivering his call sheets and sides felt like Pete was picking on me, even though, of course, that was part of my job. It was just a part I didn't want to do anymore. Chris was polite when I dropped the information off each night and even more polite when I had to make return trips because Max changed his mind about something.

Chris still whipped the door open, never allowing me to knock and run like I wanted. And his eyes stayed glued to my face as if waiting for something . . . but waiting for what? What did he want me to do? How was I supposed to act in light of the fact that he and Gemma spent more and more time laughing and talking and eating and flirting and . . .

Three more girls went home with unlit candles.

Jessica, because she was a religious fanatic who preached on her dates with Chris. She preached about the other girls' clothing, preached about Chris's love of motorcycles and electric can openers, calling them the devil's tools. She even called TV a devil tool, which made Chris widen his eyes and stare straight into the camera as if to point out the obvious.

Crystal, because she hated everyone and acted like she was better than the world—even Chris. She made it clear she was doing him a favor to be on a date with him. She had great style, and she was one of the few girls who really was well read, but it wasn't enough to overcome her majesty complex.

Jaime the Runner, because she used the other girls' stuff without asking and because the other girls complained about it. They didn't complain for themselves when they were on dates with Chris because most of them knew how he felt about gossip. They complained on behalf of each other. It made them look more benevolent. When Chris found that his handkerchief had gone missing and that Jaime was the one who had it, he determined she might be a liability who would be smart to cut loose.

Becky and Gemma were still there.

How had Becky not been kicked out? Did he not see how she manipulated and tormented Gemma? If he really cared at all about Gemma, he'd banish Becky from the mansion kingdom.

I breathed in relief when the week was all done and I was able to run away to my own apartment. They'd given me the option of staying out my weekend on the mansion property, but I turned it down, not wanting to witness any more of women dating a man I wanted to date than I had to.

The day and a half home was good for me, and it was sad when it came to an end. I spent the weekend going to lunch with my mom and Janette, as well as reading and pondering the book for book club. I'd chosen it, yet parts of me were embarrassed to have chosen it. Upon a second reading, I realized that although it was nonfiction, it was totally not a Shannon sort of book. It was too much like a pep talk given to a locker room full of football players before the big game. And while I really needed that pep talk, I didn't see Shannon needing it. I honestly didn't see any of the women needing it. Everyone had good, solid lives with either careers or motherhood or both.

Ilana had a great career doing something she totally loved. Athena had her magazine and a great boyfriend. Olivia had a happy marriage, with a bunch of kids who gave her all the joy in the world. Shannon was a pharmacist, for heaven's sake, and a mom. Paige had her two boys, and she liked what she did for a living. She was happy doing it. Daisy . . . well, Daisy was a wildcard. But I wasn't sure she was even reading the book, since she'd missed the last several meetings. She would be one who might actually appreciate the concept of meeting up with resistance and triumphing over it. Ruby had been married to a man she obviously loved, and she seemed content in her life being who and where she was.

That was what I wanted: to be content with who and where I was. I wanted to feel like I'd done whatever the universe meant for me to do.

I wasn't meant to take orders from Pete.

I wasn't meant to take orders from Max.

I wasn't meant to take orders from Darren.

I was the only one in the active book group who needed a pep talk. I was the only one at war for what I wanted. I was the only one facing resistance.

But thinking on resistance wouldn't do me any good—not when I was late getting back to the mansion.

I sighed, packed the rest of my things for the week, and raced out to my car, praying for good traffic, but my neighbor called my name. "Tori?"

I stopped, accidentally swinging my duffle when I turned to look at her and almost knocking her rat-dog that had followed her out of her apartment off the curb into the street. It yipped as if I had actually bumped it, and Mrs. Saxton scowled at me as if I'd tried to hit the mangy little rat on purpose.

With a sour look, she held out the envelope in her hands.

It was a letter from MoonLight Studios.

"I got this in my mailbox by accident during the week. I knew you were gone again because your car is hardly ever here, so I kept it until I saw you."

I could have bothered telling her she could have just slipped it inside my mailbox, but it wouldn't have mattered. She did what she did, and no reasoning made sense out of it. And what did she care if my car was there or not?

"Thanks. That's nice of you," I said instead and tried to take the envelope from her. She hung on to the end for a few seconds before finally letting go, and then she called to her rat-dog to come back from sniffing the hedges.

I threw my duffle to the backseat, where it made a soft *oomph* as it landed on the pile of clothes already there, and waved to Mrs. Saxton, hoping her dog wouldn't come out into the road. If it got hit, she'd blame me—even though she was the one who never obeyed leash laws.

I pulled out and rushed to the mansion, hating that I couldn't open my letter at home. Why did they always have to come just as I was leaving? Couldn't one come when I was already home so I could mope and mourn properly?

Of course, this one would have been in my mailbox when I'd come home the night before if certain nosy neighbors had just dropped it back into my slot like they should have.

The traffic and the panic and hope the letter represented, along with the lameness of my neighbor, all added to my irritation. I yelled and shook my fists at the other drivers like any good girl from LA knew how to do.

Once at the mansion property, my phone was already chirping with four messages that I was needed on set right away. I should have gone back the night before instead of sleeping at my apartment, but it was late, the drive sounded crummy to have to make, and I wasn't sleeping very well on mansion property—not with knowing that a short walk away someone else wasn't sleeping, even if that was only a pillow malfunction for him.

I scowled at the clock on my phone. Call time wasn't for another thirty-one minutes, and I already had messages?

Pete must have screwed something up. He only texted when he made a mess of things.

I stuffed the letter in my back pocket and hurried from the parking lot to work.

And there was plenty of work to be had. The mansion was incredibly expansive, and the next four hours consisted of my running every square inch of it. Back and forth to Max, to Pete, to the rooms of most of the cast, giving new instruction, hurrying the girls who were taking too long at make-up, and yanking the ones out of bed who didn't feel any sense of urgency that particular morning.

It always happened by the third week.

They'd get tired of the erratic hours, and then they'd whine about not getting enough sleep—like they had any idea what not enough sleep was. They lounged around a pool for half of the day most days. Their call times and wrap times were an hour after and before mine. And all they had to do was flirt with the bachelor and fight with each other.

I was ready to put them all in a time-out.

Everyone but Gemma.

Gemma remained grateful. She remained polite. She remained happy to be there.

She actually hugged me when she saw me and asked my opinion on her outfit.

I didn't dare look too closely to see what Chris felt or didn't feel for her. It was easier to stay hidden in my work and to hide behind my book.

By that evening, the entire mansion had driven me crazy. I sneaked away when they were taking another break before Chris's big date with Terri—the one allergic to hot tubs.

Terri took longer than any of the other girls on set, so there would be lots of time to read and be alone.

I found a place of solitude by the duck pond, way at the back of the estate. It was far enough back that no one ever thought about it anymore. Being there felt like a midday vacation. Away from the mansion and the bungalows, away from the bachelorettes with their bikinis and sunscreen.

It was March, for crying out loud. Who wore a bikini in March? I'd had enough of them after all the cajoling I'd done just to get them to their places on time.

Becky had been an absolute monster that morning. I'd had to strip her covers off her bed entirely, even though she was still in them, and after that, I'd threatened to get a bucket of ice. I wanted to ask Chris why he hadn't eliminated her, but it wasn't my business. This was his bachelor party, literally, and if he wanted to keep a girl with not enough kindness and too much cleavage, what did I care?

Except, I did care . . . very much. It made my teeth grind just to think of it.

"Book any good?" It was his voice at my ear, the Icy-Hot shooting through my veins, making me shiver.

He had scared me, sneaking up on me like that, but I didn't want him knowing he'd scared me. I casually looked up from my copy of *The War of Art*. I wanted to ask if he'd already read it, but what if it had been someone else who'd taken it from the library shelf? It was a shock all by itself that he was willing to have a discussion with me.

"I don't know," I said.

"Another book club book that isn't quite your thing?" He scooted aside the bread I'd been feeding the ducks and sat down next to me on the stone bench, where he could peek over my shoulder.

"Actually, I chose this one. I've read it before. I just don't remember being hit this hard with the author's philosophy. Maybe I'm at a different place. It started out being exactly what I needed, but now I'm feeling talked down to a little."

"So it isn't doing any good?"

My shoulder lifted in a half shrug. "That's not it either. I actually got the motivation to send out more feelers regarding my screenplays."

"Then I'd say it's exactly what you need *now* as well as before."

I nodded, remembering the letter folded up in my back pocket. The itch to open it made my fingers actually stretch, but then I checked myself. No. Not with him right here. Whatever the letter said, he couldn't be here with me for it. Good or bad, my success and failure belonged to me alone.

He straightened his shoulders and looked me straight in the eye. "So tell me about the book."

I gave him a confused look. Had he really not been the one to have taken the library copy? He waited, and I shook myself, realizing he must not really know what the book was about, so I explained it to him. I explained resistance and the importance of not letting anything become resistance.

He listened carefully. And he sat close; our legs were touching again. I wanted him to stay. I wanted him to have read it as well and to be able to discuss it with me. Then he asked me something unexpected. "What kinds of resistance are you facing?"

"I . . . I don't really know."

He gave his half smile. "Come on, Tori. You know." His words were low, a whisper that was more felt than heard.

"What do I know?" I asked.

His half smile spread to a full one that made him look like a kid, playful and full of mischief. "It kinda ruins it for me to tell you that you know and then you have to ask what it is you're supposed to know."

I grinned at him. "I see the issue there. It makes you seem less knowing to tell me I know something I don't."

It felt good to be smiling with him—to know that his smile was for me and me alone, not for one of the girls, not for the camera.

"Any news on your scripts from Max?" he asked after a goofy moment of us staring and smiling.

"Nope. Maybe he's waiting until the filming season's done so he doesn't have to work with me when I'm hating him."

"Ah, a grudge holder, huh?"

I put out my hands. "I only hold grudges against people who offend my soul. Not many people dare to go there."

"I see. Your scripts are your soul? Hmm. I might want to get a copy of one of those, then. It might be interesting to read your soul." He took one of my hands, making my heart thud like crazy. Could he hear it? It felt like the whole world could hear it.

He inspected my palm. "Some people believe you can read a soul by looking at a person's hands." He squinted as if trying to make out something more clearly.

I peeked over until our foreheads were nearly touching. "Oh yeah? What does mine say?"

He traced his finger down the lines in my palm. I willed myself to not shiver. "It says you're a hard worker." His finger ran along the callous below each of my fingers, and then he turned my hand over to view my nails, which were in need of a trim to tidy up the rough edges. "It says you don't take enough time for yourself." His gaze locked on to mine.

I wanted to look away. What had started out as fun and a little silly had moved into something else, something I didn't understand, something that made it hard to breathe.

While holding my gaze captive, he brought my palm up and against his cheek. "It says you're warm and caring. That you put others before you."

He held me there, with my hand cradling his cheek, my eyes bound to his, for eternity. Or maybe it was only a moment. I couldn't tell. He finally released me as he cleared his throat and gave his head a barely perceptible shake as if he'd been held as spellbound as I had been. He settled my hand back down on my leg.

His face broke into that mischievous grin. "You know, it's normally twenty dollars for a whole hand reading, but I'll give you the palm rate."

The magical moment, whatever it had been, had passed. I was sorry to see it go, but I complied and smirked at him. "What's the palm rate?"

"You have to be nice to me when you see me from now on."

"I *am* nice to you!" I swatted his shoulder.

"Oh yes, because hitting me is a great way to prove you're nice to me."

"I do that to everyone. It's a love tap." I inhaled sharply, not meaning to say the *love* word—not out loud—not to him.

"And you're a huge liar. You are *professional* with me. You treat me like you'd treat your UPS driver. No, wait. That's not true either. You laugh and joke around when the UPS driver drops stuff off here and you have to sign for it. We were doing fine, and all of a sudden you went into robot mode with me. It's rare when I can get you to smile for me."

"I smile!" I insisted, feeling a little sullen that he'd noticed how I'd stepped away from him after the whole Gemma episode.

"You don't smile. You stretch your lips over your teeth like this." He made a grimacing, snarling sort of face.

I laughed. "I do not!"

"Well, not anymore, because now you owe me for a hand reading. You owe me one genuine smile every time I see you. Deal?" He put his hand out for me to shake it.

"What? I don't have to sign for it in blood?"

"That's the cost for a lip reading. We can arrange that if you want." His grin turned wolfish.

I laughed again, feeling heat crawl up to my ears. "I guess it's good for a man to have dreams." I shook his hand.

He nodded and stood. "There. Now we're friends. And there isn't anything you can do about it."

"I wouldn't try to change anything."

He nodded again and looked back at the mansion. "I ought to get back. I can't believe Pete hasn't bellowed for me through that headset of yours. That guy keeps me on a pretty tight leash."

"They've invested a lot in you. They can't afford to cut you loose now. How'd you get away this time?" I asked, genuinely curious because Chris was right. Pete knew Chris's location every second of the day.

"Told him I was going to take a nap. It's a good thing I don't have an ankle tracker on me, or they'd know I lied and came to find you instead." He glanced around with a look like he half expected a SWAT team to come out of the bushes at us.

"You know," he said, "I couldn't have picked a more perfect spot to make this friendship transaction with you. We should hang out here more often." He ducked his head in a way that felt like he was bowing to me and left before I could say anything.

Only then did I allow myself to shiver.

Chapter 10

THE LETTER IN MY POCKET was a rejection. Two more similar rejections came through my e-mail. I read *The War of Art* with fervor, trying to battle away the immediate feelings of inadequacy and stupidity. It helped a little. But not a lot.

Another week went by. Another candle ceremony. Four girls were eliminated this time. It was a little against protocol, but Chris had insisted he didn't want to see any of those four girls again.

Max had relented. I think Max secretly loved the shake-up. There would be suspense while everyone waited to see which of the four would get her candle lit, and then none of them would. It added flair and drama. It helped keep the girls from becoming too casual with their situation at the mansion.

I watched the girls Chris was sending away as they cried and hugged the ones who would be staying. Those staying patted the backs of those leaving as if they somehow cared, but none of them did.

Nancy was going because she'd flat out talked bad about Gemma while Nancy was on her date with Chris. The girl obviously had no game skills because Chris had told her at the beginning of the date that the one thing he hated more than anything was a girl who insulted other people to try to make herself look good. He'd said it to all of the girls at one time or another.

Had she not heard him say that? He'd made it pretty clear.

Traci was eliminated because she swore a lot. Chris had explained to her that his momma had raised him to speak with manners and that swearing at a nice dinner would not be considered nice manners.

She still hadn't stopped.

Laura was eliminated because she'd been caught in the snare of my library. She had claimed to be very well read. She had claimed she'd read over half the books in the library, so he'd set up a date with her in the library so they could talk about the books.

She tried to get out of the discussion by turning it into a make-out session, but he didn't kiss her and wouldn't let her kiss him. The guy had some major dodging moves. It was almost acrobatic the way he avoided her advances.

He told her she could earn a kiss if she could give him one accurate synopsis of one book. I sucked in a deep breath when I heard that. Seriously? A kiss for one synopsis? He wasn't giving her any kind of challenge with that. Most people in the world would have read at least one of those books for some class or other. I could tell him a synopsis on every one of those books!

She tried to get out of even that, which was weird. It seemed she'd be better off just giving him what he asked and then getting some lip action, which made me gouge nail prints into my own palms just considering him doing it. The bachelorette finally realized he wasn't going to give in to the wiles of her womanhood and then tried to tell a loose sort of synopsis of one of the books by looking at the cover he held up for her. He wouldn't let her see the back.

And she got it wrong. The triumphant look on his face when she failed said that he'd known she hadn't read a single book there. How had he known? Even I believed she'd read a few.

And personally, though I had no proof, I believed he sent Kimberley away because her laugh sounded more like a bray, and she laughed at *everything*. You could tell that girl that your mother had died, and she'd laugh. It was the sort of noise that made anyone in listening range have the visceral reaction of cold chills and cringing.

Everyone on set was glad to see her go.

Gemma's was the first candle lit again. Becky's was second. The two girls were so opposite one another in temperament and personality that it made no sense that they were both placed on the same playing field. It was like putting a viper next to a songbird.

I had started taking my lunch break and any other spare moment at the duck pond. It was secluded—surrounded by trees. No one ever went there because none of the girls was adventurous enough to explore the grounds that thoroughly. The pond was small enough and far enough away from the mansion that it remained well hidden. And none of the camera guys had thought to place a camera there because none of the previous *Vows* players had ever gone there.

They thought, in the beginning, that it would be perfect for the bachelor to meet up with a lady of his choosing for secret kisses. But none of the bachelors ever found the duck pond.

At least . . . not until now.

But he wasn't meeting one of his bachelorettes.

He was meeting me.

Chris showed up every now and again, usually with some joke or some sort of gift, like the orange he'd swiped off the craft services table so he could tell me to have a sunny day or the Smarties he handed off to let me know he'd heard Pete call me a know-it-all when I'd resolved a problem in two minutes that Pete had stewed over for several hours without the ability to come up with a solution.

Chris told me about his family. His brother and two sisters, his mom and dad. He asked me questions about mine. He was surprised to hear I had mixed-race parents but was not bothered by it. He asked strange questions, like what my favorite Christmas tradition was or whether or not I liked Tabasco sauce.

Another week went by.

Three more girls were eliminated.

Mckenna, because she was always sending someone else to fetch her some water or to change the music selection or to hand her a towel. It raked over everyone's nerves to be treated as though the whole cast and crew were there to serve as her minions.

June, because she really was a know-it-all. She had an answer for everything. And usually her answer was wrong. No matter what anyone did, June had a way to do it better. And if the person being chastised didn't change to her way of thinking, she'd explode. People did her bidding, small sacrifices of will made to the goddess of the volcano, just to keep her from erupting. Chris had called her June Bug. Everyone thought it was a cute, endearing nickname, but he confessed to me that he called her that because she bugged him.

Everyone thought he had some feelings for her because of that nickname, and all were surprised when her name came up on the elimination list. Surprised and elated. No one was sorry to see her go.

No one really knew why Heather had been chosen. Not even I could figure that one out. She was perfect. Organized, smart, funny, beautiful. I'd have given my right arm to be half the amazing she was, but he'd released her with an unlit candle.

Another week.

Chris came with a marker and paper one day and traced my hand, saying he needed to keep copies of all hand-reading contracts for legal reasons. He talked about college. He'd been a business major. I wanted to press about why he was working on a farm when he had a business major but decided it wasn't any of my business. I told him about going to Barbados to visit my granny there and talked about the intense blue of the water and spending the whole time learning to swim. I brought him a sucker on the day he let one of the girls talk him into karaoke. He had a semicrummy voice, but his discomfort was worse than his voice.

Four girls gone again.

Karen, because she believed the whole moon landing was a government hoax.

Ronda, because she belched after dinner and then yelled, "Home run!" Max had grinned and said some things just couldn't be scripted. He was sorry to see her go because he had loved that she was borderline insane. Chris . . . not so much.

Luisa, because she'd been a snob. When Chris had explained his work on the farm, growing peanuts, she'd scoffed and said she'd help him find more meaningful work.

Amanda, because she'd tripped Gemma in the hallway and Chris had happened to be passing by and witnessed the event. Amanda had no idea Chris had been present, or she wouldn't have made such a fatal mistake. Amanda had really liked Chris. It was obvious she'd intended on sticking it out to the end. It was obvious she'd planned on being the one with the ring box. But that one moment of cruelty had been seen and couldn't be unseen. Chris had been furious. He'd called her out on the act at the very moment it had happened. Even my own mother had never given such a tongue-lashing.

No one was surprised to see Amanda go.

Gemma continued to climb in popularity. Twitter feeds filled with her name. The world loved her.

I worried about how the bachelor felt about her.

But I never asked when he came to visit me by the duck pond. I was too busy asking him about his hometown, his farm, how early he liked to get up. I was too busy answering his questions of where I wanted to live for my whole life or if I planned on traveling everywhere. He wanted to know if I felt it necessary to stay in LA because of my writing. He wanted to know how many kids I wanted and if I liked dogs.

On the occasions he showed up when I was working still, he left me notes taped to the swan statue's beak so it looked like the swan was holding the message for me. They were silly mostly; sometimes they were anagrams, and I had to unscramble the nonsense words to find the real message. Sometimes they were lame knock-knock jokes he'd pilfered from some milk carton somewhere. Sometimes they were just a few simple words like:

I am so sorry I missed you because it makes me miss you.

I taped them all to the back of my clipboard and tried to plot out other ways this could all end, except the one that was inevitable.

On the day before I had my weekend, Janette had me meet her down the street from the mansion to deliver me my mail and to assure me she'd watered my plants. In the pile of mail was a letter. It was from Grand Production Agency.

I held it like scorpions were locked inside the envelope. "So this is why you were so insistent we meet, even though I go home tomorrow afternoon."

"Open it!" Janette said. "The suspense is killing me."

I tried to hand it back to her. "Then you open it."

She wouldn't take it back.

With a grunt, I slid my finger under the flap and opened it.

No scorpions scrambled out of the envelope, which I took to be a good sign. I opened the trifolded paper and read aloud. "Dear Ms. Winters, I don't normally respond to submissions personally but felt, in light of your unique position to irritate my sensibilities, that perhaps you deserved a personal explanation."

Janette's smile had fallen to a look of disbelief. I felt like I might throw up. I didn't read the rest aloud but raced through it silently, my eyes picking out words that felt like a punch to the trachea.

Cheesy.

Trite.

Embarrassing.

Depressing.

I gasped, trying to take in enough oxygen to make up for the fact that I was holding my breath for so long.

Janette shook her head. "I'm so sorry, Tori! I would never have let you open that if I'd had any idea. I thought that maybe it was an acceptance letter. It felt different from the others somehow. I'm so sorry. Are you okay?"

I didn't answer her question. Instead, I wadded up the letter and stuffed it in my front pocket. "I have to get back to work."

She apologized continuously as I shut my car door and backed out of the parking space. I knew that a glance back in my rearview mirror would show her standing there with her mouth still repeating those two words: "I'm sorry."

I collected myself enough once inside the mansion gates to realize I'd been rude to Janette. She'd only been trying to help me achieve a dream. She hadn't known what that envelope contained. I texted her a quick message, telling her I loved her and that I would be fine.

I didn't go to the duck pond.

I was in shutdown mode. Talking to anyone would mean powering up again, feeling again. And if I did that, I would be feeling everything to the point of emotional overload. There would be crying, screaming, perhaps throwing things. I still had a job to do. Going crazy wouldn't help me at all.

Chris found me wrapping up cords for the lighting equipment after we'd shot the final scene for the date he'd had with Krista by the pool.

Krista had kissed him. She was the first of the bachelorettes to get a real lip-on-lip kiss out of Chris, and she'd done it by trickery. No one had seen it coming. Least of all me.

It had only added cyanide to an already toxic day.

I wanted to scream. Wanted to throw her in the pool. Wanted to jump in the pool myself and never resurface.

"Hey, assistant director lady." He called me that a lot when other people were around. Or sometimes he called me writer lady, though after today, he'd have no more reasons to call me that because I couldn't do it anymore. I never wanted another letter like that again. I was done writing. He lowered his voice. "You haven't been around all day. I was worried. You okay?"

I shook my head and swallowed the sob in my throat. Was that still cranberry-colored lipstick at the corner of his mouth, or was I just imagining it?

His look went from one of light humor to one of concern. "What's wrong?"

Gary, the lighting tech, took the cord I'd wrapped and hauled it inside. That left us effectively alone.

"Seriously, Tori . . . what's wrong?"

I sniffed, and instead of answering that while he'd been kissing undeserving women, I'd been beaten up emotionally, I took out the wadded rejection letter from my pocket and handed it to him.

He read the first sentence out loud, but then, like me, he began reading silently once he realized what he had in his hands. He lifted his head to meet my eyes and ran his finger under his nose. It had been a cold evening for a poolside dinner.

"Come on, Tori, no sad eyes like that."

"It's the last one of all the queries I've sent out. There isn't anything left." I took the letter back and stuffed it into my pocket again.

He scrubbed his hand through his hair. "Of course there's something left. There's always something left. It's just a rejection letter. It isn't the end of the world."

I stared at him, feeling my jaw go slack in shock. How could he say that? How could he not see the comparison between my failure and the end of the world? *Of course* it was the end. The end of *my* world! I'd lost my war with my art. I had tried and failed. I put my hands up to block whatever else he was preparing to say to me. "You know what. Talking to a bachelor actor who's getting paid to flirt with and kiss flippant, nearly naked females is like . . . I don't know. I'm such a bad writer I can't even come up with a proper metaphor, but it was obviously proof of poor judgment on my part. Of course it doesn't matter to you." I stood up and started down the stairs, hating myself for having told him. Hating myself for being angry with him for doing what he was supposed to be doing in this ridiculous house. He was being paid to date and kiss and flirt, and that had nothing to do with me.

Only, it had everything to do with me.

While he called our little meetings at the duck pond friendship, I felt so much more. I couldn't even deny it anymore, wasn't even sure I wanted to deny it. So it really felt like I'd lost two loves that day. Writing, through this letter, and Chris, through that kiss. How had I thought he'd be a shoulder to cry on? How had I thought he'd care at all? He wasn't really my friend. He was the *talent*. And the *talent* didn't care about anyone but themselves.

He stood and jumped several stairs before reaching out and grabbing my hand, nearly making me trip over the last stair—which I would have if he hadn't steadied me as fast as he'd unsteadied me.

"Whoa, little missy. Back up just a little. I never said it didn't matter. I only said that one little rejection letter wasn't the end of the world."

"Just shows how little you know. How many people are dead because of one rejection letter?"

His concerned look turned to one of amused confusion. "Is this a trick question because I—"

"Millions, bonehead. *Millions!* Like over eleven million!" I yanked my hand out of his grasp so I could throw my arms in the air in exasperation.

"Wow. And you just called *me* an actor. This reaction is a little over-dramatic, don't you think?"

"No. It isn't dramatic; it's the truth."

"Oh, really?

"Hitler's sketches were rejected when he applied to an art academy. If he'd been able to go to art school, World War II would have never happened. So don't tell me there isn't power in a rejection letter. One little rejection letter was actually the end of the world for a lot of people."

"Two."

I closed my mouth a second, trying to process his response, which was certainly not what I'd expected. But no matter how many ways I turned his one word over in my head, it still didn't make any sense. Finally I asked, "What?"

"Two. Hitler was rejected twice at that art academy."

I blinked.

Then blinked again.

Then balled up my fist, punched his arm, and stomped down the final stair and toward the pool with an exasperated growl.

I hated that his laughter followed me. "Don't tell me," he called after me. "That was supposed to be a love tap?"

I broke into a run, feeling tears of frustration building in my eyes, tears he could not be allowed to see because he'd already seen too many of my weaknesses, and they weren't his business. I'd been so wrong to let my guard down in front of that *actor*! I hoped my knuckles left a bruise the make-up department would have a hard time covering up when he was on his hot-tub date tomorrow afternoon.

"Hey!" He wasn't going to make this easy on me. He'd caught up to me. "Hey." He grabbed my arm for the second time and all but yanked me off my feet in his effort to stop me. "Hey." This time the word was soft, a single beat from a butterfly's wing. "I'm sorry. I'm not trying to make light of this situation. This is obviously a big deal to you, and the very last thing I want is to hurt your feelings."

"You didn't hurt my feelings," I snapped. But he had. He'd hurt them quite a lot. It had been unexpected that I cared so much what he thought of me and the crumpled rejection letter stuffed into the front pocket of my jeans.

Worse than the fact that he'd hurt me was that he knew he'd hurt me. Stupid betraying eyes with their stupid traitorous tears.

"Tori, I really am sorry. Please don't cry. I wasn't saying that this letter wasn't important. But it isn't important for the reasons you think it's important."

I was too tired to try to translate that into something intelligible and admitted as much. "I don't even know what that means."

He reached his hand down and tugged at the slip of white still sticking out of the top of my pocket. The gesture felt intimate as his fingertips brushed against my jeans, and I stuttered something that wasn't exactly a word but more of a sound.

He pulled the paper all the way out until he held it in both of his hands. He straightened it out and then rubbed it over his thigh to smooth out the wrinkles so they weren't quite so dramatic. "You have to have noticed that your little book, *The War of Art*, is missing from the library. You have to know I was the one who took it, which means you know I read it. Which means I know where you read that bit about Hitler's rejection, but your rejection isn't anything like his."

I rubbed my temple. "It isn't?" Everything inside of me knew I should leave, walk away. He was the bachelor, for pity's sake. He was scheduled to be on a date in less than fourteen hours with Terri, whose entire wardrobe consisted of three teensy triangle-shaped pieces of cloth. He wasn't a confidant. He wasn't a nice guy who could be counted on with confessions of lifelong dreams. Yet my feet kept their place on the paving stones. My eyes stayed on his. I really wanted to know whatever it was he was about to say.

Some part of me hoped he had a different answer for me than the one I'd given myself. Some part of me hoped he could stitch up the wound that had been torn open with the words on that crumpled paper.

"It isn't at all. Hitler's two letters—for him, they represented the end of the world. This one here . . . this represents the beginning. The war for your art isn't with this agency who said your dialogue is"—he looked at the letter and read it word for word—"'cheesy, trite, and embarrassing to intelligence.'" His eyes flicked up from the paper, bright with amusement and something else . . . compassion. "If you make the war about this one company, then you're right, it's over, and you lost. But . . ." He took my hand in his and faced it palm up, placed the letter on top of it, and then covered it with his own so my hand and the letter were cupped between his hands. "But if the war is waged against the right enemy on the right battleground, you'll know the truth."

I shook my head, feeling my lip tremble and hating it. "Who is the enemy?"

He leaned in closer and whispered, "You are. This is just one letter with one company. If you choose to let this be the only letter, *then* you lost the war. But if you decide to submit another script or to at least keep writing, well then, I'd be the first to ring the bell, raise your hands over your head, and declare you the champion. And *that's* the truth."

"It's all just so . . ." I wasn't sure what I was going to say. *Overwhelming, terrifying, stupid.*

As if he knew my thoughts, he said, "'Fear is good. Like self-doubt, fear is an indicator. Fear tells us what we have to do.'" He'd quoted the book exactly. His fingers lightly touched my arm, careful like one might do an animal they didn't want to scare away. He rested his cheek against mine so his lips were almost touching my ear. His warm breath washed over me as he whispered. "Tell me, Tori. What is it you're afraid of?"

"Everything." I whispered back, not sure the word came out loud enough for him to hear.

He pulled away enough that he was looking me in the eye, close enough that I felt every breath he exhaled on my cheeks. "That's what *I* was afraid of."

"What are you doing here?" I asked softly.

"Just checking to see if you're comfortable yet."

"Comfortable?"

He swallowed. This time he lifted one shoulder in a shrug. "Comfortable with me. You asked me not to make you uncomfortable." He bit his lip for a second before adding, "You told me when I first met you that the best thing I could do was be real. Can I tell you something real?"

I nodded, afraid of what reality he might have to tell me.

"There's more to you than you believe. And I came on *Vows* to truly, sincerely find love. And here I am finding you."

"What are you saying?" I asked, my voice quaking. My mom's words replayed in my head: *someone worth finding.*

He had both of my hands in his. His eyes seared through me. "I'm saying . . . what I'm trying to say is that . . ."

I felt myself leaning in. I felt him leaning in as well.

Christopher Caine was going to kiss me.

"I care about you," he whispered. "So much it hurts . . ."

I didn't answer. Not out loud.

Please, I thought. Whether I meant *please no, we can't* or *please yes, I care about you too* was anyone's guess.

"There you are, Tori!"

We broke away from each other before I could even register the voice those words belonged to.

Robert.

I swept my gaze over him and his camera, praying the red light wasn't on.

It wasn't. Only then did I remember to breathe.

"Robert," I said. "What's up?" My voice sounded too chipper, too innocent, too totally caught.

Robert's expression remained wary and concerned. "Pete's looking for you."

He lied. If Pete was looking for me, he'd be shouting in my headset already. I didn't call Robert on the lie but nodded and made a lame sort of wave of farewell to Chris.

Chris ducked his head in his bowing motion. "I'll see you later, Miss Tori."

Robert cut Chris a glare and started walking back with me. I slowed for a fraction of a second, long enough to answer Chris with a smile behind Robert's back.

The grin he returned made my stomach flutter. And the smolder he'd put into the words *Miss Tori*?

I hoped he meant it. I hoped he would be seeing me later. I needed to know what was on the other end of that lean.

Chapter 11

"Torı!" Robert had hauled me to the back of the electrician's truck and made me climb inside so he could yell at me where no one would hear. He put down his camera. "Did I walk in on what I think I walked in on?"

"Tell me what you think you walked in on so I can adequately answer your question." I was trying to play it cool and not give in to him as though he was the adult and I was merely the child being scolded. I was an adult too and didn't need lectures.

"Were you really dumb enough to be out in the open kissing the star of a show that doesn't exactly allow for on-the-side romances?"

I couldn't give a single good answer to that precise question, so I didn't try. "We weren't in the open . . . exactly." Truthfully, we were out where anyone could have seen from the majority of the windows in the mansion.

Robert whirled on me. He didn't have his camera, and his hands looked empty and fidgety without it to balance him. "Are you *trying* to get fired?"

That slammed me back into reality. Robert was right, but he didn't need to know he was right. "We weren't kissing. We were talking about a letter I got. I don't know what you saw, but it wasn't what happened." I didn't add that it wasn't what happened only because he came on to the scene too soon.

Dang it.

He sat heavily across from me on an apple box. "What's going on with you? I thought you were serious about this writing thing."

I shifted uncomfortably on the pile of extension cords that made up my seat. "I am serious."

"Then stop acting like some teenager, and act like a professional. You've never been like this before, which makes me wonder what he's doing. Is he forcing himself on you somehow? What's going on?"

The idea of Chris forcing himself on me was laughable. He'd been nothing but a gentleman. The only one forcing anything was bachelorette

Krista forcing kisses on my guy. I still wanted to rip off her lips for that. "Nothing's going on. I only . . ."

"What? You only what, Tori?" Robert had lost a little steam. At least he wasn't shouting anymore.

"I like him, Robert."

He dragged his hand down his face. "I can appreciate that. But right now I'm thinking of only one person. You. I like you, Tori. I'm your friend. And this can't end in any way that's good for anyone. He's a player."

"He is not."

"Come on. A guy goes on a dating show and then starts making moves on the second AD? He has plenty of other girls to choose from. What can he possibly gain from messing with you?"

That made me mad. "Exactly, Robert. He has nothing to gain from it, which is what makes it *real*." I stood and picked my way through the cords and fixtures to the exit at the back.

"Just be careful, Tor," Robert said to my retreating back. "You know how this all works. If you get caught in this little web you're spinning, you lose your job, but you'll lose so much more too."

I looked over my shoulder at him. "What more?"

"A chance to have your scripts bought. And not merely optioned and then shelved for forever so no one sees them but green-lighted and produced. Max and Darren—they like you. You know that makes all the difference in this business. You have an in here that you don't have anywhere else. They won't be green-lighting anything by an employee who betrays them."

I nodded, acknowledging the truth of his words. "I'll be careful, Robert, and I know you're just trying to help. I appreciate your friendship. I really will be careful."

Climbing out of the truck and not immediately going to look for Chris to see if he was okay took all my strength. I forced my feet in the direction of my bungalow.

Christopher Caine was going to kiss me.

He had feelings for me.

What did that mean? Robert said this could only end badly. I tasted the situation from all angles, trying to come up with a way out of contracts, a way to make it all be okay for me to explore these feelings.

No solution presented itself to me.

My emotions felt hopeless, much like I'd felt with the rejection letter, but amazingly, I no longer wanted to stop writing. Instead, I wanted to write and write and write—until my fingers bled and my computer blew up. Chris had restored my faith in myself and in my work with just a few words. I couldn't give up my dreams because one agent had written me a mean letter.

No matter what happened between Chris and me, he had given me back to myself.

I couldn't waste that gift.

I would win the war for my art.

That night I had my own candle ceremony and took my rejection letter out to the fire fountain. I leaned on the stone pedestal and held the rejection letter over the flame flickering from the top. I held on to it until the last possible second, when the flames were nipping at my fingers, before letting the paper fall to the paving stones and wrinkle into black, curling ashes.

Then I felt it, the prickling at the back of my neck when I knew someone was watching me. I turned and looked up. A shadow stood in the window of Chris's room. The shadows of his hands moved together. He applauded me.

I smiled and took a bow.

He bowed back, and then his shadow moved from the window.

Robert might have been right. It might get me fired, but that changed nothing. My feelings were what they were. I was pretty certain I was in love with my audience of one.

Chapter 12

I STAYED UP LATE AND finished the book for book club, then wasn't sure what to do about it. It had felt pushy and demanding. It had felt in some ways demeaning and made me feel stupid. I'd read it before, and it had done nothing but inspire me. This time around?

This time I wanted to scream and yell at it that I'd already tried all those things, but it didn't matter because I was still a failure working in a job that made me an accessory to creativity but *not* a creator.

The second reading had also made me stop to think about things I hadn't considered before. It nudged me forward, took away my excuses.

I wasn't sure. Had I liked it? Had I hated it?

I was at war for my art.

And who was I fighting against? The studios, agents, other writers?

I still wasn't sure. Chris said I was fighting against myself.

But it was hard to think about Chris because of the day's filming. We'd shared a moment last night, a moment that had made me think we might have something between us, but today?

Today another bachelorette had kissed him, and no matter how many times I watched the rushes from that scene, I couldn't excuse Chris.

He'd kissed her back.

There hadn't been any dodging like he'd done with Laura in the library. He hadn't moved aside or backed away. His lips had moved in response to hers.

My heart shattered as I watched it all play out.

He'd told me there was more to me than I believed.

But nothing he said mattered anymore. He had kissed her! How could he have done that? Yet, I knew how. I had only held out hope that he cared more about me than the message he'd been given.

Max had done it. He was tired of the reluctant bachelor, so he'd turned up the steam. It had been in the sides I'd delivered. Where had my head been not to register the meaning of the words "Kiss date good night"?

Last night I was pretty sure I loved Chris. Today I hated him, even if it wasn't his fault. And who knew what I felt about the book? Yet the one leading the conversation for book group tonight was me. What was I going to say? *I loved it the first time reading it, but things are different now . . . Sorry to do this to you guys.* I liked it, hated it, felt put out by it, was inspired, was depressed. How was that for a wishy-washy book report?

One thing was certain: they would never ask me to choose another book. I considered again that the only one in the active book group who needed a pep talk was me. Who else was at war for what I wanted? I was the only one facing resistance.

I reached into the backseat of my car before turning onto Ruby's street and felt around for my fleece, tunic-styled jacket to cover up a grease spot on my shirt. I tried to put it on while still driving but ended up tangling it in the seat belt and gave up. The only woman who showed up straight from work the way I did was Shannon. I really envied how it never bothered her to not change before book club.

I pulled up in front of Ruby's house a few minutes late, which embarrassed me to the tips of my in-need-of-a-trim toenails. Pretty much everyone else had already arrived. *Perfect.* I was the one leading the discussion, and the one providing the refreshment, and I was late.

Always doing the classy thing.

I escaped the seat belt, put on the jacket, and retrieved the refreshment bags from the backseat. If that checker had actually been doing her job and had checked me out of that line, I would have been on time.

I took a deep breath and swore vengeance. Next time I shopped there, I'd use a hundred different coupons and *definitely* go through *her* line.

I took a moment to make myself smile. And left it there another moment until it felt real. *Okay. Good. Now I can go in and act human.*

Ruby answered almost before I'd finished knocking, which meant she'd been hovering at the door, waiting for me to show up. Her lavender blouse billowed in the breeze as she swept back the door to allow me entrance. "Oh, honey, I am so glad you made it. I was worried about you." She enveloped me in a hug, forcing me to hold the bags carefully to the side to keep the doughnuts from getting squished.

Normally I loved Ruby's hugs, but today? Today, when Chris had actually *kissed* that bubble-headed Terri? Today, when everything fit wrong and even the sun looked a little too small for the huge expanse of sky it had to cover? Today even Ruby's hugs felt too tight, more chafing than loving. I pulled away much more quickly than I'd ever done before and held out the bags.

"Mind if borrow your kitchen for a minute?"

"Not at all. Do you need help?"

"Nope. But I'd love it if you'd tell everyone I actually made it and will be right there." I really needed a moment to myself to arrange the doughnuts on the plastic tray I'd bought and to force myself to pull it together.

Ruby wasn't fooled by my excuse, but she left me to my business without protesting or prying. Guilt hit hard. Had my tone been abrupt? I hoped not. Making Ruby feel unwelcome in her own home would be the absolute worst thing I could do.

I shook it off, made my way to the kitchen, unloaded my bags on the counter, and started organizing the plastic tray. I'd been around craft services long enough to know how to make even a simple tray of doughnuts look pretty and appealing. Covering the tray with plastic wrap kept the doughnuts from drying out and kept me from fiddling with the tray anymore. My feet were killing me, so I slipped them out of my shoes to allow them a little freedom. The world usually looked better from the perspective of bare feet, but even that didn't calm me. I stood there drumming my fingers on the counter in a steady staccato.

It was just a kiss, Tori. It wasn't like he'd done something wrong. He was *supposed* to kiss her. He was basically *contracted* to kiss her. I'd seen the sides before I'd delivered them to him. Once Krista had opened that door by forcing a kiss on my bachelor, Max had wanted to keep it open. Why did it bother me? Why did I care? Why had I closed my eyes the moment his lips met hers and wished it was me? What was wrong with me?

I really didn't like Terri. She'd better hope I was never put in charge of her Starbucks order because I would be too tempted to spit in it or stop at the grocery store on my way back and buy rat poison.

No.

Not rat poison.

Maybe some protein.

Protein that bulked a body up, that made it necessary for a person who wanted to keep her size-four buttocks in her cute polka-dotted bikini to buy a size six or eight or *sixteen.*

No. Of course I wouldn't do that. But thinking about it made me smile for real.

Good. Now I was ready to join the group. I left my shoes in the kitchen.

"Hey there, everybody!" I said with my smile of vengeance as I entered the room and tapped on my iPad. I noted Shannon hadn't shown up yet and was glad to not be the only late member of the party. *Way to take one for the team, Shannon.*

Arriving late left me with nowhere to sit aside from the metal fold-up chair at the edge of the room. I eyed the seat with a scowl. One unhappy backside would be the result of choosing the wrong checkout line at the grocery store. I resigned myself to it and sat. At least the kitchen was closer for when it came time to serve the doughnuts. I shot a smile at Livvy. That woman was rubbing off on me if I was finding something to be glad about in sitting on a metal chair.

"Thought you'd gone no-show on us," Athena said.

I laughed. "Yeah, well, you know how I like to make an entrance."

Livvy grinned at me. "It must be a side effect of working with all those egos in Hollywood."

I really liked Livvy. She had a great sense of humor. "You're not lying there, Liv. You would not believe the egos I've had to deal with recently. Those bikini-bottomed bimbos are killing me."

"I bet," Athena sympathized.

"Want to tell us about it?" Ruby asked.

I shook my head sadly, wishing I could tell them the grisly details. A lot of the stuff that happened on set was just funny. And I knew that since Ruby had started watching the show, she'd become an avid fan and would love the insider details. "Sorry, guys. The almighty contract has forbidden me to speak of what I know. Ask me next season about what went on this season, and I'll be able to tell you some of it."

"Dang." Ruby snapped her fingers. But I could tell she still hoped she'd be able to wear me down sometime and make me fess up details. *Not gunna happen, Ruby darling. Not gunna happen.*

"So let's get this party started!" I said, trying not to feel bad at having shut Ruby down.

"*The War of Art*, by Steven Pressfield. I'm really glad I read this book again," I said and then realized the words were true. Good or bad, liked it or hated it, it had been good for me to read it. "Really, the subtitle kind of takes away the mystery of why I was glad to have read it: *Break through the Blocks & Win Your Inner Creative Battles.* I don't know how many of you know this, but I'm a writer. This is why I work in the film industry. I don't want to direct film or produce it. I want to write it. I want to change people's lives and minds with the words I put into the mouths of good actors." I didn't mention how much I really hated reality TV and believed with all my heart that *those* actors could never be considered *good* actors. They could be considered manipulative, sneaky, cruel, lame, dumb, and a lot of words my grandma would have me thrashed for thinking, let alone saying out loud. One actor in particular bore the brunt of my frustration. That man was going to be the death of me or the death of *him* if I didn't keep control of myself. He could have told Max no. He could have just not done it.

I shook myself back into the conversation. These ladies didn't get together to watch me have a mental breakdown over an actor.

Several of the ladies met my small writing confession with varying degrees of surprise. Not Athena or Ruby, who both already knew, and not Ilana, who looked like she'd hardly heard me and certainly didn't care, which was strange. She'd been distant pretty much every single time we'd met, but she'd never been outright apathetic. I looked at her more closely. She looked like she was actually sick. I glanced down at Ruby's white couches and rug and worried a little that they weren't safe in the presence of a sick lady. Did she need a bowl?

But she looked up and offered me a brief smile. Okay, then she was probably fine. She was a big girl. She'd likely know when she was going to be sick and give herself enough time to make it to a bathroom.

I hoped so anyway.

I turned my attention back to the ladies and accepted their exclamations over my desire to be a writer as wonderful with a nod and a thank-you. I actually felt embarrassed saying it out loud. What was I thinking spitting that out? By telling them all, that meant they'd hold me accountable— especially after having read the book.

"Anyway," I continued. "I'm really glad I read it. And this is going to sound dumb, but the thing that struck me the most was something mentioned at the very beginning of the book." I turned my iPad on again, since it had gone to sleep. "There's a line here where it said it was easier for Hitler to start World War II than it was for him to face down a blank canvas every day. That was kind of powerful to me because I really do let the blank computer screen get to me. Sometimes I worry I won't be able to fill it with the right kind of words or that the world won't see my words the way I see them." *Or that an agent will call me cheesy, trite, and embarrassing . . .* I refrained from saying that out loud and continued in a way that didn't make me sound like a bitter, raving lunatic. "So I let that resistance thing get to me and find other things to do. Find my job to do. I tell people I work on *Vows* because I need it to help me break into the market, but really, that's the biggest excuse of them all. I hide behind my job so I don't have to face the blank computer screen. It keeps me so busy and leaves me such little time when I'm actively involved in filming that I can't be bothered with reaching out and achieving my dreams, you know?"

I took a deep breath. Wow had I ever just said a lot. A. Whole. Lot.

But the ladies were nodding.

"I really liked the book too," Ruby said. "I liked how it showed resistance for all the things resistance really is. At the very first of the book, I was grabbed by the line"—she looked at her book, where her thumb had been holding the place—"'Most of us have two lives. The life we live and the unlived life within us. Between the two stands Resistance.' How many of us have an unlived life?"

I stared at Ruby as if seeing her for the first time. I would never have looked at her and thought, *There is a woman with an unlived life.* I'd definitely look at her and think, *There is a woman with a full, complete life.*

"There are lots of things I want to do," she continued. "Maybe not artistic things, necessarily, but things I want just the same, and I let resistance get in my way. My whole life, I've let other things define me. I was the spouse who supported her husband in all of his stuff but never had a—" She cut herself off from saying anything more, but her words were a surprise. A huge surprise. I had always thought she had loved every single itsy bitsy aspect of her marriage to Phillip. This was the first time it looked like that perfect marriage might have had a few splinters. It reminded me of how a person could never really know what went on in the headspace of another person. Ruby was far more complex than I'd first thought.

I frowned at the thought. Just one more reason to stay focused on my job and writing. Getting involved with *any* guy in a world filled with reality shows like *Vows* could only lead to the haunted sort of look on Ruby's face. Yet Ruby had made her marriage work. She'd been happy.

"I had that same thought," Livvy said after a moment of Ruby struggling to find words she actually wanted to say out loud. "Joining this book club in the first place was a huge step for me overcoming resistance. And some of the things I thought had been holding me back were really nothing more than my own fears, insecurities, and excuses. By me taking charge of my own life, I found happiness. I found happiness in my marriage." Livvy laughed. "I mean . . . Not every day. Some days I still want to strangle the man with his own tie, but most of the time, there's happiness where there'd been only silence before. Reading this book reminded me to be cautious not to sabotage myself by turning good things into resistance."

"I'm so glad you've found happiness in your marriage, Olivia." Ruby sounded ready to bawl right then and there. I stared at her, feeling overcome with the incredulity at such a thing as a sad Ruby.

What had happened with Ruby? I realized asking her directly might make her feel bad if it was something she didn't want to share. It definitely had something to do with marriage because of what she said to Livvy. Maybe I could ask Shannon about it at some point. It was then I realized Shannon still hadn't shown up. "Where's Shannon?" I asked.

"Oh, she had to work the night shift tonight. She tried to get it off, but you know how jobs can be so demanding," Ruby said.

Dang. That meant I really was the last one to arrive. *Thanks for nothing, Shannon*, I thought.

Athena cleared her throat. "You know, I didn't exactly love the book. I mean it had some good points. But ultimately, it wasn't my sort of thing. As a businesswoman, I could totally appreciate the way the author gave a real motivation to just sit in the chair and get the work done, but really? Artists aren't all-powerful beings who shape the future of the universe. It's a little egomaniacal to imagine that a bit of poetry or a bit of color on canvas can do all that."

Livvy smiled in her nonconfrontational way. "Actually, I can bet that a lot of works of art do just that. A piece of literature can help reshape someone's viewpoint. I have to say I'd never thought about what life might have been like for the maids in the South all those years ago. It had never occurred to me to think about their lives. By reading *The Help*, my eyes were opened, and I thought about other people who sometimes come into our lives. It's like they stay in this place of being underappreciated or unseen because they're simply doing their jobs, and we aren't thinking about them because we *expect* them to do their jobs."

Livvy leaned forward like she was excited to share what she'd learned. "You can bet that since reading that book, I pay much closer attention to the waiter refilling my glass or the woman cleaning my hotel room. I see them now when I hadn't before. It taught me to be more generous with tips, to make sure I say thank you. It taught me to be a little kinder. There is power in the words we find in books. Some paintings have moved me to awestruck silence and sometimes even tears. And so much music has brought me to my feet and forced me to dance. Art creates action in the person participating with the artist."

"Which is why it's just that much more tragic that some artists face that blank canvas of their work," Ruby said. "If they never express themselves through their art, that means there are people who aren't moved to dancing or to awe over beauty or to gain a self-awareness of literature. That resistance can actually lead to the detriment of the world's future."

Athena grinned wide. "I'm not arguing. I can actually agree with all of that, and like I said, I really understood and appreciated the lessons of how to avoid resistance or wage war on the resistances in your own life. I think that a person learning how to control the friction that opposes them accomplishing the things they desire is a great thing. But it almost feels like the writer is passing judgment on all of those who allow nonart-related activity to continue in their lives. It seems out of proportion to me. He purports that a person isn't really a professional at whatever their art is until they give up everything else in their lives that isn't art. That seems unhealthy and like the author is snubbing those who strive for a balanced, comprehensive life. Keep in mind . . . I was exactly this sort of person a few months ago, but now I can see how it can get out of hand. There needs to be a balance."

Ilana hadn't said anything.

But Paige jumped in. "There has to be balance—a kind of moderation to all things. But sometimes my life gets out of balance the other way, so this really helped me remember to grow that artistic part of myself. My favorite quote in the book was that resistance is directly proportional to love." Paige scrolled through her Kindle and read aloud, "'If you're feeling massive Resistance, the good news is, it means there's tremendous love there too. If you didn't love the project that is terrifying you, you wouldn't feel anything. The opposite of love isn't hate; it's indifference.' I'd never considered how powerful a little apathy could actually be."

"Absolutely!" Ruby agreed. "I mean, that makes a lot of sense. Things that are good and true in this life take a lot of effort to maintain. If they aren't something you are passionate about, you won't care enough to make it work."

Ilana began rocking gently, rhythmically, like she was rocking an injured child or something. For a moment, I stopped listening to Ruby and watched Ilana. Was she okay? Was she sick?

She caught me watching her, and instead of looking away due to my embarrassment at being caught staring, I sent her a questioning look.

She smiled, but her smile looked like something that didn't naturally belong on her face. The smile didn't fit with the haunted eyes that seemed watery and sad or the furrowed brow. The smile didn't belong with the nose that flared out as if she was about to cry.

She turned her eyes away from me, but I didn't stop watching her or worrying about her. She raised her hand after another few minutes. "Hey, um . . ."

We all fell quiet, and finally, everyone else turned to her. I wondered if they saw what I saw. She raked her fingers through her hair and rubbed at her forehead as if trying to drill holes into her temples. Paige must have picked up on the body language because she looked worried. So did Livvy. "Can I use your restroom?" Ilana asked.

Ruby put her hand on Ilana's arm. Ilana stared at it as if the last thing in the world she wanted at that moment was to be touched by anyone. Ruby must not have noticed Ilana's mouth tightening because she didn't remove her hand right away. Instead, she patted Ilana's arm and said, "Of course, dear. A half bath is just down the hall past the kitchen."

"Thanks." She snatched up her purse and stood. She passed me, and I tried to catch her eye to convey my worry and to offer her some support. That was when I noticed how dilated her pupils were. The fingers clutching her purse had a slight tremor to them.

She was definitely *not* okay. The way she refused to meet my eyes made things seem even stranger.

Paige said something else about the book. I didn't catch the comment. It could have been anything. Ruby responded, but the words had all turned to static as I shifted in my seat so I could view the hallway better.

If she was sick, she might appreciate a glass of water or something. I thought about following her to the bathroom and asking if she wanted some water when I realized she hadn't gone into the hallway bathroom.

She'd continued past the bathroom toward the stairs.

Now that was weirder than anything else. I cast several looks down the hall to see if she'd realized she'd missed the bathroom and come back, but she'd gone up the stairs quietly—as if sneaking—and had not come down again.

I leaned forward and tried not to worry—tried to remember why I was at book club. It was my book they were discussing, and I felt a moral obligation to actually pay attention, but my eyes kept straying to the hallway.

I finally caught Ruby's eye and mouthed, "I'll be right back."

I had barely stood and made it into the hallway when Ilana returned. She seemed a little calmer, so maybe I'd been reading more into her previous reactions.

Except . . .

Except her eyes were still dilated, and her actions weren't *normal* as she passed me in the hall. It was as if she hadn't even seen me.

I contemplated what all of that might mean and finally had to go investigate for myself. I'd been on enough sets with actors who required Visine to help get the drugged-out look from their eyes to know that when something seemed wrong, it usually was.

From the sounds coming from the living room, everyone else was in the midst of a great conversation about their own dreams and goals and the ways they could help each other achieve those goals.

I loved the support they showed each other and told myself that was why I had to check. Ilana might need support too.

I passed the hallway bathroom and slipped up the stairs in the same way Ilana had. A light glowed faintly from inside a room that had the door partially opened. I peeked inside to find that the room was the master bedroom and the light was coming from the master bathroom. Why would she use the bathroom up here when the one downstairs was where she'd been directed to go? How would she have even known there was a bathroom in this room?

Without allowing myself to think too much about what I was doing, I slipped into Ruby's room with a backward glance to make sure no one had followed me. No one could have seen where I'd gone from the living room, since the only chair that had a view of the hallway and stairs was the one I'd been sitting on. The tidy room didn't look like it had been ransacked in any way, so I followed the light to the bathroom.

The mirrored medicine cabinet hung slightly ajar. Not that an open medicine cabinet proved anything, but it made my stomach drop just the same. I opened it all the way and peered inside. A small iodine-colored pill bottle with a white label sat a little off the edge of its shelf. I picked it up. Percocet.

I shook it, glad it still seemed pretty full.

You're just projecting the lifestyles of the lame people you work with onto a really nice woman. I was satisfied with my own stupidity until I turned to go and my bare toe felt a slight lump at the edge of Ruby's blue rug. My toes curled around the lump and then folded the edge of the rug over enough to reveal a little white pill.

I pressed the palms of my hands against my eyelids, hating what it likely meant but hoping I was wrong. I picked the pill up and matched it to the ones from the Percocet bottle.

Great job, super sleuth. Now what?

I looked back in the direction of the living room, even though I couldn't see through the walls. *Ilana . . . what are you thinking?*

The wall gave no response, but Ilana *wasn't* thinking. The pill was in the driver's seat now. Ilana was just a passenger. I stood a moment, wondering if I'd need to throw up with this new discovery. Suddenly, my problems on set seemed smaller.

Ilana had the great clothes and nice car. She was smart and interesting and had a cool career. How did a woman like that get tangled up in pills?

I popped the bottle top, slid the pill inside, then tucked the bottle back onto the shelf, not sure what to do about the situation. Leaving a nearly full prescription bottle seemed like a bad idea. Would Ilana go back for more? Should I take the thing, go back to the living room, and chuck it at Ilana's head while demanding an apology for Ruby?

No.

A little too much reality TV in your life, Tori . . .

I liked Ilana, and no matter how mad it made me that she'd taken pain meds from an older woman who might actually need them, putting her on the defensive wouldn't help.

If only Shannon had shown up to book club. Shannon would know what to do. She worked with these things every day of her life, and she was Ruby's niece. She'd have been able to help me figure out how to handle the situation.

Which decided things. The only real option was to visit Shannon at her pharmacy. Ruby had said she'd be working late, which meant she'd still be there when book club was over. With a growl, I grabbed the bottle and shook out one of the pills to show Shannon. Maybe the bottle didn't really have Percocet in it. Maybe Ruby reused bottles and this pill was a generic ibuprofen or whatever. Maybe.

I knew it wasn't, but the benefit of the doubt was the only gift I had to give Ilana.

I tucked the pill into the pocket of my jeans and hurried back to everyone else so they wouldn't wonder if I'd died.

Of course I hadn't.

But as I avoided meeting Ilana's gaze, it felt like a small part of me had.

Apparently, I wasn't the only one facing resistance after all.

Chapter 13

THE WIND HAD BEEN RIPPED from my sails as I presented the dessert to the ladies. I'd meant the doughnuts to be a fun tie-in, but the message of finding ways to make time for the important things by taking the stress out of our responsibilities fell flat, along with the corners of my mouth, which wouldn't stay turned upward.

I tried though.

I was grateful when Ruby took the attention off of me and my doughnuts so she could show us pictures of her trip to Greece.

The pictures were amazing, and the guy who had been their tour guide was totally hot for being an older man. Ruby seemed a little flushed as she looked at the pictures with him in them.

Huh. Interesting.

Ruby finally shut the book, acting almost hasty with the motion as she announced she'd bought us all presents.

An evil eye bracelet and earring set. Adorable.

Ilana even seemed to have caught the spirit of things as she accepted her gift with a grin.

Ilana was a good woman—a nice woman. Whatever she'd gotten herself into didn't make her bad. It made her someone who needed help. I watched her while we ate doughnuts. She'd calmed down a great deal. The tremor in her hand was almost steady. Her eyes didn't seem so dilated. But she seemed pretty out of it. Her answers to other people's questions were *wrong* somehow, as if she hadn't really heard the question and was merely saying whatever came to mind to say.

I probably acted as distracted as she did for the final moments of the meeting, and I was relieved when it was over and people began to leave.

"You okay, darling?" Livvy asked. She was cleaning up for Ruby while I found my shoes in the kitchen and stuffed my feet back into them.

"Sure I am," I said. Total lie.

"Sure you are . . ." she said back in that way that let me know she knew the lie for what it was.

Ilana had left first, escaping the house as if it had caught fire. Paige and Athena had hung around a bit, talking in the foyer, but they'd gone before I could try again at being social with them and at least apologize for my lack of enthusiasm there at the last.

Ilana's situation had really rattled me. These ladies had become my escape from the drama of my job. They were the ones I depended on to be normal, to prove to me that people lived regular, happy lives. And now?

Now, I felt trapped in a reality TV nightmare.

"What's been bothering you tonight, honey?" Ruby asked once there was only Livvy and me left.

I smiled. "Nothing." My voice was too high-pitched. The answer too fast.

Livvy leaned on the counter on one side, and Ruby took up space on the other—effectively sealing me into some sort of confessional.

"You seem frazzled, and frazzled isn't nothing," Ruby said with a wave of her hand as if dismissing my denial.

"And you were frazzled before you walked in the front door," Livvy said. "Is something going on at work?"

Work.

So many things were going on at work.

But my current concern could not be pinned on Chris and that kiss. I'd shoved aside the ache that went along with all thoughts of Chris because of the pills. But with these two women staring me down, that ache came right back to the front of my heart. "I think I'm in love." It seemed to me that the words had been merely a thought in my head—a silent admission of guilt. But the reaction on Ruby and Livvy's faces told me I'd actually said them out loud.

"With who?" Ruby asked, her eyes widening in delight and her hands clapping.

"Wonderful!" Livvy exclaimed in perfect time to Ruby's clap.

"Yeah, wonderful," I muttered. What was it about these women that made me spill my guts like I did? How had I said that out loud? At least I hadn't said his name.

Ruby's look had turned positively rabid. "Tell us everything. If you won't tell me about Christopher Cain's love life, I can at least hear about yours!"

Christopher Cain's love life. *My* love life. The two were absurdly connected. The way he looked at me . . . the way he smiled and his fingers grazed my arm when he was trying to talk to me, the way he lowered his voice as if we were star-crossed lovers meeting in the dark—meeting for a kiss that could never happen.

How could that no-talent bubble head have stolen *my* kiss like that?

But then . . . Chris had never really said anything that offered hope that he felt for me what I felt for him. He said he cared for me. You could care for almost anyone. You could care about your dog or your pet fish. What did caring prove? He was always nice to me, but he was always nice to everyone. He was even nice to Pete, who was as smarmy as a human being could get. The fact remained that Terri hadn't stolen my kiss. She'd been given a kiss that belonged to her. It wasn't her fault, yet I still despised her for it.

"There isn't anything to tell." I clutched my paper bag of leftover doughnuts until my knuckles whitened. "He doesn't even know I'm alive." At least, he didn't know how alive I felt when he was near.

"Nonsense!" Ruby said at the same time Livvy made a face and blew a raspberry. "No one could overlook a woman of your beauty and intelligence."

I allowed a smile, loving that they were so quick to assume I was something amazing when they had no idea what kind of women competed with me. With all of the eliminations and the season moving toward the finale, the studio had brought in the hair stylists, make-up artists, and wardrobes that cost more than five years' worth of my personal income to all be at their beck and call twenty-four hours a day.

I had my dollar-store tube of lip gloss.

Gemma didn't need my help anymore.

And there was also the matter of the pill in my pocket. I glanced at my watch. "Oh, hey, guys. I'll take a rain check on you all telling me how great I am and how lucky he'd be to have me because I really need to get going. Don't worry about me. I'm a little distracted, but I'll be fine. I promise." I smiled wide, showing all of my teeth like when I was little and my mom was making sure I'd brushed properly.

They didn't look convinced, but I squeezed past them, determined not to allow the way they'd caged me in to intimidate me into staying and saying anything else I wasn't wanting to confess.

"Thanks for the great book group, Ruby. I appreciate you letting me come to restore my faith in humanity."

"You're welcome, dear." Ruby gave me a hug. "Though we're certainly not perfect, we are perfectly human."

I patted the pill in my pocket. "You're more right than you know." I hugged Livvy and hurried out. Time to go to Walgreens to figure out some humanity.

* * *

The parking lot at Walgreen's had four cars in it due to the late hour. Fewer cars meant fewer customers, which meant Shannon might have a moment to talk to me and help me out. With a heaving sort of breath, I shoved open my door and stepped out of the car. No sense delaying the inevitable. If I waited too long, Shannon's shift might end or the pharmacy might close. She could slip out some back employees' entrance, and I'd miss her entirely.

The quiet in the store had a library feel to it. I hurried to the prescription counter while clutching my doughnut bag and relaxed when I saw that Shannon hadn't left yet. She wore a blue scrubs top underneath a white pharmacist smock. The bright computer screen on the counter reflected in her eyes as she stared into it and tapped at the keyboard.

I suddenly felt stupid.

What if I was wrong? What if Ruby had been the one to drop the pill on the carpet in her bathroom and Ilana was just . . .

Was just what?

I didn't imagine her sneaking into Ruby's room. I didn't imagine the tremor in her hand or the watery eyes. The signs were all there, and something had to be done about it. But interrupting Shannon's work now felt like a wrong move. What would Shannon be able to do about it?

I hovered near the counter, torn between clearing my throat to get her attention and turning around and walking away.

She picked up a pen and made a notation of something and then noticed me waiting nearby. Her facial expression went from one of concentration and focus to smiles and relief at getting a break. "Tori! What are you doing here?"

I smiled, feeling foolish and paranoid. Yet I'd come this far . . . might as well go the whole way. But edging into the conversation made me cringe inwardly. Blurting out that Ilana stole Ruby's pain meds might be more than awkward. Polite chitchat might be better to begin with. "I was planning on giving you grief for no-showing tonight at book club. When I got there, I hoped you were late too so I wouldn't have to be the only miscreant in the group."

"You were late, huh? Bet Aunt Ruby worried you died on the 405 somewhere." Her fingers flew over the keyboard, but she didn't act like she was distracted. Divided attention from Shannon felt like the full attention the rest of the world gave. I could take a few lessons from her.

"She'd worried a bit, I guess," I said, leaning against the counter.

She hit her enter key and then turned fully to me. "So how was book group tonight?"

"We had doughnuts for dessert." I shook the sack at her.

Her smile widened into something that could only be described as epic. "Any chance you have a cruller in there?"

"Are you kidding? Any self-respecting purchaser of baked goods would get plenty of crullers. Can you eat back there, or will you get in trouble?"

"I'm actually about to turn things over to another pharmacist. Give me a few minutes to get things squared away, and I'll meet you out there."

I agreed to wait.

She went back to the computer screen, and I sat in the chair at the blood-pressure cuff. I put my arm in the cuff and fiddled with the screen until Shannon showed up.

"Having fun?" she asked with a smirk.

I yanked my arm out and felt heat in my cheeks. "Sorry. Just . . . you know." I waved at the machine and shrugged.

"It's the most popular seat in the store. So what's up?"

"Uh . . ." Here it was, the moment I could just spill it. Instead, I handed off the bag of doughnuts.

"Thank you," she said. "I need to pick up a few things. Want to tag along with me?"

I agreed, feeling relieved to have an excuse to stay with her awhile longer, and fell into step beside her. She fished a doughnut out and bit into it as if it was the first thing she'd eaten all day. "So . . . how was book group?" she asked around a mouthful.

It took a moment for me to process the question. I wasn't really thinking about book club any longer. "It was fine." A fine night for drug theft in the home of a friend. "Ruby doesn't know I'm here. But she's the reason I came."

"Oh yeah?" She tugged a shopping cart out of where it nested with the others.

I followed her as she headed down the aisle. "Well, kind of. And Ilana."

"Ilana?" She took a bottle of nail polish remover off the shelf.

I took a deep breath. This would take some serious explanation, though it was possible she already knew there was an issue with Ilana. This was her profession, after all. She'd probably seen the signs way before I had. Had Ilana taken medication from Ruby before now? That was possible too. But I spilled everything in chronological order.

The whole thing sounded so dumb when I explained it, but I forged ahead. "The light in the master bathroom was on, and then when I looked around to try to figure out why Ilana would have gone up there, I found this on the floor. I thought maybe you could identify it for me."

I held it in my palm for her to inspect.

"Mallinckrodt oxycodone," she said after barely a glance. "Percocet." Her forehead had furrowed into frown lines.

I sighed out my last bit of hope that maybe it was an aspirin and I'd been making a big deal out of nothing. "It's possible that Ruby just left the cabinet open and dropped this pill, right? It's possible that it wasn't Ilana who dropped it at all." I wanted to make sure we explored every explanation. Ilana deserved for us to be fair.

"Possible . . ." Shannon said, taking the pill from my palm. "But Ruby never takes anything that isn't absolutely necessary."

"Maybe Ilana has her own prescription?" I really wanted some other reason. I wanted anything but the logical conclusion. "Is that what you're thinking?"

"But why use Aunt Ruby's private bathroom for that? And a private bathroom on a different floor than the guest bath?"

All excellent points. I was out of excuses for Ilana.

I pressed my palms over my eyes—my frustration habit. "Right. She just seems too classy for this sort of thing. Ilana isn't the type."

Shannon gave a humorless laugh. "Everybody is the type. I've seen some really fabulous doctors and other pharmacists destroy their lives and families because they thought they weren't the type."

I leaned on Shannon's cart, needing the support. I felt like a tattletale for running to Shannon about Ilana, but what other option existed?

"What should we do?"

"The first step is trying to make sure we're right about this. If we're not, it could be devastating to confront her about it."

"Okay." I nodded, glad to have someone coming up with rational ideas—at least ones more rational than chucking a pill bottle at Ilana's head. "Good point. How can we find out?"

Shannon shrugged. "Spend time with her, ask her how things are going since her surgery."

I considered the situation and Shannon's interpretation of it before saying, "I need to get a birthday gift for my mom. Maybe I could invite Ilana to go shopping with me."

"That's a good idea," Shannon said. "Do you mind letting me know how it goes? Maybe I could invite her to lunch or something."

"Do you think we should talk to Ruby?" I gave an apologetic smile. "And by 'we,' I mean you."

"Sure," Shannon said.

What a relief. Talking to Shannon about it had been hard enough. I gave Shannon a huge hug of gratitude. She seemed a little surprised and stiff with the return embrace. That girl needed to be hugged way more often. My mother wouldn't ever let anyone return a hug with such floppy, uncertain arms. She'd stay there hugging on them until they got the practice they needed and returned the hug properly.

I didn't do that to Shannon. Instead I said, "Thank you so much. I knew you would be the right person to talk to. I'll let you know how things go. Can I get your cell phone number?"

We traded numbers. Going to Shannon had been a good idea. She was smart. She understood the ramifications. All of my experiences with drugs had been from watching actors come back to set wasted and stupid, but they had their agents working with them to help them stay clean. None of that had ever been any of my business.

Ilana felt like my business. Her problem seemed personal to me. I couldn't just let it go without trying to help in some way.

I was glad Shannon had taken me seriously and that Ilana's problem felt as personal to her as it did to me. Ilana was one of us. And we would help take care of her.

I'd joined that book club for all the wrong reasons. And now? Now I was neck deep in friendships that were starting to feel like family. I'd be staying in the group for all the right reasons. It was good to be able to step back from my problems for a moment to see that there was a bigger world out there. Focusing on Ilana might help me take my focus off one certain man.

Chapter 14

I CALLED ILANA FIRST THING the next morning. The mansion required me to be back that night, so there wasn't time to waste.

The phone rang once. *Is this a stupid idea?*

Twice. *What if she hangs up on me?*

Three times. *She'll think I'm a lunatic.*

Four times. *She's not home.*

Five times. *Or she's passed out in bed, having crashed from her high the night before.*

Six. *I should really just hang up. This is—*

"Hello?" Ilana finally answered.

"Hey there. Ilana?"

"Yes?" She sounded . . . exhausted. And super bugged to be on the phone.

"Hey, it's Tori . . . you know from book club?"

"Tori, right. Hi. What's up?" She sounded better now that she knew it was me, which I took as a good sign. At least she liked me enough to not want to be rude to me.

"I was just thinking about you and hating that we really didn't get the chance to talk last night. I had some things going on with work that kept me pretty distracted. Anyway, I was thinking about you and your style."

A sigh came from the other end of the line, so I picked up my pace in case she decided I was worse than a sales call and hung up.

"Anyway, it's my mom's birthday coming up. I've been thinking a lot about my mom since we read the Henrietta Lacks story, and I really want this to be special. You always look so nice and have such great ideas about things. I was wondering if maybe you'd come with me to buy her a present. I would love some professional advice." I stopped talking and held my breath, waiting for her decision.

"I don't know about today. Could we do it some other time . . . later?" she asked.

My heart sank. She was going to say no. "Um . . . sure. I guess later would be okay. Her birthday isn't for a month. I have to work all this week, and the hours are pretty intense, but you know, the show goes on hiatus in a few weeks. We could do it then."

"Hiatus?"

"It's where we take a break for a specific amount of time. It just means we're not filming."

A long pause—long enough that I wondered if she'd hung up anyway. "Okay," she finally said. "When you're on hiatus, then. Call me then."

We talked for a minute about where we might go and then hung up.

I did a mental victory dance at the same time I frowned in concern. She agreed to go but also put me off. Ilana needed a friend to help her before it was too late. There had been too many sets of dilated pupils parading through my life to ever want that for Ilana. I'd seen lives destroyed and lives hanging on by threads. If I could be her friend and let her know she wasn't alone, maybe she could stop this roller coaster before it made it over the first hill.

And maybe she could help me too—keep me from thinking too much about Chris and the things I could do nothing about in my own life.

* * *

I awoke to a text message from Max.

Darren made some good comments about what he's read so far. Keep your fingers crossed, kid

My conversation with Robert felt like it was on repeat in my mind. Max and Darren had my scripts. Darren had said good things about them. Robert had told me to act like a professional, to be serious about my writing.

I had to do the right thing by Chris. He had a contract. I had a contract. Steeping ourselves in a situation from which there could be no good ending just made things worse. Any flirting I did with Chris was unfair to him. And it was unfair to me. Watching him kiss the ultrahot Terri made that clear enough. I couldn't handle thinking I might have a chance when there were no chances available to either of us—not with each other.

I had to go back to being professional.

Returning to the mansion filled my stomach with boulders. I stayed away from the duck pond and didn't have to interact with Chris until I had to stop by his room to deliver mail to him. He smiled, and when I didn't smile back, he stopped and said, "Hey, we have an agreement. You owe me payment for a hand reading."

Instead of making a snarky comment about all the lip reading he'd done with the various bachelorettes, I reminded myself that my current situation was my own fault and smiled for him before trying to escape.

His hand grabbed mine, pulling me back. "Hey there, writer lady. What was that? That wasn't any smile. That was more like you were showing off the fangs you were planning on biting my head off with. What's up?"

"Nothing." I reached inside my own head, thinking of Livvy and her way of finding things to be glad about. The season was more than half over, and then I could forget—something to be glad about. I gave a real smile.

"There it is. I knew you had it in you. See you at the duck pond later?"

The smile fell. "I . . . don't know. There's lots of work to do and . . ."

Chris lowered his voice. "Don't hold this against me. You know I had to."

"Had to what?" My voice was strained, too high-pitched, too tight.

His eyes filled with some unreadable emotion, almost a pleading for understanding, for forgiveness. "Had to kiss her. Max talked to me personally. He said I had certain obligations that I wasn't fulfilling. And he's right. I agreed to certain things—after-date kisses for some girls were included in the package. Robert told me it looked strange to have me not interacting more with the girls. He told me it could cause trouble for you. I don't want to cause trouble for you. You know what my job is here. You of all people should understand that."

Robert—always looking out for me.

I did understand, more than Chris knew.

And understanding allowed me the strength to say, "Hey. We're just friends. We did the secret handshake and everything. I'm fine. We all have contracts here. I told you that from the beginning, so I'm the last person you need to worry about. We're just friends." I gave a real smile, one I had to dig deep to find.

He frowned. Mercy, even a frown looked good on that man. "Right." His nod was slight, and his jaw muscles flexed. "Friends. Got it."

I held up the handful of call sheets and sides. "Got to get these delivered. I'll see you later."

He didn't respond. But it seemed his door shut a little harder than normal.

I flinched at the noise.

"You're doing the right thing," I whispered to myself.

But I'd never known the right thing to hurt so much.

* * *

The week passed. It felt like the world had been shrouded in fog. Focusing on anything felt impossible. I delivered the wrong things to the wrong rooms more than once. One bachelorette missed her cue because I forgot to go get her when it was time for her to come down.

Max cast strange looks in my direction.

Pete growled and acted as though my actions were to purposely make him look bad.

Chris . . . Chris stopped looking at me.

I no longer felt his gaze on me when we were in a room together. It felt as though he held his head tight to keep it from turning my direction. His jaw muscles were always working like he was grinding his teeth.

His hurt and anger came at me in waves.

Which wasn't fair at all.

I hadn't kissed anyone in front of him.

I wasn't the one on date after date after date.

With the passing week went three more girls.

Sara, because she hated all music except Irish drinking songs. She interrupted him anytime he tried to sing anything else.

Annette, because she continually corrected his grammar when he spoke. And I think it bugged him that she was usually right.

Josephine, because she hated Disneyland, and Chris had called that un-American. He nearly fell apart when he found out she didn't like Miracle Whip either. He was just being petty on that one.

Though part of me was glad to see them go, to know they weren't what he wanted, it made me sad to see them cry and ask what was wrong with themselves. They analyzed their bodies, their hair, their opinions like crazy after they walked away with the unlit candle.

And I wanted to reach out to them and tell them to stop it. In middle school, when I'd gone home crying over a boy making fun of my super curly hair and demanded my mom figure out how to straighten it, my mom bundled me up and held me. Then she quoted me the saying she had on our fridge: "In a world where you can be anything, be yourself."

These girls were trying to modify themselves, to tailor make themselves into something a guy they barely knew wanted. It was petty of me to dislike them until they were castoffs. Then I only wanted to commiserate with them.

Another week.

Three more girls.

Becca, because she confessed to finding things to tick her boss off on purpose. She was apparently hard to get along with. I hadn't ever had a problem with her and thought the bachelor was being lame on that one too. Her boss probably deserved it.

Julie, because all she ever did was talk about how she'd met Ewan Mc-Gregor on a movie set and how he'd kissed her, as if that lip connection somehow made her famous—annoying.

Melanie, because she wore a lot of black and talked enough about vampires and zombies to worry about the reality in which she lived.

Seven girls left. Gemma still among them. Becky, who exclaimed great relief in no longer having to deal with anyone confusing her with Becca, was also still among them.

And I missed Chris.

Crazy missed him.

How could I miss someone who usually stood less than fifty feet away from me for hours a day?

But I did.

Another week.

Three more girls.

Rachel, because she laughed at his drawl and told him she believed a British accent made a person's IQ go up five points, but a Southern drawl made it go down five points. She was trying to be funny, but Chris didn't laugh.

Krista, because she tried to trick him into more kissing. I was glad to see her go. That was one grudge I couldn't seem to shake.

Tristi, because she admitted to reading tawdry romance novels. He likely would have been fine with her reading choices, but she also admitted that she didn't think any real, living, breathing man could ever compare to the guys in the books. She called it the great tragedy of humanity that real men were stupid.

Four girls left: Gemma, Becky, Terri, and Jennifer. By that time, Chris had kissed all four of these girls to some degree or another. I was counting down the days until I no longer had to deal with this being tossed in my face. I never watched the episodes when they aired. Watching it in real life had eaten enough of my soul.

With only four bachelorettes left, it was time to get exotic. We were going to Dubai. Due to the change in scenery and the need to prepare for all eventualities, we had a two-week delay. Which meant I had two weeks off—mostly.

I had two weeks to breathe before I had to go back to a world where Chris would have to pick a girl and give her a ring.

I had two weeks until my world ended for real.

* * *

Cleaning up the mansion took a few days. We had to do all the paperwork and make sure it was in order. And there was all the camera and lighting equipment that had to be packed up and put away. Chris and the four bachelorettes were still on the premises but not in filming mode. They were in hang-out-and-wait mode.

I worked hard to pretend Chris hadn't gone back to watching me every now and again. He'd be sitting idly by the pool with a book from the library in his hands, but his eyes weren't on the pages. They were tracking me as I inventoried and cataloged the equipment.

It was because I was watching him watching me that I didn't see the dolly sitting at the bottom of the steps leading down to the pool. I stumbled over it.

I ended up body slamming the dolly onto the cement stairs, hitting my head hard with the metal handle of the dolly and twisting my ankle around it in a way that ankles weren't meant to go.

Chris was on his feet and at my side faster than I could cry out in pain.

"Are you okay? No. You're not," he said after looking me over. He then shouted, "Medic!"

Several other people rushed toward me, Gemma among them. They all made noises of commiseration and asked me stupid questions like, "Does it hurt?"

Would I be crying if it didn't hurt?

The medic showed up a few minutes later. Chris scooped me up and carried me over to a padded lounge chair so the medic could check me out.

He declared the head wound superficial and told me it might bruise but not to worry about it. After pulling on my foot and moving it in ways it really didn't want to go, and making me wince and cry, the medic declared it a sprained ankle, maybe a slightly torn ligament but not bad. "It'll heal on its own if you're careful with it for a couple of weeks," he said. "In the meantime, it's gonna hurt like crazy. Let me write you a prescription for something to help with that."

Chris and Gemma stayed at my side, even as the others drifted away, realizing the drama wasn't very interesting after all.

"I don't need a prescription," I said, waving him away.

"Pain management is very important at the beginning of an injury. If pain isn't properly managed, you might injure it worse."

Gemma nodded as though that decided everything.

Chris agreed with her, which just made me mad. Being mad made me incapable of speaking because I'd just say something that would not be nice. So I stayed silent while the medic wrote a prescription for Lortab.

Robert showed up as the medic wrapped my ankle in an ace bandage and told me to be more careful.

"I am being careful," I muttered.

Robert chuckled, though it sounded humorless. "Tori? Careful? Not a chance."

The medic gave me a stern glance and said, "For today, just stay off the foot. No running around packing up. Let the rest of the crew do it. You go back to your bungalow and rest. That's an order. I'll call Max and report the accident and do the paperwork there."

I nodded, feeling deflated. My work was what kept me from thinking too much.

Chris moved to pick me up again when Robert said, "Hold on. What do you think you're doing?"

Chris looked confused. "He said she had to go back to her bungalow so she could rest."

"Yeah. But he didn't tell you to take her."

Chris looked back and forth between Robert and me before shrugging and saying, "He didn't tell you to take her either."

"I can take myself so you guys can stop posturing like cavemen." Only it wasn't true. I didn't believe I'd make it a single step.

But Chris scooped me up again. "Looks like since I've already got her, I guess I'll be the one to take her."

Robert did not like that one bit, but Chris refused to put me down. I was tempted to try to get down on my own and walk while they fought about it, but my ankle hurt so much that the very idea of putting weight on it made me want to throw up.

Robert and Gemma accompanied Chris and me to my bungalow. The guys continued to argue about how I was going to get home since it seemed unlikely I'd be able to drive.

"It's my left foot. My car's an automatic. Why couldn't I drive?" I tried to reason, though the two men seemed past reason, and Gemma was taking whatever side Chris happened to be on.

I had to admit where I hid my key—not that it mattered since we weren't ever coming back to this location—not this season.

Once Chris entered my living space, I was super grateful that I'd already packed away my dirty laundry. That could have been embarrassing.

Several scripts were spread across the table—extras I'd printed when I'd gone to print copies for Max. Robert glanced them over as he walked past.

Chris went straight to the bed and gently laid me out over the covers. He sat beside me, his arm crossing over me and his hand resting against the other side of me closely enough that his thumb rubbed lightly on my arm. He smoothed my hair back from my face with his other hand, and his eyes filled with concern. "Do you need anything? Can I get you anything? Does it hurt much?"

The energy of his closeness made me forget that there was any pain. "I need . . ." His eyes locked on mine, pouring out so much emotion I wanted to cry. It took a great deal of focus not to tell him I needed *him*. "Ibuprofen."

Instead of leaving my side, he looked up at Gemma, who was watching us with a curiosity that made me feel guilty. "Will you get me some ibuprofen and water?" He looked back at me. "Where will she find it?"

"In my purse." I pointed to the yellow leather purse I'd left by my luggage at the front door.

Gemma seemed hesitant to leave Chris's side. Her brow was furrowed. She finally did as directed, but she wasn't happy about it, and her attention remained on Chris. She ended up dropping my purse by the front door. Robert had to help her pick everything up and stuff it back into my purse while figuring out where the ibuprofen bottle had rolled to.

As if pulled by the energy of his stare, I turned back to Chris. Tears leaked from my eyes, but I couldn't say if it was the pain in my ankle or the pain in my heart. *Stay with me,* I wanted to say.

His eyes seemed to be pleading, *Please let me stay.*

A universe of conversations passed in the moments we held that gaze.

It was all over when a plastic cup half filled with water appeared in my vision.

"Here, Tori. Sit up as much as you can." Gemma abruptly edged Chris out of the way.

She'd been through a lot over the last two months. She'd been targeted for torture by twenty-nine other women. Her eyes, as they looked down on me over the glass of water, said everything. She'd made it through twenty-six of those contestants. She was in the homestretch. She had no intention of losing to me.

It amazed me how much she understood with such little information to go on. We hadn't done anything or said anything inappropriate, but she knew something wasn't right.

I sat up with Chris's help and took the drink and tablet she offered me.

"I'll drive you home tonight," Chris said after taking the cup from me.

"You can't!" both Robert and Gemma said at the same time.

They shared a startled look, but Gemma calmed herself enough to give a more reasonable reply. "You can't be offsite until after the last episode has aired. You know that. Robert can take her, can't you, Robert?"

"I can take myself!" I shouted, making everyone jump a little. "I'm fine. Really. It'll be healed by Dubai."

Gemma's eyes widened. She must have been considering the fact that I would be going to Dubai with them. I felt her panic surge through the room. "Are you sure? Maybe you should go out for a medical leave of absence. You don't want to injure it further."

Just like that, I had become the competition instead of the friend for Gemma.

"I'll definitely be going to Dubai," I assured her with a steadiness that made her look down.

Robert backed me up. Whether he knew a power struggle was taking place or not, he said the right thing. "She's absolutely going. Max and Pete wouldn't know how to function without her."

That's right, little girl, I thought. *Don't challenge me on this. Don't try to eliminate me like the others. I can't be eliminated. I am part of the crew, and I'm going.* I'd survived the whole season, which earned me the right to go to one of the coolest places on the planet. I'd been looking forward to it since Max had announced the location.

Chris was oblivious to the interchange. "I could call someone if you won't let one of us take you. You don't have to do everything yourself. You can let people in."

I gave a weak smile. "I can call if I need someone to take me home. Don't worry."

"We should go, Chris. Pete will wonder what happened to us." Gemma shot an impatient look at the door.

"She's right," I said. "The last thing I want is to get you in trouble. You have a contract. You don't have to worry about me."

Chris's eyes widened as if he were considering something he hadn't thought of before. He stared at me as if seeing me for the first time, and then he nodded, much to Gemma's relief.

But then Gemma gasped, a small sound, so quiet it was hard to hear over the thundering of my own pulse racing past my ears.

She gasped because Chris leaned over me, his breath warm, his eyes alight with something that could be described only as fire. His hands cradled my face, and his lips gently pressed against the place just below my ear. "But I do worry about you, writer lady," he whispered.

He stood then, leaving a fiery mark on the place where his lips had been.

Gemma all but dragged him from the tiny room.

Robert stood silent, leaning against the wall.

"Don't, Robert," I said.

"Don't what, Tori?" He sounded tired, beaten, worried.

"Don't say anything."

"I won't. And I won't tell you to be careful anymore. We're way past that warning, aren't we?"

I didn't answer. We were *way* past that.

Chapter 15

THE MEDIC WAS WRONG. My ankle was fine, mostly. Within a couple of hours, I could put partial pressure on it and only wince a little. Not that I was stupid about it. As soon as I did drive myself home, I Googled treatments for mild sprains and found that a regimen of alternating cold and hot packs would help it heal faster.

I didn't get to say good-bye, which made sense. Gemma would be smart enough to find ways to keep Chris busy. I hadn't given her enough credit. She'd be just fine in this death match against Becky.

The girl had game after all.

Poor unsuspecting Becky.

Max called, not even texted but actually called, which sent a chill through me. I answered immediately. Did Robert say something? Did Gemma?

"Hey, Tori. Heard you got hurt. You doing okay?"

He didn't sound angry.

"Yeah, I'm fine."

"The medic said you might be out of commission for a few weeks. Is that right?"

I laughed and kept any tremor of pain from my voice. "He's exaggerating. I'm great—already up and walking and everything." I wore an ankle brace I'd picked up from the drugstore just to make certain it stayed in place, but I wasn't about to admit that to Max.

The whole conversation smacked of Gemma interference. She must have told the medic to recommend a medical leave for me. *Nice try, Gemma. I may not get the guy, but I'll be darned if I miss out on the vacation.*

Max sounded relieved to know of my good health, likely also relieved to know a lawsuit wasn't on its way. "Glad to hear it. I actually need you at the mansion sometime at the end of this week, maybe the beginning of next.

Paperwork mostly, but Pete can't make it in. He's out of town . . . I guess with a girlfriend."

"Seriously?" I said, unable to keep the incredulity out of my voice. How did Pete get a girlfriend?

"I know, right?" Max said. "Kinda surprised me too. I didn't know he had it in him. I know we're on hiatus for two weeks until we leave, but you can come in, can't you?"

"Sure, just text me the times."

"Good girl. And, Tori? Darren says he might have a decision soon. It's lookin' good, kid. He's actually thinking of doing one of them fast. He says the timing is perfect for it to come out this next winter, which means we'd need to be in preproduction by July. Not sure which script he's meaning, but anyway, thought I'd give what information I did have. See you in the morning."

He hung up, leaving me with a phone cradled in my hand and a wild, frenzied, girl scream coming out of my mouth.

Preproduction by July! A green-lighted script!

The possibility of everything hung above me. I only had to jump up and snatch it.

* * *

A script. I might have sold a script! It was happening for me—just like I'd always wanted.

I grabbed my phone to call Chris and tell him when I realized I didn't have his number, and even if I did, his phone was in lockdown. He couldn't answer a call.

There wasn't anyone else I wanted to tell as much as him.

Before even calling my own mom, I had wanted to call Chris—to tell him first, to have him share in the moment with me.

What did that mean?

I'd gone back and forth, vacillating between love and friendship.

But wanting to share this news with him before anyone? That was love. It had to be. The real kind. Christopher Caine was the first person I wanted to share any kind of news with—good, bad . . . everything.

I loved him.

I stood numb in my apartment, staring at my phone, unable to move.

I was finally certain of it, finally couldn't deny it. No more excuses.

But what could be done about it?

Nothing.

Which left a hole in my middle.

Feeling a little less excited about the news that an offer to make my script into a movie might be in my near future, I called my mom and then Janette.

Janette's girl-scream was louder than mine when she heard the news. Mom cried and shouted over to my dad, "You see! Tori's *my* smart girl."

After hanging up with them, it occurred to me that I hadn't thought much about anything *not* work related in the time I'd been at the mansion. Grief while Chris and I shared our silent standoff had consumed me so thoroughly that thinking of anything in the outside world had proven impossible.

Grief that felt so much worse now that I had named the thing I'd been feeling.

Getting away from the mansion and making the couple of phone calls reminded me of responsibilities neglected there. My parents, for one. My siblings for another. I hadn't contacted any of them in the month previous. I'd even neglected Janette, and she was my best friend. Even my decision to check in on Ilana every few days had been a bust. Some friend I turned out to be.

With this free time and my desire to not think about my feelings toward Chris, I tried to call Ilana. Her machine answered. I decided to call and text her every day until she agreed.

Remembering Ilana reminded me about the new book I was supposed to be reading for book club: *Zen and the Art of Motorcycle Maintenance.* I had to actually go back and check the notes I'd made at the last book club meeting to even remember the title. I hadn't downloaded or bought myself a copy. Which meant I hadn't bought a copy for the mansion library. Chris wouldn't be reading this book with me. Maybe there would be time to slip a copy into the library when I went to help Max pack his office.

I wanted to see Chris, wanted to hear his voice—even if it was someone else he spoke to. But going to visit him was one of those things on the forbidden list. I could visit only if I was summoned by Max. That summons wouldn't come until the end of the week.

So instead, I barricaded myself in my apartment, downloaded the book, and tried to throw myself into reading.

I read the first chapter with interest. A guy taking his kid on a long-haul motorcycle ride and then the spectral mystery of seeing something of his past. It seemed interesting, but after a while, I put the book down and said out loud, "Who chose this book?"

The philosophy annoyed me. The guy talked about being accepting of people at the same time he was looking down on his friends who traveled with him. He didn't like how they traveled just because they experienced the world differently than he did. It struck me as pretty narrow-minded to assume your way was the only way. I hated the main character by chapter four, hated feeling like he was talking down to me. This guy would never be on my Christmas card list.

I tried to keep reading, but with my self-admission of being in love, the book held no interest. The only thing that interested me at that exact moment was love. I finally put my iPad down and determined to fake my way through the next book club meeting.

Since I ended up ditching the book, I spent the rest of the week watching Jane Austen movies and gardening with my mom and Janette.

By the following Monday, after a full week of vigilant phone calls, Ilana finally agreed to go out with me.

We decided to meet at Bloomingdale's. I hadn't been to a real store to pick up something for months. After dressing in a pair of black jeans and a fitted black T-shirt, it occurred to me that I didn't have to look plain. An accessory or two might be downright elegant on my assistant-director body. It might even make me feel human for a minute. I pulled out an off-white scarf, thinking about how nice it would be to not have to worry about it getting caught in the wheels of any dollies, and then pulled big hoop earrings from my jewelry box, thinking how nice it would be not to have to worry about them getting caught in my headset.

Definitely human again.

I found Ilana staring off into the crowds and smiled. It really was great that she'd finally agreed to hang out with me. Maybe she was better. She looked better. Maybe I'd imagined the whole thing at Ruby's house. Of course I hadn't, but the woman standing in front of me looked healthy and happy.

"Look at you. You look fabulous." She actually smiled when she said this.

I laughed, looked down, and shrugged. "I'm on set six days a week, sometimes for sixteen hours straight. I rarely wear anything nice or bother with accessories. Might as well feel almost like a woman one day out of the week, right? In spite of gorgeous fashion statements like this." I hiked up the pant leg to my jeans to show off the robin's-egg-blue ankle brace. "You aren't the only lucky one to have an accident at work. I tripped over a dolly."

"Oh no." She looked genuinely sympathetic. "Are you in a lot of pain?"

"Fortunately, no. Aleve pretty much takes care of it. The medic on set gave me a prescription for something stronger if I felt I needed it, but I've been okay."

Her head shifted slightly at the mention of the prescription. "You should totally let me borrow a few pills. Heaven knows Aleve isn't cutting it for my injury. What do you have?"

I blinked in surprise. Awkward. "Lortab, but I think it's against the law to share prescriptions," I said, trying to make it sound nice, but there weren't many nice ways around this conversation. I thought of the pill bottle in Ruby's house again.

She laughed like she'd been joking.

I laughed too and hoped it sounded real. "I haven't bothered filling it. The pain isn't that bad." It seemed like a good idea for her to know that no actual medication existed on my person. I didn't want that coming between us when today was a day meant for real friendship.

"Well, that's good," she said. "So do you want to go in here first? Any idea what kind of thing your mom would like?"

She seemed fine. I was just being hypersensitive about Ilana and pain medication. She had to have been joking. I led the way into the department store and heard Ilana's boots make a rhythmic beat on the black-and-white checkered floor.

"I really am horrible at gifts," I said. "But this is Mom's fiftieth birthday. I need to get her something nice that she'll *like* for once."

We'd stopped at the make-up counter, which made me think of Gemma and helping her with her make-up. I should have put clown circles on her cheeks.

"Tell me about your mother so we know where to start." Ilana pulled me out of my mean thoughts.

"Well, like I said, she's turning fifty. I . . . I'm seriously so bad at this stuff. She's my mom; I should know what she'd love. But she seems to have everything she wants. She's one of those people who always gets herself the things she needs so no one has a chance to buy her anything for birthdays or Christmas."

Ilana considered this before asking, "Does she have any hobbies? Anything she loves learning about? Collecting?"

I thought about it. "She loves plants, but she's pretty intense about what kinds she likes. She hates fake plants."

"Does she like gardening?"

"Yes. A lot." I thought again about how our house had always felt like a greenhouse growing up. "But she already has the latest anything for her garden. She even has the accessories—gloves, shovels, knee pads—you name it."

"Perfume? Clothes?" Ilana scrunched up her forehead as she came up with ideas. "Something to hang on a wall in her house. A cool decoration for her kitchen. Shoes."

"Maybe . . ." I said, taking in her ideas and trying to process them into an actual gift. We walked around, checking out various displays for a while until I came to the handbags. Nothing smelled as good as a buttery, new leather handbag.

I ran my hand over one with purple alligator print. "I love purses. For some women, it's shoes. For me, I could have a house full of purses and still want more." I liked shoes too, but purses were my kryptonite. I showed off my newest purse, a fabulous daisy yellow. My mom had laughed at me when she'd seen it. She did not get my love affair with purses.

"Would your mom like one?"

She wouldn't, but that didn't mean they weren't worth looking at. "Hmm. Maybe." I wandered over and checked them all out, trying them on to see if they hung right. Nothing was worse than a bag with straps too small to sling properly over your shoulder or ones that were too long and made the purse bang into your legs when you walked.

I gathered a few, not nearly as many as I wanted, and checked them against my outfit in the mirror.

"Do you want me to hold something for you?" Ilana asked.

"Oh, would you? Here, just take my purse so I don't get it tangled up with the rest."

That was when I saw a black-and-white bag with a chain handle. So cute.

"I'll be over here." Ilana pointed at a chair. "Can I put anything back for you first?"

"Those three there." I indicated the pile. "Thanks so much!"

After a few minutes, I realized that not only was the clock ticking, but Ilana had also been bored into a chair. No woman should be sitting out a shopping experience in a chair meant for men who didn't get the whole retail-therapy concept.

I wandered back to Ilana, who looked flushed. "Hey, you okay?"

She startled like I'd jumped out from behind a mannequin and screamed boo at her. "Yeah. Yeah, I'm fine. Just got a bit of a head rush. Maybe I need to get something to eat."

"Great idea. Let's go to Charlie Palmer while we're in Bloomingdale's."

She handed me my purse back. "I've never eaten there. Let's do it." Then she pointedly eyed my empty hands. "Did you not find anything for your mom, then?"

My face warmed with realizing I'd allowed myself to get sidetracked by the drug of high-quality leather sewn together with precision stitching and hand-tooled metal clasps. No doubt about it. I was a purse junkie. "Nah. I realized after looking at about thirty handbags that she's never carried one in her life. Ever. It was fun for me, but I'd better get her something else. I'm sure we'll come up with an idea over lunch."

I led Ilana over to Charlie Palmer—a place Janette and I went to often when we were both blessed with free time and a desire to shop. Janette was a bigger purse addict than me. We were meant to be best friends.

Once Ilana and I were seated, we talked. Really talked. I dumped on her about my frustrations with the world of the silver screen. It wasn't intentional, but it was hard not to vent when she seemed eager to listen. I apologized for choosing The War of Art, since the only one in the group who'd needed a kick in the pants had been me, but she assured me she'd liked it and had been glad to read it.

Thinking about the book reminded me about the pills she'd taken, so I changed the subject. No reason to throw a cloud over a nice day. We talked about her job, and she told me she'd been laid off. I asked her to tell me about what she did before the layoff, and for the first time in months, she seemed animated and excited. She went on and on for a long time, but then she said, "Yeah, well. Anyway. That life is over." And her whole countenance changed.

I shrugged, uncomfortable with her rapid descent into depression.

My phone vibrated in my pocket as the salads arrived, but I ignored it, not wanting Ilana to think anything was more important than her at that moment, especially when she obviously felt crummy about not working anymore. Whoever it was could wait.

My phone vibrated again as the main courses came. Ignoring the phone might be a bad plan. The last thing I wanted was Max hollering at me for failing to do something he deemed urgent.

"Excuse me a moment. I need to use the restroom."

Ilana waved me off. I scooted out from behind the table and hurried to the restroom so I could check my messages. Oddly, it wasn't Max at all but Ruby whose name appeared on my screen.

I bit my lip. Was she calling me about Ilana? I paced around the tiny bathroom a moment before deciding I should call Ruby back. I needed to know if there was something specific they needed from me in this situation. Handling it wrong would be bad for everyone, especially when Ilana wasn't more than fifty feet from where I stood in the bathroom.

I dialed Ruby's number. She picked up immediately and was all cheerful hellos and queries about my day. She didn't say anything about Ilana. I relaxed, realizing this was nothing more than a social call. She wanted to set up a lunch date, but our schedules didn't match up, so we put a rain check on that.

"I've been thinking about your mystery man," she said.

I leaned against the sink, grateful it was clean. "Oh really? And what is it you've been thinking?"

"I've been thinking I wished I knew more about him."

I laughed. Ruby was fabulous. "Hmm, let's see . . . He's tall and handsome, and he reads more than any of us in the book club, and he likes saltine crackers with peanut butter and dill pickles."

"Is that all you're going to give me? Nasty snack preferences? No name or location for where he works?"

"Sorry. That's all you're getting for now." The snack preference would have been a big hint, except he'd never mentioned it to anyone else on set—only to me.

"Dang. Then tell me something about Christopher Caine."

I smiled to myself. She had no idea I had done exactly that. "Christopher Caine is an off-limits topic, but I will tell you this. He's as nice in person as he is on TV."

"I'm so glad. Nothing is more disappointing than finding out about actors who play great people in their roles but are really scabs of humans themselves."

I turned around and inspected myself in the mirror while we talked, tugging back a loose curl so it was part of my messy bun. "I agree. And when the season is over, I'll give you details on which of the bachelorettes are exactly those kinds of people.

I wanted to bring up Ilana and the pills issue but couldn't find a way to do it. Shannon knew and had already agreed to take care of that part. Where was Ruby sitting at that moment in her house? My thoughts kept straying to the bathroom at the top of those stairs, where pills were missing. The house was now a crime scene, and Ruby didn't even know it.

Ruby sighed. "It's too bad all people aren't more like Gabriel."

"Gabriel?"

She hesitated and stammered a moment before saying, "Oh, the tour guide in Greece. He was one of the most genuine people I've ever met."

I grinned at my reflection. Sounded more like Ruby was hiding a crush of her own. She clammed up when pressed for more information, which made me realize we'd been talking for several minutes and Ilana had been left hanging at the table. "Hey, Ruby, I gotta go, but I'll call later so we can make plans for lunch, okay?"

We hung up, and I made my way back to the table.

Ilana blinked as if startled to see me back so soon, which was weird, since I'd been in the bathroom forever.

I steered the conversation to her by asking how she'd met her husband, Ethan. Ilana was animated again, telling me about the romance, the jokes, the cute things he did, and his proposal. I listened with rapt attention, not only because hearing the unique stories of how people got together always made me happy but also because another proposal looming on my horizon kept trying to edge its way into my thoughts. I couldn't think about Chris being engaged to one of the girls.

"You said your mother likes plants," Ilana said after we'd finished off dessert.

"Yeah?"

"I have the perfect gift."

We paid our bills and took my car, ending up at a florist-greenhouse place Ilana had used frequently during her time in the trade-show business.

"The right plants and flowers add a lot to the entire tone of a trade show," she said. "You'd use different plants for a garden show than you would for one featuring whimsical children's toys. These guys know their business."

Ilana was right. The cute little lady with the name tag identifying her as Shirley took charge as soon as we walked through the door. She asked all kinds of strange questions regarding my mom's likes and dislikes before walking me straight to a huge potted plant with long, rich green leaves and delicate flowers. "The plumeria," Shirley said.

The plant was lovely, fragrant, perfect.

I bought three of them. And because Ilana had done a lot of business with Shirley in the past, Shirley gave me 15 percent off.

Perfect indeed.

The lunch date had ended well. Ilana had acted healthy and even happy, except for those few times where a shadow had passed over her features and she'd had to shake herself to come back to our conversation. It had happened when I mentioned my mom having four kids and how it had been fun growing up in a loud and busy home. It had happened when we talked about her job. It had happened when we walked past a baby boutique in the mall on the way out to my car.

Shannon was right about Ilana.

Ilana yearned for motherhood. I wanted to ask if there were medical reasons or if maybe her husband didn't want kids, but I decided some things were simply not my business. Everyone had their secrets.

I had mine.

It was okay to allow Ilana to have hers.

Chapter 16

MAX TEXTED ME A LIST of things he needed me to purchase and then deliver to him at the mansion. I dutifully made the purchases and drove through the gates, feeling like a flock of birds had taken off for winter migration in my stomach.

Somewhere on this property, Chris existed. Somewhere he breathed, and his heart beat a steady rhythm, and maybe he was talking or reading. I wanted to see him so badly I ached.

Robert and Max were in the study discussing the footage they expected second unit to get before the rest of us arrived.

I waited outside the door until they were done. Max walked Robert out and saw me there waiting.

"Tori! Great. Good to see you, kid. Hey, I'll be right back; don't go away." Max hurried off, leaving Robert and me alone.

Robert rested his camera on the corner table, sat in the chair next to mine, and tapped my leg. "You feeling okay?"

I nodded, not really feeling okay. But he meant my ankle, not my heart.

Robert furrowed his brow and shifted in his chair so he could view me better. "All right. Spill it. What's going on with you?"

I bit my lip. Telling Robert might be a good thing. He might offer perspective I wouldn't have on my own. He had a good marriage and a happy life. He knew about love. I really wanted to ask my parents, but they were so close to me that if I mentioned to them that I was in love, they'd freak out. Their advice couldn't be trusted.

But Robert's advice?

"If I tell you, will you promise to keep it between us?"

"Do you really have to ask that?"

I grabbed at his collar and wrenched it to the side like I might strangle him. "Yes. Promise me, or leave me alone."

He laughed in that way that said he was trying not to be offended by my abruptness. "I promise."

Once he'd promised, finding the words to say out loud to *someone else* proved nearly impossible, even though Robert already suspected the truth. I swallowed several times, fidgeted with my hands, and then closed my eyes so I didn't have to see Robert staring at me, waiting for me to confess.

"I may have a problem . . ." I started.

"Does this problem have anything to do with the bachelor?" he asked.

"Yes. It may have everything to do with the bachelor. I think . . . I might be a little in love with him."

There. The words were out. More importantly, they were out to someone who wasn't me.

"I . . . figured," Robert said slowly, calculating what he would say next. "And what do you plan on doing with this information?"

"I hardly know. What can I do?"

"Let it go."

That was not the answer I had anticipated. "What? How do you just let something that important go?"

Robert swiveled so he faced me full on. "What would happen if you told him?"

"I don't know . . . Maybe he'll love me too. Maybe it'll be the match that *Vows* has never managed to make before now—something real, something that will last." Desperation tainted my words. Robert heard it too.

"Tori, you can't go through with this." Robert's voice was pleading, a tone I'd never heard him use before. He sounded as desperate as I felt.

"I love him. And I'm pretty certain he loves me too. I'm sure of it. What kind of guy gives a girl lotion-laced tissues when she has a cold? What kind of guy reads what she's reading? Or carries a girl all the way to her bungalow? One in love, that's who. I've never met anyone like him. I need to at least try because I might lose the only thing worth having if I don't."

Robert was already swinging his head back and forth in a violent shake. "You'll lose your job. You'll never work in the film industry again. You'd be giving up your chances to ever be a screenwriter if you do this. You're putting everything at risk for something you aren't even sure about."

He was right. I wasn't sure what would happen. But he was wrong too. "I know you're just trying to help, but I've weighed the options. I don't want to live a life alone. I don't want my career to get in the way of the things that make people really happy. Relationships. Relationships, Robert. Those are the things that make people happy. A better job, a better car, a better house—that's all just . . . nothing."

Ilana staring at that baby boutique with such desire had shown me that.

And even the book *The Help* showed it. Skeeter had chosen a career over relationships. She had nothing in the end except her new job. But I didn't think that would make her happy. Though I didn't think the loser-guy option would make her happy either, I knew she'd end up miserable if she didn't get some solid people in her life. I knew *I* would be miserable. Athena and Ruby were right. I needed real people.

Robert took a deep breath, then put his hands over mine. "You love him?"

"Yes," I answered.

"Really love him?"

"Yes." It was such a relief to say it out loud. I wanted to repeat it over and over and over again.

"Love him enough to throw your career and life away?"

"Robert, I'm not—"

He held out his hand to stop me midsentence. "Just answer the question."

"Yes."

He measured me with his eyes. "I believe you. But here's another question, one you need to take seriously. Is this love worth throwing *his* life away for?"

I yanked my hands out from under his and scowled. "Thanks a lot. You think being with me is akin to throwing a life away?"

Robert was shaking his head again. "That's not what I mean at all. You know I think the world of you. What I mean is the guy signed a contract—one that looks a lot like your contract. The studio isn't going to stand for the second AD taking off with their cash cow. The penalty will be intense. You know they'll take him for everything he's worth."

"He's a farmer. What are they going to take? An old broken-down tractor? A pig? A box of corn or whatever it is they grow in the South?"

Robert's head was still shaking. I wanted to put my hands out and hold his head still before he drove me crazy with all that motion. "You are so naïve, Tor. You still don't know. You're the only one on set who hasn't figured it out. Even the idiot bachelorettes are on to him. A guy that well read, that well mannered, that well cultured? You think he's some hayseed farmer who runs a failing farm when nothing could be further from the truth. He's rich. He's a gentleman plantation owner."

"Then he's a liar because he said he makes peanuts for wages." I was tired of the conversation. Robert obviously only wanted to argue with me. My mind was made up. I loved Chris. I didn't care that he made so little he'd jokingly called it peanuts. This wasn't about money. This was about love.

"Yes. Peanuts. Exactly. He owns acres and acres of land where they grow peanuts. He supplies half the world with their peanut butter. And it's all his, not something that belongs to his mom or dad or anything like that. He owns it all—in his own name. He's wealthy beyond even your overactive imagination. If you go to him with this new little plan of yours, he'll get sued by the studio. He'll lose his fortune, his land, his business holdings— everything."

I was the one shaking my head now. "No. No, you're wrong. He—"

"He's wealthy. And if you run off with him, you'll ruin him." Robert moved to his feet. "You say you love him, babe. Now I'm curious to know . . . do you love him enough to stay away from him?" Robert rapped his knuckles lightly on the table and walked away.

* * *

Max returned as Robert left, scooting aside for Robert's large frame.

I don't know what I looked like to make Max's countenance fall into one of total concern. "You really are in pain, aren't you? Do you think you'll need medical attention after all?" Max eyed my ankle with suspicion. His head likely whirred with the fear of a workman's comp claim.

"No. Absolutely not, sir. Ankle's great." I rotated it a couple times to prove the point. Beyond that, I don't remember much of what Max said or what we worked on while in the study. All I could think about was how it felt like I stood on a thin plate of ice that was splintering underneath me. A fall was on its way, and any movement I made to try to avoid that fall would only make it happen sooner.

If I told Chris the truth about my feelings, would I ruin him?

Yes.

Which meant he couldn't be told.

I figured I could leave the mansion, put off seeing him, and he'd never know I was ever there since Max's study wasn't the typical stomping ground of any of the talent.

But the day was meant to be one of ruin.

Chris showed up in the doorway. Our eyes met, and I feared he'd read my every emotion if I didn't tear my gaze away.

"Oh, good," Max said as Chris entered the room. "This proposal is going to be epic!" Max loved the word *epic*.

Chris gave a thin smile. They talked for several horrible minutes, and I tried to tune out words like *wedding, ring, dancing, masquerade, honeymoon, epic*. Max had already decided on the mob wedding concept—one of my ideas. It was to be a surprise for the bride. Max hired a choreographer that was brilliant at making simple footwork look like an elegant dance since Max didn't want to dip into budget by paying professional dancers. He planned on using the crew and a few amateur dancers.

The ice cracked under me even more to hear them talk about something I'd come up with. How could I escape this?

And then Max left, taking a private call. To Max, a private call meant at least thirty minutes—sometimes an hour.

Chris didn't waste a second of that time. He was at my side, my hands bundled into his, his eyes afire with desperation and determination.

"This has gone way too far," Chris said, keeping his voice soft and low to avoid being overheard. "Tori, they expect me to propose in Dubai. *Propose*, Tori. I have to pick one of those girls, and you know I can't. You know I can't do this."

I didn't even bother to pretend a smile. "Do you need help figuring out which one? You could always try eenie meenie minie moe."

"No!" He looked horrified. "I already know who I want to give a ring to."

Please not Becky. Please not Gemma. Please not any of them.

He pulled my hands closer to him so our hands were linked against his chest. That was when I noticed how right my hands looked in his. Our fingers were laced together. When had that happened?

"Tori, you're all I think about, all I want, the only person on this planet who I would ever consider giving a ring to and meaning it. Tori, I love you."

I stared.

Hope, yearning, love, *anger* all filling me, consuming me.

"You have a contract." That was it. The only words I said to him after he declared his love to me, after he all but proposed to me. But what else could be said when Robert's words rattled around in my head?

"I also have a good lawyer. Forget my contract."

My cheeks were wet. When had I started crying? "Chris . . ." I shook my head. "We *both* have contracts. I'd get fired. We'd both be sued. They have lawyers too."

"Tell me you don't feel the same. You tell me that, and I'll walk away; we'll pretend this conversation never happened."

There would never be a day when I'd be able to pretend this conversation never happened. *Do you love him enough to stay away from him*, Robert had asked.

"I can't do this. I'm sorry, Chris. I just . . . can't."

He nodded, his lips tightening into a firm line before he opened his mouth and said, "In my experience, *can't* means *won't*. Is it because they have your scripts? Are you afraid of getting another rejection letter?" Our hands were suddenly no longer linked. He was on his feet. He looked so hurt.

"You don't understand!" I stood as well and threw my hands in the air, exasperation and anguish filling those three little words. He didn't understand. I couldn't let the studio ruin him. He'd lose everything.

Robert was right.

His eyes narrowed. "See . . . that's where you're wrong. I do understand. I totally get it. What I get is that you're giving up a life of love in reality for reality TV. You really are already in a relationship—with your *job*!" He turned to storm out, but in a flash, he was facing me again, my face cradled in his hands and his lips pressing urgently on mine. I melted against him, kissing him back, feeling the urgency that had to be addressed. Fire and ice filled that kiss. Rage and hope. And. So. Much. Love. A person could be swept away by the wave of love in that one kiss.

He pulled away abruptly, looking angrier and more hurt than I'd ever seen anyone look. "*That*, Victoria Winters, is reality. Everything else . . . *everything* is just make believe." He turned away, with me still gasping for the breath he'd stolen with that kiss. Then he was gone, taking my heart and hopes with him.

The ice shattered underneath me.

I was falling.

Chapter 17

I RAN STRAIGHT INTO GEMMA on my way out. "Watch it," she said brusquely, and then she saw the tears, and her expression softened. She became the Gemma from the first of the season. "Hey, are you okay?"

I shook my head, not wanting to see her. The fact that I had to be sobbing in order for her to find herself again only showed how far she'd fallen as a person during the course of filming. *Vows* had ruined a genuinely good person.

Vows was good at breaking people.

I drove home and hid in my house for the rest of the day. I took no calls, though my phone rang several times.

The hurt on Chris's face ghosted along beside me everywhere I went. My eyes could be open or closed; it didn't matter. His eyes were there, staring at me with that pain.

And the kiss.

I relived it again and again and again until I thought I might die knowing such a kiss would never happen again.

The tears didn't stop.

All through the afternoon, they kept coming.

I pretended to clean my apartment, but I'd already cleaned it the day before. Nothing needed dusting or polishing, but I dutifully ran the dust cloth over the cupboards anyway. It was how I handled stress.

My phone played the chorus to Disney's "Grim Grinning Ghosts," letting me know a text message had come in.

In my rush to get out of the mansion, I'd failed to get the receipts to accounting so I could be reimbursed. Max wanted all accounting done before we left to Dubai.

I went through my purse to find the receipts and fax them over to accounting. Plus, it would be a good idea to throw the prescription away.

Ilana's strange request for me to share the pills reminded me that an unfilled prescription posed a temptation for some people.

I frowned while searching the purse for all the slips of paper.

The receipts were all there, paper clipped together where I'd put them, but the prescription was gone. I'd put it in the side pocket; I was certain of that because I'd had to reorganize the whole thing after Gemma had knocked it on the ground and dumped everything out.

Just in case, I dumped the whole thing out again and meticulously went through everything again.

Nothing.

I then took the paper clip off the bundle of receipts and went through each of them one by one in case the prescription had somehow wedged its way into the pile.

Nothing.

The only thing missing from the previous organization was the prescription. I thought back, tracking places I'd been and people I'd been with.

I closed my eyes and sucked in a breath hard.

Ilana.

It was the only explanation that made sense. She knew I had the prescription. She'd asked about it with such interest the alarm bells should have sounded for me enough to take my purse with me when I left her. She'd held my purse while I'd drooled over all the others in the store, and she had been alone with my purse during my whole phone conversation with Ruby in the bathroom. I hadn't left my purse alone with anyone else. And it wasn't possible that I'd simply forgotten where I'd put the prescription. My memory and personal obsessive-compulsive issues with everything being in its place didn't allow for errors of that nature.

Ilana had to have taken it.

I stood and paced, throwing punches in the air, feeling betrayed and used and . . . furious!

We'd gone out as friends.

She'd totally broken all friendship codes by having the nerve to search through my belongings in the first place but then to *steal* from me?

Seriously?

I didn't know what kind of crime it was to fill someone else's prescription—felony, misdemeanor—but was certain it had to be illegal.

But more than angry, I felt hurt. Hurt to have liked her genuinely when she was apparently just using me. Hadn't we had fun? Hadn't we bonded? Was I just a means for another hit instead of a friend?

"What to do . . ." I whispered, eyeing the phone, considering calling the police right then and there. But to tell them what? She might have just taken it. She might not have filled it. Accusing her without hard evidence would be the worst kind of awkward. And if she decided not to fill it, I didn't want her in legal trouble.

But how was I supposed to know if she had filled the prescription or not? Shannon.

Shannon would know what to do. She worked with prescriptions. She'd understand the ramifications of this act.

I really needed her advice. The thing with Ilana was too big to handle on my own.

I considered it for several minutes before getting up the courage and finally dialing Shannon's number.

"Hi, Tori," Shannon said, though she sounded a little depressed to hear my voice.

Rather than be offended, I jumped right in. "Hi. I hope it's okay that I'm calling."

"It's totally fine. What's up?"

"It's Ilana." My pulse quickened just thinking about it. This had to be what they meant when people talked about feeling like their blood was boiling. "I'm sorry I keep pulling you into this, but I just don't know who else to talk to."

"It's fine," she said again, only this time she sounded like maybe she meant it. "What's happened?"

"Well, I tripped over this dolly at work on Monday—totally lame, right? I know. Anyway, we have a nurse practitioner at the studio all the time, and he looked at it, told me to ice it, and then gave me a prescription, handwritten and all that."

"Okay?" She sounded distracted. She was probably driving.

"So, on Wednesday, I took Ilana to lunch. I've been texting with her a little, and she finally agreed to get together, so we went out to lunch, and in the course of conversation, I talked about the fall and the silly doctor giving me pain meds for my dumb injury. She got all intense, you know, and asked me what I'd been given. I told her I hadn't needed it, but she kept pushing. I finally said it was for Lortab, and she, well, she asked me for some."

"Oh dear. Did you give her any?"

"Of course not. I hadn't even filled the prescription. I told her that and then added that I wouldn't have given them to her even if I had filled it.

You're not supposed to share prescriptions. It was kind of awkward to say all that, but I wanted to make a point."

"No, that's good that you set a boundary."

It felt better to know Shannon agreed with me on that. She was my guru for handling a potential junkie. Her opinion really mattered to me. "I'm glad you think I handled it right. But then yesterday I went to throw the prescription note away—since I wasn't going to use it. I looked for it and couldn't find it. I mean, I don't want to jump to conclusions—in fact, I feel horrible that I *am* jumping to conclusions—but I haven't seen the prescription since that lunch with Ilana."

"Was she alone with your purse after you told her you wouldn't give her the meds?"

"Yeah, she was."

Shannon let out a deep breath as if the whole affair made her as tired as it made me. "Can you text me your full name and birthdate? I'm going to head over to the pharmacy and look it up. If she filled it or even tried to fill it, it will show up under your name."

"Really?" I said. "You'd do that?"

"Isn't that why you called me?"

"Oh, I don't know." I felt a little dumb, like maybe it wasn't as big a deal as it seemed to me. "I just needed to talk to someone about it who could tell me if I was overreacting. I'm not so organized that I couldn't have lost the prescription or something." A lie. I was very organized. Things were never misplaced in my world.

"It will take me a few minutes to check it out, and then we'll know for sure. Just send me that info, and I'll let you know what I find."

"Okay, thanks so much."

I texted her everything and waited. An hour later, she called me back. I was making myself a late-night snack to calm my nerves. Between Chris and his kiss and Ilana and the pills, my brain felt like it might explode. My heart felt like it already had.

"The news isn't great. She filled the prescription." Shannon sounded exhausted by this.

I wasn't exhausted anymore. I was furious.

We'd shared chocolate cheesecake and talked about purses and love. How could someone betray a person they'd shared chocolate cheesecake with? Was nothing sacred?

"I can't believe this. She stole my prescription. She is in deep, isn't she?" At least she was in deep trouble as far as I was concerned because this wasn't going to be ignored.

"I can't get into details," Shannon said.

"It's obvious. Why else steal from me if she weren't desperate? So what do I do now—call the police?" I was prepared to hire a hit man.

"That might be taking it too far."

"Why? Isn't it illegal for her to have done that?" I slammed the microwave shut and tossed the steaming bag of kettle corn on the counter to cool off somewhere where it wasn't scalding my fingertips. "I mean, she had to pose as me, right? I don't know how she even got it filled. Aren't there supposed to be all kinds of safeguards in place to keep people from doing that?"

"There are lots of safeguards. But nothing's perfect. Calling the police is opening up a whole can of worms though."

"No, stealing my prescription is opening up a whole can of worms. You think I should do nothing?" Shannon didn't know me at all if she thought I was going to let this go.

"I didn't say that. We don't know for sure that she did this."

What?

"Yes, we do." I said, feeling indignant. "She took *my* prescription and I'm taking that seriously. I've watched too many talented people in my industry flush away their lives for drugs and too many people turn a blind eye because they didn't want to kick up dust. I want to kick up so much dust about this that she never, *ever* dares do anything like this again. I mean, you see this stuff too, right? In your work, you've got to deal with junkies."

"Ilana's not a junkie." But she didn't sound certain. "Junkies use street drugs; Ilana is showing some serious drug-seeking patterns—it's different."

"Well, whatever the title, she needs to face the music for it." My parents never let me or my siblings get away with anything. I credited the fact that we all grew up to be nice adults to my parents and their tough love.

"Tori, you just have to think this through. We don't know her very well, and her husband is a doctor. Prescription fraud is a felony; she'd face fines and jail time. It would follow her for the rest of her life."

"So you want me to do nothing?" Doing nothing felt like throwing Ilana out on the streets to freeze in the dead of a Detroit winter.

"No, that's not what I'm saying." But it was what she was saying. I could feel it in her tone. "Can we just sleep on this? It's not going to change by

Julie Wright

tomorrow, and maybe if we can take a few hours to think it through, we can come up with the right approach."

I took a few calming breaths before agreeing to sleep on it. "I'll call you in the morning. Maybe Ilana will come over tonight and confess and ask forgiveness. One can hope, right?"

"One can always hope." Shannon didn't sound like she was talking about Ilana anymore, but I didn't ask what it was she hoped for.

Instead, I waited until the next morning, after sleeping on it and changing my mind about nothing, and called Shannon immediately. She didn't answer but sent me a text saying she'd call later. I was glad when she called me back that afternoon.

"So what do you think we should do?" I asked, hoping she'd come around to my way of thinking.

"I think we should talk to her."

That was not the anticipated response. "Really? We barely know her."

"I know. But the most important thing is for her to get help, right? Isn't your ultimate goal for her to get better?"

"Well, of course it is," I said, feeling a little penned in from the fact that talking to her would require a confrontation. "I'm just a little . . . uncomfortable with the idea of talking to her. What are we going to say?"

"I'm not sure. But I think I can present it in a way that maybe she can admit what she's done instead of us accusing her."

That worked for me, a little anyway. Accusing someone of a crime sounded so volatile. Yet, not accusing her allowed her to get deeper and deeper into this world no human could possibly control on their own. She needed help. "That's a good idea," I agreed. "When should we do it? I don't think we should wait very long. Strike while the iron is hot and all that." Plus, I was leaving for Dubai soon. This needed to be rectified before I left.

"Good point," she said, then paused. "Do you think you could see if she'll go to dinner with you Monday night? I kind of have a crazy idea, but I think it will make an impact."

"Impact is good," I said quickly. "I'm all for impact. What's the plan?"

Chapter 18

THE PLAN HAD MADE MY jaw drop when Shannon laid it all out for me. Was she serious? She wanted me to trick Ilana? How was Ilana supposed to know I was her friend? How was she supposed to trust me if I was pulling a fast one on her?

But Shannon's idea was good—even if it forced me to be a creep for a little while.

I really hated being the creep.

But I called Ilana and set up the dinner date. And then hated myself as soon as we'd hung up.

The only upside was the fact that all of my anger and fear for Ilana's safety drove away the intense pain of the situation with Chris.

I ground my teeth and yelled at traffic to make me feel better as I drove the distance to Ilana's house the next evening. In spite of the idiots on the road, I was in front of her house at exactly six.

She came out with her ponytail swishing happily as she walked to the car. She looked glad to see me, which made me feel even worse. *Forgive me for this*, I thought over and over again.

I offered an apologetic smile when she settled into the car. "Hey."

Please forgive me.

She smiled. "Hey."

I tried to find things to talk about while we drove, but it felt as though my tongue had lodged itself firmly in my throat. I made a few attempts and gave up. Fake was not my thing. I couldn't pretend that there wasn't a weight on my chest, so it felt easier to not say anything at all.

I nearly climbed out of my skin when a car in the other intersection honked at the car in front of it. Did Ilana see me freak out?

"You okay?"

Yes. She'd seen it, all right.

I flicked my eyes briefly from the road to this woman I cared about. "Yeah. I'm fine." I owed her something for what I was about to do. When I was younger and had done deep cleans of my bedroom, I always pulled everything out because it felt easier to really organize that way. It allowed me to deep clean all of the cracks and recesses of my shelves and toy boxes. My mom would laugh and tell me I'd made everything worse. She laughed even harder when I told her that sometimes things had to be broken in order to get fixed.

Was I breaking Ilana in order to fix her? I didn't want her broken. I pulled deeply from inside of me, trying to be like Livvy and find something to be glad about. But there wasn't anything. I forced myself to smile anyway.

She smiled back, but like an animal, she tensed, sensing danger but not knowing what the danger was or where it came from.

I was glad to see the restaurant, glad to be distracted by waiters and menus and eating.

I hardly knew what we talked about while we ate. I picked at my food, my stomach twisting at the sight of it. I checked the time on my phone several times—discreetly under the table, where Ilana wouldn't notice my clock watching.

"I can pay for my own food," Ilana said with a laugh when the bill finally came. The phrase seemed comfortable coming out of her mouth—something she probably said a lot. She and her husband had earned good incomes through the years. Her husband was a doctor, so even with her out of work, they had to be well off. I imagined she usually paid for lunches and dinners for other people because she could afford it.

But not this time.

I signed my name to the credit card receipt as my last cry for absolution in the whole affair of what had to happen next.

Without saying anything more, we headed back to my car and got in.

Come on, Tori-girl, you know what you have to do now. I finally found my voice. "Up for another stop before I take you home?" Did Ilana hear the tension?

She shrugged and smiled. "Sure." She actually sounded happy to spend more time with me. Would that opinion be dust in another hour?

She seemed comfortable in the silence that followed. The silence was anything but comfortable for me. My finger hit the button for some music, which at first sounded too loud amidst the words I couldn't say, but after a moment, the music soothed me. We were doing the right thing—Shannon and I.

So why did it feel like we were about to send a favorite pet to the butcher's block?

I glanced at Ilana. She'd actually dozed off, which made me feel worse. She felt safe enough with me to fall asleep.

Her eyes opened when the keys jingled out from the ignition. Here sat the moment of truth. I didn't allow myself to consider it, afraid of too much pondering, where I might change my mind and take her home like a good friend would do.

But a good friend wouldn't take her home.

A good friend would break her in order to fix her.

I got out without explanation, assuming Ilana would follow me. It wasn't like she could go anywhere else. I had the keys.

She did follow me. I'd gone several paces ahead of her, but ahead of her wasn't where I needed to be.

I needed to be beside her—every step of this long walk to the truth.

I stopped and waited until she fell in step beside me.

"Come on," I said softly.

She looked up then, noticing the cross at the top of the church, and she took a step back.

"I'm not Christian, remember?"

"I know. I'm not trying to convert you or anything." I smiled. There was so much more I could say. I could wrap her in a hug and explain that I loved her and that she was sick and needed to get well. But I could see from the sudden fear in her eyes that she was nowhere near ready for that.

When I finally picked Shannon's form from the shadows, I wanted to run to her in relief, but I kept the pace casual as we approached.

I shot Shannon a meaningful look when we finally reached her, one that said, "Okay, Captain. Lead on."

"I don't understand." Ilana's head gave a slight shake as she looked back up to the top of the church again.

Shannon smiled. "Hi, Ilana."

I felt Ilana's gaze burning a hole in my cheek, but I refused to meet that gaze, instead focusing on Shannon, who said, "I found a place we can talk."

"Talk?" Ilana repeated the word, panic in her voice.

Shannon headed for the church entrance. I waited for Ilana to follow. When she didn't, I nudged her forward, walking behind her in case she decided to flee the scene. If she didn't go inside and hear us out, there would be no getting her back to this point. And then things would get ugly.

We made a small procession through the building. Shannon gave an air of confidence I lacked but was able to borrow from her. With Shannon's help, I could get through this. With our help, Ilana could get through this.

Ilana looked at her watch, then turned to me. "I really should get home . . ." Her fear was tangible. Almost feral. She seemed to shake with that fear.

I gently took her arm to steady her, to comfort her, and to keep her from bolting.

Shannon sat down and offered Ilana the chair next to her. Ilana sat, her movements stiff; she was prepared to run. Fight or flight. We penned her in so she couldn't flee. I half wondered if she'd throw a punch at one of us.

Too much reality TV, Tori.

Shannon pulled out her cell phone and silenced it; Ilana did the same, which was a good sign. She wasn't running, and she wasn't hitting us. She'd resigned herself to whatever it was we'd planned for her.

Shannon leaned toward Ilana and smiled. I leaned in as well.

"Ilana," Shannon said. "I'm sorry for the trick we played to get you here."

Flight kicked in. She snatched up her purse from the floor, and her leg muscles tensed, her whole body poised to leap up.

"But we're really worried about you." Shannon's tone said it all. I actually heard the echo of my concern for Ilana in Shannon's voice. I felt the worry and the hope too.

Ilana darted a look my direction. I nodded in agreement, feeling tears building in my eyes. *Please,* I wanted to say. *Please know we care about you.*

"Worried about me?" She turned to me, the question in her eyes. "What are you talking about?"

"I know you took some of Ruby's pain pills last month," I said, finding relief in saying it out loud to her—not just to Shannon like some gossiping girl but to Ilana herself—the only person who could make it right. "I found one on the floor of the bathroom after you left."

Her eyes went wide, and her mouth fell open as if about to protest, but Shannon didn't give her the chance. "Percocet. From a prescription bottle in Ruby's master bathroom."

Ilana's gaze went back to Shannon. I felt Ilana weighing and measuring her words. Ilana wasn't stupid. She was searching for the way out of the maze she'd created for herself. "I don't know what you're talking about," she said finally, picking at her slacks as if she didn't care. But she couldn't hide the tremor in her hands. Or the tension in her voice. Her face flushed, and she straightened, looking enraged and indignant. I'd expected that. I'd seen it before. Rage was a common addict response to confrontation. I'd seen agents actually get punched out for trying to coax their actors into sobriety.

She hitched her purse strap over her shoulder and rose to leave. But I was ready for it—was even ready for her to swing at me if it did, indeed, come to that. I put my hand around her arm and urged her back down. I didn't hold her tight enough to leave bruises or even a red mark on her arm but had her tight enough to let her know I had no intentions of letting go. I met her gaze with defiance and a strength that came from being right and watched some of the fight and rage drain from her. She eased back to her chair.

Shannon leaned closer, hands clasped. "There's a meeting going on in the next room," she said, pointing behind Ilana. "And I'd like you to attend it with us. Then we'll talk, and we'll take you home."

"I don't have to stay." Ilana cast her gaze back and forth between us, caged and pleading for release. "I can call my husband to come get me right now." Her voice rose. "You can't do this!"

Part of me wanted her to call her husband. From everything Ilana had said about him, he loved her. He was a good man. He would want to help his wife. "You *can* call your husband, Ilana," I said, figuring it was unlikely that she'd really do it. "But we're trying to do you a favor. We could just have easily gone to your husband about this or your doctors or the police."

"You're *threatening* me? You have no proof of anything, and you're threatening me. Great. I just—I need to go." She was up and heading for the door before I could stop her this time.

But Shannon called after her. "It's illegal to possess someone else's prescription."

She stopped.

"Either the paper script or the actual fulfilled product," Shannon said.

Ilana turned so slowly it was painful to watch. She had her purse in a white-knuckled grip, as if that little bit of leather was all she had to tether her to reality—to sanity. We waited while she worked through the implications of the moment.

Shannon rose and walked toward the door, motioning us to follow. Ilana looked back at me and gave her head another small shake. *Please help me,* her eyes said. But I couldn't help her like she wanted. I wouldn't take her away from all of this and turn a blind eye to her drug issues.

I am helping, I thought and smiled, waving Ilana along in front of me.

The other room was much larger and was filled with rows of chairs. Shannon guided us to where a young man had saved us seats. We settled in next to him, taking care to keep Ilana between us, and waited.

Her hands shook.

She rocked back and forth as though comforting some phantom infant.

I thought again about Shannon's concern over Ilana wanting a baby and not being able to have one. I turned to Ilana, feeling more sympathy than ever before. Did she know she was rocking, or was it something so subconscious that she wasn't aware of the movement?

She caught me staring and stopped immediately.

A woman began the meeting of Narcotics Anonymous. I felt Ilana pull back at that word, almost as if the word itself stung.

The room erupted in cheers when the woman announced she'd had tea instead of wine at some function or other. She raised her hands over her head in triumph. I thought about *The War of Art* and considered that this woman had overcome resistance for herself.

Resistance didn't just stop us from being artists. Sometimes it stopped us from being human. Sometimes it stopped us from living.

The guy who'd saved our seats stood and headed to the front, where he took the microphone. "Hi, my name is David, and I'm an addict."

"Hi, David," the audience said.

Some demented part of me wanted to giggle at that. The words felt like bad nighttime television.

He grabbed the sides of the podium and spoke with power. "Life is hard. And each one of us encounters things in our own lives that we simply can't handle. It's not because we're stupid or weak or less than someone else; it's simply a fact that every person in the world deals with things that are too much."

I considered that. The last couple of months had felt like too much. Finding the perfect guy and then watching him date half the world felt like too much. Especially when it was heaped upon by so many agents and studios telling me I wasn't good enough when it came to writing.

Maybe my *too much* would be nothing to someone else, but to me, it felt like a mountain had been dropped on my head.

He continued. "And when we encounter these things, we are offered a variety of ways to cope with them." David listed the ways people coped: God, other people, and the bottle—of the pill and alcohol variety. He confessed that his coping mechanism had been drugs.

A brave admission.

"And maybe I'd have never been able to truly feel the fear I should have felt in the beginning. I don't know if that's how it would have happened, though, because I chose my path, and I can't go back and change it. But I *can* change how I handle stress now and my obsessive compulsive disorder and the abuse from my childhood and the girl who broke my heart and the college I didn't get into and the loss of a grandmother I loved so much who died when I was too young to process my emotions."

I felt a little guilty to hear him tell about all he'd had to cope with. My problems were so small in comparison.

But it didn't change the fact that my problems felt huge to me. I sneaked a peek at Ilana, not really knowing what she was going through in her life but knowing that whatever it was, it all had to feel huge to her—a mountain on her head.

Everyone applauded David's two-year anniversary of sobriety. Ilana applauded too. She'd become entirely engrossed in his story. These all seemed like good signs. Shannon and I shared a look over Ilana's head. Shannon gave a small smile and a nod. Her eyes were moist.

We've done the right thing, those eyes said.

Yes, we have.

Ilana suddenly sucked in a deep breath, shuddered, and began rocking again. I wasn't sure what to do at first. Was she going into some withdrawal or something?

Shannon led the way by taking Ilana's hand in hers, squeezing it lightly in support. I reached for her other hand, glad she didn't slap me away.

We sat like that for a long time. Three women linked together by an awful truth. But linked also by the possibility of a victorious outcome.

Ilana could beat this. She wasn't that far gone. If she was willing to get help—to let us help her—she could find herself again.

She pulled her hands away from both Shannon and me so she could wipe at her eyes. She did it automatically. I wondered if she even knew she was crying.

At the end, Shannon took Ilana's hand again. "Ilana," she said, giving Ilana a look so sincere, so filled with conviction it made me swell. "You're going to be okay."

Ilana took her hand from Shannon's. She shook and hugged herself as if she could stop the trembling if she held on tightly enough.

"You are going to be okay," I echoed Shannon. "And you aren't alone. We brought you here because we care, and we want you to be okay."

We got up since everyone was putting away chairs and talking quietly in groups. We thanked David for his words and then went outside.

"Can I go home now?" Ilana whispered.

"Yes. Except . . ." I looked again to Shannon for help. I didn't want to be the bad guy but hated continually making Shannon be the bad guy.

"Except what?" Ilana asked.

Shannon licked her lips and shot me another look over Ilana's head. This was hard for Shannon too. "As a medical professional, it's my duty to report . . . these kinds of things."

Ilana looked like she might drop to the ground right there and never get up again. "Please, no. I'm going to stop. I swear."

"I can give you a week," Shannon said. "You have until Monday to find help on your own. If you don't, I'll have no choice but to go through professional channels to enforce the law."

We had to do it. We had to play hard here because the results of our actions today would have ramifications too horrible to consider. Ilana had to know we were serious, that we weren't going to let it slide.

Ilana nodded and followed me to my car.

I didn't say anything on the way home. Ilana still hugged herself. Tears streaked her face in a continual stream. She looked so fragile I was afraid that talking to her would make her explode.

When I pulled up in front of her house, there were a million things I could have said.

Sorry for ganging up on you.

Hope I don't have to visit you in jail.

I really do care. Call me if you need anything.

Please get help for this. Please don't be like all of those other wasted-out people who gave their lives to some stupid substance.

Please see how wonderful you are.

I said nothing. Ilana nodded at me. I nodded back, afraid to do anything that would send her over the edge. Her eyes were filled with something desperate, something terrifying, something I didn't understand.

She got out of the car as if on autopilot.

One more thing I could have said—*should* have said—but didn't say.

Please don't do anything stupid.

* * *

I went home and found an e-mail from Shannon to Ilana that she'd cc'd me on. It was a good note, one that said we were on her side, wanting to work with her, not against her. It helped me feel better about the whole thing.

I wrote back to both of them.

Dear Ilana,

You have so much to be happy for in your life. I've never seen anyone so obviously in love with their husband the way you are. After listening to you talk about him, you have to know you aren't alone in the world. I know it seems like we ganged up on you, but you have to know we wouldn't have gone to such extremes if we didn't care. We're your friends. We want to see you happy.

Love, Tori

I worried about Ilana the whole next day, picking up the phone to call and then not knowing what to say and hanging it up again. To take my mind off of things, I called my mom and asked her to go to dinner with me, grateful to know there was no trickery in my invitation. It was simply dinner.

Between the drama with Ilana and the drama with Chris, I felt emotionally spent. And now that I was in a sit-and-wait mode with Ilana, all of my focus returned to Chris, to his hurt, his anger, his kiss . . .

Getting out of bed Friday morning felt pointless. Why bother? Everything I thought I wanted was too stupid to waste energy on, and the one thing worth my energy, I had already ruined.

I contemplated staying in bed all day, but the shoe-repair shop, where I'd sent my favorite slingbacks, called and left a message that my shoes were ready for pick up and had been ready for over a week.

They were always grumpy when shoes stayed orphaned for too long.

Ignoring that message was not optional, which meant I had to get out of bed.

Finding a pair of shoes that fit perfectly and looked amazing didn't happen every day.

Once I had picked up the shoes and paid for them, I walked out the front door and stared down the street. Ruby lived in this neighborhood— Ruby, with her good marriage and her love of matchmaking, Ruby, who would understand my troubles and perhaps make sense of them.

I was in my car heading to her house before I could stop myself.

I had to do this. I had to tell someone, someone who could help me figure out the twisted psychosis in my mind. Someone who wasn't my mom and wanted grandbabies. Someone who wasn't Robert, with his studio mindset.

As I pulled into her driveway, a nice-looking older gentleman was leaving. I hoped she didn't have other guests. The topic was too sensitive to discuss in mixed company.

Ruby would at least give me a hug. I really needed a hug.

I stepped up to the door and rang the bell.

"Please be home. Please be home." I almost started crying again but kept myself in check.

She answered the door. *Thank you so much for answering that door, Ruby,* I thought. I wanted to fall into her and unload the entire drama, but I didn't have to say anything before she bundled me into a hug. I must have looked like a hurricane hitting land—as my dad always said.

"Come in." Her soothing voice calmed me. "What brings you to my neighborhood?"

"I had to make a stop at the shoe-repair place up the street that I love. And I still feel bad about cancelling our lunch date, so I thought I'd stop in and say hi."

"Wonderful," she said.

I watched her. "Who was the man I saw leaving here?"

She immediately looked guilty, which made me smile. *Finally* . . . something to smile about.

"Gabriel." She stopped me before I could ask the obvious questions. "Yes, he's back from Greece. Although, I'm not sure for how long." She positively glowed.

"He is seriously good-looking, Ruby!" One of us ought to have a love life. That Ruby caught a hottie? Fabulous.

She started toward the kitchen. I followed because I still wasn't sure how to say what needed to be said.

"It's so great to see you. Do you like brownies?" She looked like she was dying to ask real questions, but she remained careful to let me take my time.

"Do they have chocolate in them?" I tried to laugh. It sounded wrong, and I gave it up.

Ruby poured milk to go with the brownies as if she was my mom and I was five years old and coming home after crashing and skinning my knee.

It felt like I'd crashed and skinned my heart.

She set everything on the table, and I stared at it, feeling incredulous. What kind of person had fresh baked goods lying around their kitchen? I finally voiced my thoughts. "Really? You just happened to have homemade brownies on hand?"

"I woke up extra early this morning. And maybe I sensed I'd have such a lovely visitor."

I sometimes woke up early enough to get to the bakery when the doughnuts were their freshest, but that was about it. "Oh, Ruby, you always say the sweetest things. I wonder what it would be like to see the world from your perspective for just one day." My voice cracked. Embarrassing, but I finally had to say something or I'd die. "I am not a good person. Not good at all." *The pain in his eyes . . .*

Ruby shook her head as if I'd told a huge fib. I wasn't fibbing. I was a horrible person. She reached out and patted my hand, then finally asked *the* question. "What's wrong, honey?"

That's when the tears started.

Again.

As if there hadn't been enough tears in my life recently.

"It's Christopher."

"Christopher Caine?"

I nodded. "He's the one I'm in love with." I had meant to ease into this conversation, not blurt it out like that.

"Oh my goodness," Ruby whispered.

That pretty well summed things up. "Yeah." I laughed and cried a little harder. "*Oh my goodness.*"

"When . . . did this happen?"

"I don't know when it happened, but it did, and I'm a complete mess." When had it happened? With him sitting by me in the warmth of the window? Him sending me the box of tissues? The many meetings by the duck pond? Or was it really that first glance and I'd been too stupid to see it? I should have grabbed his hand and turned him around before he ever went into that final audition.

"Oh my goodness!" Ruby said louder.

I dropped my head in my hands on the table. If only I'd recognized that first moment for what it was. If only I had taken him away, asked him to take a walk with me, then asked him to be a part of my life forever. That wouldn't have broken any contracts. That wouldn't have resulted in the current mess.

"What are you going to do?" Ruby asked, eyeing me closely.

I shook my head, not knowing. Going back was impossible. Dwelling on going back made me a fool. "That's why I'm here. I need your advice. You had a good marriage." I took one of the napkins on the table and tried to clean up my face. Then I unloaded the whole of the mess to her—explaining everything—even the kiss. "You know what it takes and the sacrifices required to make a good life. That's why I'm here. To know how you made it all work. To know if it's possible to make things work if love is the central ingredient. Because . . ." I hiccupped. I always got the hiccups when I cried. "If I tell him how I feel, it could ruin everything—the show, my career, his reputation . . . my reputation. He'd lose everything."

How could three little words affect so much? He had said them to me. Did he know what he was giving up by saying those words?

Ruby's countenance changed. She looked determined when she finally said, "My husband, Phillip, was the worst person I could have chosen to marry."

I gaped at her. "What?" Surely I heard her wrong. Surely she hadn't said what it sounded like she'd said.

"It was never right, not even in the beginning. The chemistry wasn't there. I was always trying to force it or to justify why I didn't feel it. And when I realized what was truly wrong, it was too late. I had a son by then who needed his mommy."

"What do you mean, Ruby?" My mind reeled at the very idea. Ruby had everything so *together.* "I thought you had a wonderful marriage."

"Everyone thinks that. But it wasn't just the lack of chemistry. It was a lack of something more important. Trust. Respect. And the idea of another person making you want to be better, to love deeper, and to cherish more."

I genuinely could not have been more surprised. Ruby hadn't had trust in her marriage? She hadn't had respect?

"Just the fact that you're sitting here in my kitchen, your heart breaking into a million pieces because Christopher is dating other women, tells me you're deeply in love with him. The only way it will work is if *both* of you are willing to sacrifice for each other. If it's one-sided, like it was in my case, you'll be miserable."

Chris had proven he'd make the sacrifices for me. But could I let him? Did he really understand the ramifications of loving me? There was also the part of me, the evil part, that worried *I* hadn't been willing to sacrifice for him. If I'd told him I loved him, Darren would never buy my scripts. "How will I know?" I whispered. The question meant so many things. How would I know if he was willing to sacrifice? How would I know if *I* was willing to sacrifice? How would I know if this was the kind of love even worth sacrificing for in the first place?

But it was that kind of love. I felt it in every look and in every touch. It was the kind of love that would last and last and last.

"You might not know until you tell him how you feel," she said. "But it's a risk you need to take . . . to find out his feelings. If he's not willing to risk everything he's committed to in order to be with you, then you'll know, and you'll know it won't last."

"I'm just so scared."

She squeezed my hand. "If you don't tell him, you'll regret it."

She couldn't know how much regret already existed. "Is that how it's been with Gabriel?" I asked.

"Gabriel? What do you mean?"

I smiled again. "You know what I mean. You can't deny it. It's so obvious on your face when you talk about him."

She blushed but hurried to stand with her milk glass and take it to the sink like she planned on rinsing it even though it was still full. "He's a very nice man, and I really care for him. But I have no plans to remarry, if that's what you're thinking."

I laughed at her. "Look at you. Telling me to sacrifice my career to go after a guy who's completely unavailable, and you are avoiding the real thing standing right in front of you."

"You don't know anything about Gabriel. He's a friend to everyone."

I joined her at the sink and put my hands on her shoulders. If I had to confess, so did she. "Ruby, I saw the pictures from Greece. He was smiling at you in every single one. He didn't even care that someone was taking pictures. And . . . you were smiling back."

"Maybe the pictures were doctored." She finally turned to face me.

I snorted, folded my arms, and lifted my eyebrow.

"All right. I like him," she said finally, as if admitting to liking a guy was the worst thing ever. "I can't even describe why, but I feel like my whole self when I'm with him. And he only knows the basics of the . . . problems . . . I had with my husband. He doesn't know the whole story."

"So tell him!"

She took her turn to laugh. "Listen to *yourself*."

I covered my mouth, feeling like somehow she'd tricked me into this circular reasoning. The whole thing was insane, which made me laugh out loud. Ruby laughed too. We were both being ridiculous. Telling Chris might make him lose everything, but then at least he'd know. He had a right to know the truth. Even if it still couldn't work out, I owed him that much. I finally grew serious enough to be rational. Something she said resonated within me. *I feel like my whole self when I'm with him.*

That was how Chris made me feel.

"Let's make a deal, Ruby."

She frowned at me.

"You tell Gabriel about your marriage, and I'll tell Christopher my true feelings."

"Are you serious?" She looked like she might faint at the very idea.

"Unless you want to back out," I said. "It will be really tough to tell Christopher I—" Oh man, would it *ever* be hard, especially after having already denied him.

She took my hand as if sensing my dwindling resolve. "Deal."

I stared at her only a moment before pulling her into a tight hug. Going to Ruby had been exactly what I'd needed. "Thank you so much. You have no idea how much you've helped me."

She nodded as if she *did* have some idea.

She wrapped the brownies for me to take with me. If nothing else came of this decision, at least I got brownies.

I was going to tell Christopher Caine I loved him.

Chapter 19

WITH EVERYTHING GOING ON, I hadn't put together that the day the cast and crew of *Vows* left for Dubai was the same day as book club.

This meant I wouldn't be going. This meant there was no way to get an update on Ilana—assuming she showed up.

I hoped she did. And I wanted to be there for her. How would I know if Ilana was okay if I couldn't see her for myself, hug her for myself, prove to myself that she was okay?

I didn't care at all about missing the discussion on *Zen and the Art of Motorcycle Maintenance*. I did end up reading the book—sort of. I read a chapter, skipped a chapter, read a chapter, skipped a chapter. If I was being honest, I skipped more than I read.

I felt too out of sorts to hide any more feelings than I was already hiding. If I couldn't be honest about loving someone, I hoped to at least get the satisfaction of being honest about not liking the book.

But I would be on a flight to Dubai while they discussed the philosophies of the uptight motorcyclist.

I texted Shannon to let her know.

Hey, Shan,
Not going to be at book club due to work. Sorry for dumping all of this on you. I know you already have a full plate and could have used some backup, but I can't get out of this. Will you keep me posted?

She texted back.

No problem. I will definitely keep you updated, but I think everything is going to be okay. Don't worry about it.

I thanked her for her awesomeness in general and drove to the mansion to meet the shuttle so I could accompany the cast to the airport. That meant

Chris would be surrounded by the final girls, but maybe a moment would present itself where we could talk privately.

He wasn't at the mansion.

I stared around the piles of luggage and girls, feeling confused as the driver loaded the bags into the back of the shuttle. "Where's Chris?" I asked.

"He's already gone," Gemma said, her tone a little too wintry for the warm weather.

"Gone?"

"To Dubai," Terri said pleasantly when Gemma turned away, not seeming to notice the frost settling between Gemma and me. "Pete picked him up yesterday."

"Oh, right." I pretended that I'd just forgotten but had to go back over my e-mailed instructions to see what I'd missed in the first reading.

There it was; Max had placed Pete as Chris's handler. It was under Pete's name, so I'd skipped the instructions, figuring they didn't pertain to me.

Stupid, since Pete's job always pertained to me. Where was my head? In the clouds somewhere.

Feeling sullen and annoyed to be stuck with all the other girls like some kind of chattel, I took my seat in the van and tried hard to ignore the girl talk behind me.

The girls really did seem to be friends, pointing things out to each other, sharing inside jokes, talking about their homes and their excitement to see Dubai.

At the airport, I bought a bag of Bit-O-Honey to give as a peace offering.

I dug around in my carry-on for ear buds and my iPad. I would not be listening to the girls' chitter and chirp the whole way to Dubai, not when I had to plan the great takeaway when I stole Chris out from under their noses.

Arriving at the Dubai airport was a relief. Soon I would see Chris. Soon I would tell him. Soon I'd have an answer either way. From the air, the long airport had looked like a silver caterpillar to me with its planes nested against their boarding gates like little legs. Inside, it was a modern, clean environment. It made it easy to forget that Saudi Arabia, Iran, and Iraq were nearby neighbors. I herded the girls to where our driver waited for us with my name on a big sign, then herded them into the hotel, trying to get them to stop gawking and flashing their cameras at every single little thing. If my mind hadn't been so thoroughly immersed in spilling my guts to Chris, I would have joined them in taking pictures and staring at this city that felt like so much more than simply a foreign country.

Didn't the girls know we were in a hurry? Didn't they understand how much I needed to get inside that hotel and find Chris?

I finally unloaded the burden the girls represented to their rooms with a warning that I'd be back to take them sightseeing. There were a lot of laws in this part of the world. The dress code of the country meant the girls couldn't run around Dubai in the little bikinis they'd used for the mansion—not unless they wanted to be arrested for indecent exposure. Max was in no way going to let them wander away on their own. They needed to be babysat.

I hurried away and dumped my own belongings in my room—one I would share with Monica, who handled all make-up for the cast.

I really loved Monica. She was half Navajo and had the most beautiful hair any girl ever had a right to. Sharing a room with her was normally a pleasure. But with all of the secrets bubbling around inside my gray matter, sharing a room was not my favorite plan. If my bank account would have allowed it, I'd have bought my own private room.

She was in the shower when I dropped my stuff on my bed.

"Tori? Is that you?" she called out from the bathroom.

I tsked to myself for not being quieter when entering the room. "Nope. It's a hottie sheik looking for some love."

"Tell him he better have brought a razor with him because these legs need shaving, and I forgot mine."

I dug around in my bag until I found the ten-pack of disposables. I opened it and tossed one over the shower curtain to her.

"Thanks, Tor!"

"No worries." I eyed the room door with need. "Hey, I'm stepping out for a bit to stretch my legs and see some sights before we get going tomorrow. Any idea where Pete is? I ought to check in with him."

"Pete took the bachelor sightseeing to some places he wouldn't be able to get to with any of the girls. You know, the boring places: all of the historical forts and stuff that would kill a decent date. They won't be back until late."

"Oh." I slumped against the bathroom counter. Those places would be interesting to see and wouldn't destroy any kind of date at all but rather enhance it with information and discovery. I should have been glad the girls were all too shallow to want a date of that variety. Chris was seeing it without me, but at least he was seeing it without them too. *There goes that plan.* "Hey, wanna come with me to babysit the bachelorettes? I could use some intelligent company."

"Love to! Can you wait another thirty minutes while I finish getting ready?"

"Absolutely. The girls will take at least that long. You know how Jennifer is."

Monica made a noise that indicated she did indeed know. I left the bathroom to give her privacy and wandered to the hotel window and looked out. Somewhere in that city was a man who needed a message.

And the message would have to wait.

Again.

* * *

Sightseeing with the girls didn't turn out too bad. They were funny and almost cute as they touristed through the streets of Dubai. They bought matching gold anklets at a little shop and dared each other to sample some of the local food. Gemma was the only one who didn't embrace the idea of me as their tour babysitter. In spite of everything, the other girls really liked me. Gemma was the only one who had any idea that I wasn't just a buddy along for the ride. I was the usurper.

Monica noticed Gemma's cool behavior and commented on it while we got ready the next morning for filming.

"One would imagine she'd act better toward her fairy godmother," Monica said as she expertly wove her hair into an intricate set of braids.

I rolled my eyes. "Why are you calling me that?"

"Everyone calls you that. Even the tabloids suggested the girl had to have had a fairy godmother to have produced such an exquisite look for that first candle ceremony. None of the other girls could hold a candle to her." Monica smiled at her own pun. "Some people are crying foul play—that the studio has been playing favorites the whole time."

"Huh. Didn't know that." I winced when a bobby pin poked into my scalp.

"Well, anyway. She acted like a perfect monster yesterday toward you. I almost had to pull on a sweater with her ice-princess behavior, and it was a hundred degrees outside!"

I laughed, glad to hear someone finally call Gemma anything except angelic or adorable or lovely or whatever the Twitter feeds were saying as praise.

The day went horrifically. I bustled Terri off to her limo and somehow missed ever seeing Chris. By the time I caught a glimpse of him, the date was already well underway. Robert winked at me. Chris acted as though he'd never met me before.

A whole day passed, and not one opportunity presented itself to talk to Chris alone.

The next day belonged to Jennifer.

Another day passed. It almost seemed like Chris had left strict instructions to everyone on crew that he wanted me kept as far from him as possible because every time an instant presented itself where we could be alone, someone tugged me another direction.

I still had not told him the things I wanted to tell him.

The third day was Becky's.

She simpered and smiled and acted as though she was some sort of Arabian goddess. Wardrobe put her in some shockingly revealing attire, and I expected her to be arrested at almost every turn. I wondered if Max was hoping for it because his eyes glittered with glee anytime someone looked askance at Becky's bare shoulders.

Max was grumpy at the end of the day. Becky had not been arrested.

It surprised me how much that fact disappointed me as well.

Chris remained surrounded by people. Was he doing it on purpose? Had he surrounded himself so he didn't have to talk to me?

Gemma's day came.

This time Gemma was the one who kept Chris's attention. She made certain his eyes were on her almost every moment. At one point, she gave me a half grin. *I win*, the grin said.

As I watched Chris watch her, it occurred to me that she might be right.

Pete took it on himself to deliver Chris the sides and call times. I handled the girls. Pete handled Chris.

Five days from our arrival in the Dubai airport, after I'd seen Chris take his dates to Dubai fountains, ride in wooden boat taxis, stand on the top of the Burj Khalifa, and attend camel races, I'd had enough.

At three in the morning, I sneaked out of my room with the bag of Bit-O-Honey, careful not to wake Monica, and knocked on Chris's door.

"Chris, please. You have to answer." Keeping my voice low so as not to call attention to myself but loud enough to hope to be heard by a sleeping man felt impossible. But the door swung open.

Max stood in front of me, looking tousled and confused—in his boxers. "What's going on? Is there a problem? You said something about Chris?"

I stammered, looked at anything but him, and stammered some more. "Sir! I . . . apologize for disturbing your sleep. I'd just . . ."

Just what?

"Was just thinking of the wedding, if the girl he proposes to actually accepts," I said finally.

"It couldn't wait until morning?"

"Just thinking the flash mob wedding might be better visually if it was done entirely in black and white."

I hadn't been thinking that at all, but it was the first thing that came to mind.

Max considered it. "That could be visually interesting; however, it's a little hard to hide a mob that's all dressed the same."

I nodded, horrified at my own stupidity. "Excellent point, sir." I fidgeted with the bag of candy in my hands.

He saw the bag. "Is that for me?" he asked.

Startled, I held it out to him. "Um . . . sure?"

He took the bag and looked down, finally waking up to the fact that he was standing in his boxers and a ratty old T-shirt. He tried to hide himself behind the door. "It can wait till morning, Tori. I appreciate your enthusiasm, but look at a clock before coming up with great ideas." He firmly shut the door.

It took several long moments before I remembered how to breathe, and then I practically crawled back to my own room.

Where was Chris? How had they changed rooms without informing me?

The next morning I awoke late. The room had a quiet, empty feel. I sat up straight and glanced at Monica's bed. Empty.

I checked my phone. Eleven in the morning! Eleven! How had that happened?

They were leaving for Dolphin Bay at ten.

I did not brush my hair or my teeth but, instead, threw on clothes and grabbed shoes without bothering to put them on my feet, then ran to the elevator. By the time the elevator landed on the ground floor, I'd stuffed my feet into the shoes and yanked my hair back in a ponytail holder.

No one was in the lobby—at least no one from *Vows*. I went outside, where not one shuttle or taxi waited to take me anywhere.

"They left me," I said out loud, then checked my phone. Two texts and one missed call.

The text was an assurance that all was well, to enjoy the day off, and not to wait up. That one had come from Max. The other text told me to get expense reports finished. That one had come from Pete. They'd made a last-minute decision to travel to the palm islands. They needed only a skeleton crew. Basically, only Max, Robert, and the cast went.

Monica showed up outside the front lobby. "Hey, Tori. I had no idea you had bad hair days, but really, you look terrible. What's wrong?"

"They left." Shouldn't it have been obvious what was wrong? Shouldn't she have already guessed that being left felt like absolute abandonment? Watching Chris go on dates had been torture, but the idea of him on a date I couldn't see?

Agony.

She shrugged. "Yeah, didn't you get the texts? I got mine. I had to be up an hour earlier than the call sheet said, but I got the girls and that hunk of a man all gussied up and on their way before seven this morning. I thought you knew because you were sleeping in." She gave me a look that indicated she thought I might be ill or something, and she took a step back as if desirous not to be infected.

"Yeah, right. Texts. Got them." Dazed, I went back into the hotel, back into the elevator, back into my room, back into my bed, and wondered what Chris was doing at that exact moment.

Monica returned to the room for a moment to grab some things from her bag.

"Do you know Chris's room number?"

The bold question should have tipped her off that I had personal reasons for wanting the information, but she didn't act suspicious as she gave me the number.

I nodded, committing it to memory, then went to the bathroom to get ready.

And then I planned to wait at his door until he returned.

* * *

He didn't return until after midnight. I'd had to duck into an alcove with a statue because Robert walked down the hall with Chris. Seeing Robert ruined a little of my resolve.

Do you love him enough to stay away?

I had loved him that much—still loved him that much. But I also loved him enough to be honest.

Robert had his hand on Chris's shoulder. They talked too quietly for me to hear, but they both looked somber, as if they'd received bad news. Chris nodded and went into his own room. Robert went back to the elevator.

The time to talk had come.

Before I could change my mind, I ran to the door and thumped hard enough my hand hurt.

Chris answered. "Robert. I swear I get it . . . I'm not going to—" His eyes swept up from the floor and locked onto mine. "Tori." He looked around to make sure we were alone, then quickly pulled me into his room and shut the door.

I was alone with Chris, finally.

"What are you doing here?"

Tears skewed my vision. I hadn't planned on crying, on being weak. I'd planned to put it out there boldly. So much for plans.

"I had to see you. I'm sorry for what happened before, for not telling you the truth. But there was so much to be afraid of. I was so worried you'd be sued. You'd lose everything just because of me. But I can't do it. I'm too selfish. You have to know the truth. I love you. There. I said it. I mean it. I love you." And then I stepped up and kissed him.

He stood frozen, not returning the kiss in any way. I opened my eyes to find that his were open. I frowned and stepped back, shaking my head. "What's the matter?"

"Tori . . . I'm sorry. I know what this probably looks like, but I . . ." He scrubbed his hand through his hair and looked toward the door as if seeing through it to something else. "I'm engaged. Robert had an idea about the last candle ceremony being a little more snazzy visually on the palm islands. I chose a girl. I proposed . . ." He trailed off, carefully keeping his eyes away from mine.

My breathing came in rapid, shallow bursts. I tried to process the words, but no matter how many times I repeated them in my head, they didn't make sense. "You proposed?" I asked. My voice sounded like I was drowning in sand.

Falling.

I was falling again.

I staggered back against the door and shook my head. It suddenly felt like someone had shut off all the noise. Why couldn't I hear anything?

Chris's mouth moved, but no sound made it to my ears. He reached for me, but I scratched my fingers into the wood grain of the door until I found the knob and wrenched it open.

In the hallway, sound returned to me again. Chris called me back. I started to move away but turned and asked the question I didn't really want an answer to. "Who?"

His eyes brimmed with shame. "Gemma."

"Right. Of course." I whirled around and staggered away.

"I had to, Tori." His voice pled for absolution from behind me. He sounded as though he sat at the end of a long tunnel. Was he two steps away? Ten? A hundred? "Darren's going to buy your script. A scandal would ruin that for you. I couldn't let that happen."

Darren is going to buy my script.

It didn't occur to me to ask which one. Did it matter?

I ran to the end of the hall, pounding the elevator call button over and over until the doors finally slid open for me. I climbed inside the metal box, watched the doors close on the view of Chris's face a few feet away, sank to the floor, and tried to remember how to breathe.

* * *

Engaged.

He was engaged now. Gemma Mays would become Gemma Caine. I finally exited the elevator on Robert's floor, stormed to his room, and pounded on his door hard enough that several other people on the floor peeked out of their doors to see what was wrong.

"You did this," I said as soon as the door opened. I pushed my way past him, into his room. I couldn't hide the shock in my own words. "How could you do this to me?"

He didn't ask what I referred to. The guilt swathed him like a second skin. But still, he tried to defend himself. "I was doing you a favor, Tor. You know I'd never try to sabotage you. You go with that pretty boy actor, and you'll be blacklisted from every studio. You'll never get your scripts green-lighted if he makes you break your contract. But you have a guarantee if you play nice in the sandbox. Darren called Max last night. I heard the whole conversation. He's planning on buying a script. Loved it. Wants it bad. I knew I had to get the proposal pushed up to today. Waiting till tomorrow would have ruined you. What did you want me to do? Let you give up something you've worked your whole life for? It's like you said about that book. This is *The War of Art*. I just couldn't bear to watch you fight another battle only to lose to the production company when they fire you because you broke your contract. "

My hands shook. My whole body shook. I wanted to pound Robert into paste. "You're seriously using that against me? That was your valiant reason for ruining my life? Yes, I am fighting a war for my art, but that war was never against the production studios. That war was never against Chris.

That war was against *me*. Me, Robert. I'm the one who holds me back. I'm the one who chooses or doesn't choose. How dare you think you can fight that battle for me! How dare you assume you can control my life that way. This is my life. My art. My war. Keep your nose and your *camera* out of it!"

I breathed hard, tugging in air like I was suffocating. And who knew? Maybe I was suffocating, drowning in my own stupidity for not speaking up when I'd had the chance, not *seeing* what had stood right in front of me.

And now it was all gone.

I gave a disgusted shake of my head to Robert and moved toward the door.

His eyes tracked me. "I had to, Tori. Even Chris agreed you shouldn't give up your dreams."

"You don't get it, Robert . You just don't get it. Chris *is* the dream." The quiet strength of that declaration felt as though I'd taken a final step to the top of the mountain. I could see the whole picture clearly for the first time. I yanked the door open, but before passing through it, I tossed one look back at him. "And don't ever call Chris an actor again. He isn't the actor here. You are—acting like you've been my friend all this time. Someone in the Academy . . . give that man an Oscar."

His eyes widened in surprise, and his brows furrowed with hurt. "Tori . . . I—"

"Just don't talk to me anymore. Just . . ." I took a deep breath—the kind that always came like a wind before a storm of tears. "Just . . . don't." I went through the door and slammed it shut behind me.

The tears fell—acid rain melting away any hope of changing this horrible new turn of events.

Chris had already proposed.

He'd already asked someone else to marry him.

And to ask him to go back on that proposal now would be to ask him to be someone he wasn't. Besides, the lawsuit that would follow his breaking off an engagement would brutalize him to the point that he'd be lucky to be left capable of limping to a homeless shelter.

And though I hated myself for considering it, if I got Chris to back out and choose me, Robert was right—I'd never work in this business again. I'd be lucky to find a waitressing job back home after committing an offense as big as contract breach.

But being at the top of my own personal mountain allowed me to see beyond that. I could still write. Winning the war on my own personal art didn't mean I'd be green-lighted. It meant I would write. I would never stare at the blank canvas of my laptop screen without actually doing something about filling it with words. Chris had taught me that.

And I couldn't even thank him.

Chapter 20

I STAYED IN BED THE next day, blaming it on the ankle, which worried Max because the accident had happened at work. The studio was liable. Max wanted me to have a doctor in Dubai look at it, but I insisted it would be okay if I kept weight off of it for the day. I limped and acted pathetic until Monica left for the day's work.

I was almost as good an actor as Robert.

Everyone had gone off to learn the new dance steps for the flash mob wedding—everyone but the bachelorettes. They were all flown to the hotel where they would be held until we'd aired the episode showing the candle ceremony.

Gemma had not flown with them, but she also did not go to learn the dance. For her, the flash mob would be a surprise. Chris didn't go either, since he and Gemma would be the focal point of the dancers. It would happen all around them, but they weren't required to participate the same way. They would be handed off from one person to the next until they were in the wedding position.

I received text after text detailing all that needed to be accomplished. Gemma didn't know the wedding would take place within the week. She didn't know dancers had already been hired, caterers already ordered and likely already baking. She didn't know bouquets of flowers would soon be so abundant that all of Dubai would smell like a florist shop.

She only knew that she and Chris had a glorious week of dating left in this fair city.

I texted Shannon to check on Ilana. When Shannon wrote back saying that everything with Ilana was fine and she'd explain it all when I got home, I decided to sneak out of the hotel room to go sightseeing on my own. It might be my last chance to see something exotic, since I planned on quitting as soon as my feet were on American soil again.

I never wanted to see Robert again.

I went to Jumeirah Beach, took a water taxi, visited a mosque, and took my own camel ride. I glared down pretty much everyone who tried to offer me smiles. No one really wanted to argue with me in the souk because of that glare. Thinking of Ruby and her trip to Greece, I bought gifts for my book-club ladies, my mom and dad, and Janette. None of my siblings would expect presents since they all assumed the few months of actual work each year meant I was broke, which wasn't true, but I didn't bother to correct the rumor.

A bouquet of flowers waited for me at my doorstep when I arrived back at the hotel. I didn't bother looking at the card. They could have been from any number of people: Max, to say sorry for the ankle situation; Robert, to say sorry for ruining my life; Chris . . . well, engaged men shouldn't send flowers to other girls.

I threw them in the garbage can.

"If you wanted a day off, Max would have probably given it to you. No reason to fake sick," Monica said as I kicked the garbage can after having deposited the flowers there.

"I'm not faking," I insisted. She'd startled me a little since I hadn't known she was back already.

"Bad ankles don't kick solid copper garbage cans."

I cast her a withering glare. But it didn't bug her.

"Max did tell me to tell you he wants you to learn the dance steps. He said even if you aren't on your feet tomorrow, he wants you in the dance hall with the rest of us."

"I can't dance in any wedding. I'm crew, not cast, besides the fact that I'm a cripple." I kicked off my shoes and socks and plopped down on the couch, forcing Monica to scoot over to give me room, and stretched out my legs, showing off the blue ankle brace.

"I'm crew too. They want us in it. C'mon, it'll be fun."

"I would rather go out dressed in a French maid's costume and be arrested for indecent exposure. I am not going to the wedding. Little angelic Gemma would probably be glad to not have me at her nuptials anyway."

She leaned forward and narrowed her eyes. "What happened between you two? I've never seen you be mean to any of the cast, and we've had some seriously deserving cast."

I shrugged and didn't answer. Any honest answer was unacceptably lame. But Monica was right. Missing another day of the dance practice, even with the ankle excuse, would raise questions I had no answers to.

* * *

The dance was elegant in its simplicity. Max had hired the perfect chore-ographer, and most of the local dancers were thrilled to be involved and thrilled to be paid. Some of them looked like they came from a more ghetto side of town, which softened me a little toward Max. Helping out the poor in the areas we traveled to was something I'd always coaxed him into doing.

And Max was doing it all on his own because I'd become so self-absorbed in my own problems it hadn't occurred to me.

I waved my hand up and swished it to the side, joining hands with the next man in line to create an arch with our arms that the couple next to us then glided through.

My partner and I glided through the tunnel of arms next to us before we released each other and clapped in three short bursts, then circled each other in long sweeping strides with our arms out as if soaking in the world.

Was Chris kissing her now?

Another dance partner took my hand.

Did he tell her he loved her?

Another couple slid under the arch of my arm linked to some guy I didn't know but who smiled a lot.

Worse, does he actually love her?

My partner released me.

Maybe they're discussing how many kids they'll have and what those kids will look like.

Three short claps.

Will they stay here for the honeymoon? Will they go back to his huge peanut plantation and watch the sunrise together?

"Ow, Tori! You're hurting me!"

I blinked in surprise and dropped the hand I'd been clutching with a little too much force.

Gary rubbed his hand and laughed. "Are you planning to murder someone tonight?"

"Sorry." How embarrassing to be caught in the physical manifestations of my emotional disaster.

Robert, who'd been filming the whole dance progression, noticed the interchange. His mouth was down in a sad, droopy line.

It seemed his sad, droopy line matched my own.

Three more days of dancing, clapping, stepping, gliding. Every day the movements went faster, the tempo picked up until it felt we were racing in great circles in perfect beat to a song that swelled with hope to celebrate a union that held no hope for me.

Max went radio silent on me for those three days. I did not get one text or one message. He asked nothing of me, and I offered nothing. The silence felt strange, as though he knew I planned on quitting *Vows* as soon as this season was wrapped.

I would not be going to the wrap party.

On the fourth day, Max showed up in my room after dance practice. His hands were stuffed in his pockets, and his lips were pursed. This was his standard look when he was surveying a set before filming. He liked to take everything in and rock back on his heels while he envisioned filming.

He surveyed me as though I were one of those sets. "Are you happy with us, Tori?" he asked after a moment.

"Happy, sir?"

"Happy working with us. Has *Vows* been good to you?"

I frowned. Where did he mean to go with this line of questioning? "*Vows* has been more than generous to me in pay, friendships, and opportunities."

He nodded, his lips still pursed, his hands still shoved deep in his pockets. His strange look made me wonder if quitting wouldn't be necessary after all. Maybe he planned on firing me.

"Was that botched proposal really you at the Disney Concert Hall?" he finally asked.

Heat crawled up my face. No sense in lying about something that hardly mattered anymore. "Yep. That was me, all right."

"Why did you say no?"

"Why are you asking, sir?"

"Curious mostly. Just wondering if you said no because he put you on the spot and you didn't want all that attention on you." He leaned in far enough that if he fell, he'd never have enough time to pull his hands out of his pockets and catch himself.

"I said no because I didn't want to marry the guy. Ever."

His shoulders popped up in a shrug. "Fair enough. I'm sorry for this business you're involved in now."

My heart skipped a beat.

Then skipped another.

"Sir?" What did he know? How did he know?

The answer came as fast as the questions.

Robert.

"If this other guy, our bachelor, had been the one in the Disney Concert Hall, would the answer have been different?" Max wanted to know the answer to a question that would entirely incriminate me.

But I gave it anyway. "It would have been different." The words ached as they bubbled out of my chest, leaving a hole that couldn't be filled. I wrapped my arms around my middle as if trying to keep myself from bleeding out through that phantom wound.

Max nodded. He looked tired. Tired like I felt. "Then I am truly sorry. You know I'm not the heartless director people believe me to be."

"No one thinks you're—"

"I know what they say. They say I'd throw my own mother under a train if it meant getting the right shot." He jiggled his head as if not quite certain if he would or wouldn't. "Anyway, I'm sorry, for what it's worth. And I hope you aren't thinking of doing anything drastic like quitting on me or anything. We have plans for you, kid. Good ones. Your moping around the last few days is really throwing my game off. I count on you. For what it's worth, Robert has confessed to meddling in your life, and I think his motives were pure. You might want to consider talking to him again. He really has been a good friend to you."

"Right. Talk to him. I'll put that on my list of things to do tomorrow."

Max let the dripping sarcasm in my reply go. "You will be at the wedding tomorrow?"

"Wouldn't miss it, since seeing the series through to completion is in my contract."

"Oh, good. Glad to know we can bind you by law even if we can't make you like it." His turn to be sarcastic.

Usually, Max's to-the-point straight talk made me smile, but not today, not when he wanted to talk about things I didn't even want him knowing about.

Way to go Robert, another betrayal thrown at me. That guy was really on one.

"Robert said we owed you and told us to at least get you a nice dress. But you can rest assured I was getting nice clothing for everyone in the wedding party. I'll have it delivered to your room in the morning. I want you to know I'm letting you keep yours. But don't tell Monica. All the other clothing was rented. No sense in creating discord among the ranks."

Yeah, because buying me a dress fixes everything.

Max turned to go, taking one hand out of his pocket for only a moment so he could open the door.

He didn't turn back to face me when he said, "Think about what I said, kid. Don't be too quick to leave us. You have a career here, and you have people around you who want the best for you. Just think about it, okay?"

He closed the door behind him before I could reply—not that I could find anything to say anyway. Staying with the studio wasn't an option. Doing another season of *Vows* would be like severing several limbs.

It was time to move on.

But I didn't even get to leave on my own terms. Robert had already ratted me out to the director and likely the producer as well.

I sighed and sat on my bed, wondering how my life had come to this point.

Monica came in and nearly bounced me off my bed as she leaped up to sit by me. "Want to go shopping with me?"

"Not really in the mood for shopping."

"I found a really great purse shop." She sang this to me like some siren out of *The Odyssey*.

I looked around the room, considering. I could stay here and mope or . . . get a really great new purse. "I'm just not in the mood," I said against the inner interest she had sparked.

She felt my forehead. "Are you dying tomorrow or something?"

That pretty much sums it up, I thought.

"And even if you were dying tomorrow, you don't want to go out without a really great bag on your shoulder."

She got up and tugged my hand. "You can't stay locked up in a hotel room in a foreign country you'll probably never be able to come back to because it costs a fortune to *get* here let alone *be* here. We're going out. Put your shoes on."

I obeyed. Monica was right. When would I ever be coming back to Dubai? Probably never. Might as well see it all before I had to leave the day after tomorrow.

We shopped until the souk closed down for the night and the vendors covered and locked up their wares.

I bought four new handbags and actually found reasons to laugh along with Monica. The experience helped armor me against the coming events of the next day.

Because like it or not, the next day was coming and a wedding right along with it.

* * *

The insistent knocking on my door came much earlier than the ring of my alarm clock, even though it was late morning. Monica and I had been out late enough that we'd agreed on a major sleep-in day. Monica didn't have to get Gemma ready until just before the wedding, and I had no duties at all except to dance at the wedding.

All of that would be this evening when there was enough dusk to be romantic but enough light to be visually stunning.

Monica groaned and stuffed a pillow over her head. "You get it," she mumbled.

I padded to the door and opened it a crack. A big box sat in front of the door. The bellhop stood to the side, waiting for me to sign for the package.

After signing, I brought the box into the room.

Monica peeked out from under her pillow when it plopped to the bed. "What is it?"

I didn't answer but instead opened the box. Inside were six more boxes. Each box was labeled to indicate who the owner was. Three for Monica. Three for me.

That woke Monica up.

She rose from the bed in a practical pounce. "We've got packages? Sweet!"

Two of them had dresses. Two of them contained shoes, and the tiniest two contained masks.

The flash mob wedding dance would start with Chris taking Gemma to the Dubai fountains. As soon as the song "Baba Yetu" came through the speakers, all of the dancers would don their masks and the dance would begin. We'd hand Gemma off from one male in the dance circle to another until she finally ended up at the front, facing Chris, with the preacher in front of them. We were supposed to hand Chris off in the opposite direction through the females in the dance.

Gemma's wardrobe selection for the day was a simple white sundress, which was the base for the rest of her wedding attire. Max had had a robe designed to go with that specific sundress so that when it was cinched around Gemma's tiny waist, the outfit would transform from a simple sundress to an elegant wedding gown . . . fairy godmother style. They wanted her to look like a storybook princess because that was what half of the viewing audience called her.

Gemma had no idea it was coming. Chris knew and apparently approved.

I thought the entire thing was absurd and moving way too fast. Chris barely knew this girl and was willing to marry her after having been engaged for only a week?

Who cared if the whole thing had originally been my idea? That idea came before I'd fallen in love with the bachelor.

Now it seemed ludicrous. Who got married after only one week?

Idiots, that's who.

My dress was a white silky thing with a sheer black and white overlay. My mask had black-and-white feathers rippling from the top and black-and-white beads hanging down to cover the bottom half of my face. My shoes were more like beaded white ballet slippers.

I hated that I liked the outfit and would have probably chosen it for myself if the choice had been mine.

Monica's was similar, only pink and black instead of white and black.

So apparently, Max had totally decided against my idea of a strictly black-and-white wedding.

But he'd allowed *me* to be in black and white. It was a small concession, but it mattered to me that he'd been listening—even at three in the morning when he was standing in the hallway in his boxers.

Monica ordered in a room service brunch that we ate as we goggled at our new gowns.

"Will you help me with my hair?" Monica asked after we'd wasted away what was left of the morning and most of the early afternoon. "Then I can help you with yours."

Monica only wanted a simple single braid going down the left side of her head.

But by the time she was done with me, I had an elaborate twist with several small braids swooping back to connect at the twist, and my tight curls loosened and draped around my head.

"How did you get those curls to do that?" I asked in wonder, loving that each braid connected at the back with a single elegant white jewel.

"It's what I do: make hair obey me out of absolute fear."

Monica insisted on doing my make-up as well before she asked, "Are you going to be okay? I can tell them you hurt your ankle shopping last night if you don't want to go through with this."

So she knew.

Did everyone know?

I was going to kill Robert. Kill him twice just out of principle.

"I'm fine," I said and put the mask on over my face to try to hide the fact that I wasn't fine—not really.

"Aren't you needing to go help Gemma get ready?" We'd spent so much time primping for ourselves that the afternoon had gotten away from us.

She nodded slowly and stood just as slowly. "Want me to make her ugly for you?"

I laughed at that. "No. A girl deserves to be beautiful on her wedding day, even if she is *that* girl."

Monica grabbed her huge make-up toolbox and headed to the door. "Max got the feathers on your costume wrong. You shouldn't have feathers on that mask but at your shoulders, because that was the most angelic response on the planet."

I laughed.

Laughing was better than crying.

"See you at the shuttle."

"Right. See you there."

* * *

We arrived at the fountains an hour before the happy couple. This helped us get into places, make sure we accounted for real tourists, and run through the routine once to check for glitches.

The genuine tourists clapped when we were done. Dozens of cameras filmed it, reminding me of someone filming Lawrence and his proposal. If I'd simply said yes to that proposal, none of this would be happening. But marrying someone wrong just to escape a future heartbreak wouldn't solve anything.

Ruby had taught me that.

A "settle for" marriage didn't work.

I'll find someone else. I'll be okay.

The repetition of these phrases was what kept my feet in their assigned spot, kept them from fleeing to anywhere else but there.

The cab arrived.

Chris stepped out and offered Gemma his hand to help her out. They wandered to the fountains. I stared at him with an intensity that bordered insanity.

His head twitched my direction, but he didn't turn to see me. I wanted to catch his eye, to have him look into my eyes, to have him call a halt to everything so he could marry the right person instead.

I knew all I had to do was get him to look at me—to see me, really see me.

And then it occurred to me that he would have to take my hand during the dance. He would have to form that arc and spin, and *then* he would have to look at me. Maybe then . . .

I wasn't sure what would happen then, but hope dared to flicker faintly in my chest. I might be able to derail this wedding after all.

They'd arrived at their first position—the one Robert had preplanned with Christopher well before this moment had come.

Gemma and Chris had their heads together as they talked. He kept her from turning to face the water like she wanted. The waters were the background. The dance was the main feature at the fountains this time.

The music started, but when Gemma tried to turn to watch the waters, Chris pointed at all of the fancy people in masquerade masks suddenly approaching.

Her mouth formed a beautiful smile, but I couldn't watch her any longer since the first dancer had a hold of my hand. We made the arc, allowed the couple next to us to go through, clapped, circled each other, moved on to the next person in the circle.

I searched for Chris's face—the one face that wouldn't be masked through the dance. But as the song progressed and neared the end, his hand still hadn't touched mine.

Where was he?

Why was he not holding my hand and looking into my eyes?

Why could I not stop this moment?

And then the song was over. I was in the center of the circle, like I'd requested, so I didn't have to see Gemma personally. I curtsied to my final partner like we'd practiced for several days prior.

When I rose from the curtsy and looked forward, I found that everyone was facing *me*.

Had I turned the wrong direction and messed up the dance? I cast an uncertain glance at my partner, who then removed his mask—a white-and-black mask with feathers and beadwork—one that was a perfect match to mine.

"Chris," I whispered.

Chapter 21

His smile filled me, even filled that hole in my middle.

I glanced around to see where Gemma was hiding in all of this. She was on my other side, and her hands went up.

Was she planning on strangling me? That would be wedding footage even Max could be proud of.

Her hands held a jeweled comb with a sheer piece of fabric hanging from it. She gently tucked the comb into the twist of my hair.

"From one fairy godmother to another," she said, then stepped away.

I whirled back to Chris, bewildered, terrified, hopeful. "What's going on? What is all of this?"

He grinned wider, if such a thing was possible, and dropped to one knee, then took something from his jacket pocket and held it in his fingers.

It caught the golden light of the setting Dubai sun. "This is me asking you to marry me."

I hazarded a small chuckle that came out with a hiccup of a sob. "On reality TV?"

He lifted a shoulder and quirked his lips to the side, giving me that half smile I loved so much. "You told me from the beginning to keep it real. So I'm really asking you—twice now, since you didn't answer me the first time. Will you, Victoria Jade Winters, marry me?" He held the ring up higher.

Tears coursed down my cheeks, making the mask stick to my skin. I peeled it off my face so I could see him fully. I dropped the mask to the ground and, for a brief second, thought about that first marriage proposal—the one where I'd run. I stared at him levelly, knowing that everyone around us held their breath while awaiting my answer.

"I have a question first."

A murmur rippled through the crowd along with a few shushes as people leaned in to hear my question.

He frowned. "What would that be?"

"Will you be the spider killer in our relationship?"

At the confusion that fell over his features, I continued. "Because in every relationship, someone has to kill the spiders, and I can promise you that person will never be me."

His grin was back in full force. "I'll be the spider killer if you agree to put this ring on."

I allowed a half smile of my own, feeling like I might explode with a joy I never dared believe would belong to me, and took the ring from his fingers and placed it on my own.

It was a perfect fit.

"Yes," I said.

And the fountains behind us exploded into the sky in celebration.

Chapter 22

We didn't actually exchange vows right then and there. We both wanted our families present when we actually married. And Janette would kill me if she didn't get to be my maid of honor.

It seemed everyone pressed in to embrace us both, to kiss our cheeks and wish us well in our happily ever after. Gemma whispered in my ear, "Sorry for the misunderstanding. I wasn't my best person at the last there. Hope you forgive me."

"Are you serious? You're not . . . mad at me?"

She gave a derisive laugh. "Oh! I was at first when Max explained the change in plans. Robert had to hold me back from running to your hotel room and breaking down your door. But then . . . I realized Chris didn't love me. He liked me. We were friends and everything, but he never looked at me the way he looks at you. It didn't hurt that Max offered me an undisclosed amount of money. I told you from the beginning that I wanted the prize money at the end so I could pay for school and help out my family. I got that. So don't worry about me."

I hugged her fiercely. "I'm so sorry for my behavior. You're a really great person, Gemma."

She gave her impish little grin. "Then it seems we're okay again."

I nodded, and she handed me off to Robert. I threw my arms around him. "You did this! You made this happen!" I cried.

"Had to fix what I broke. Are you happy, Tor?"

"Yes." I sobbed into his shirt. "How? How did you make this all work? Am I going to be fired when we get back?"

Robert laughed. "Nope." He kept his voice low so no one but me could hear. "Just wait until you see the bonus episode of *Vows*. You'll need to sign the nondisclosure agreement. And we'll be keeping you under wraps until it airs. You're officially one of the girls. I'll also need your permission to air it since most of the footage has you in it."

"You filmed us? How much did you film?"

"You know how the mansion works. Cameras everywhere . . . in window seats, duck ponds, certain bachelor doorways . . ."

"You filmed *everything*." My cheeks went hot with this realization.

"It's who I am. I convinced Max that we'd get great ratings on the bonus episode. Max had a heart attack first—yelled and ranted—but once he saw dollar signs, he was okay. No lawsuits this time, sweetheart."

He then passed me off. Monica hugged me. Gary hugged me. Max almost smothered me. People I didn't know hugged me. I think they were tourists.

Somewhere in all that hugging and celebrating, I found Chris again. His arms went around me, and then he dipped me into a perfect kiss. The warmth of his lips against mine felt right, like coming home and getting in a hot bath at the end of a hard day. It thrilled me to know this was among the first of many kisses.

"I love you, Victoria Winters," he whispered into my ear. "Love you so much it actually hurts a little."

"I love you too, Chris Caine." There. We'd both said it and said it at the same time.

I felt his lip twitch up in a smile against my ear. "Then we should definitely get married," he said.

"According to this ring and all these people," I answered, "that's exactly what's going to happen."

"Oh, good," he said. "I do love a happy ending."

I laughed. "Me too."

* * *

Later, back at the hotel, Monica stayed up with me, laughing and talking about everything. We squealed several times over the epic awesomeness the day had been. I was engaged! And I couldn't even tell my mom.

I did text Ruby right before getting under the covers.

Dearest Ruby,
I've got news about a man saying he loves me.
But don't tell anyone.
I mean it.

No one.
Thank you for your advice.
Now, your turn. Do you have news for me?
I love you,
Tori

I went to bed that night with a diamond on my hand and a smile on my face.

I loved Christopher Caine.

Christopher Caine loved me.

I had finally found reality.

Victoria Winters's Take-Care-of-Yourself Doughnuts Recipe

- Look at clock.
- Realize you're running late.
- Make decision to pay attention to what is important by letting go of the things that aren't.
- Drive to closest/least expensive/favorite bakery.
- Buy enough doughnuts for everyone in your group to have at least one.
- Then buy one extra (you deserve it).
- Place doughnuts on a serving tray (or leave in box if really rushed).
- Serve with a smile, and remember it's not about the time you spent making the food; it's about the time you spent making relationships.
- Eat extra doughnut as needed.
- Be happy.

ILANA'S WISH
COMING APRIL 2014

Annette Lyon

A NEWPORT LADIES BOOK CLUB NOVEL

Ilana's Wish

Preview

Chapter 1

As I walked down the long Exhibit Hall B corridor, I compared my clipboard with an e-mail on my phone, a message from the Long Beach Wedding Show owner about two last-minute exhibitors. The show would open tomorrow morning at nine o'clock, and the floor wasn't anywhere near set up. I had to tell the display company owner, Chuck, where to add the two additional booths. His workers would set those up—and then they'd charge the exhibitors their firstborn for additional chairs and tables. The union workers were the only ones allowed to carry vendors' products to the floor or even plug cords in outlets.

I pursed my lips while studying the floor plan. The only real place to squeeze in last-minute vendors would be at the back side of aisle three—not the best spot. I hoped the other businesses there hadn't started setting up yet; they might have to start over, depending on how Chuck worked the extra booths.

This kind of thing was exactly why I tried to get my shows to turn in their final floor plans two weeks in advance, but I'd made an exception in this case. A bigger show meant more vendors, higher attendance, and a bigger splash, making my chances of a promotion at the convention center even better.

Halfway to Chuck's station at the back of the hall, I brushed my curly hair away from both sides of my face. It was driving me crazy; I should have pulled it into a ponytail this morning. Even though my hair looked great in the mornings after I styled it, by lunch, the Newport Beach humidity made me look not unlike Napoleon Dynamite. And we were already way past both lunch and dinner.

But doing my job right meant such sacrifices. This show would be one of the most complicated I'd ever coordinated, yet the client had tentative plans to do two or three a year, so this first show needed to do well if Ethan and I were to pay off our medical bills.

Or rather, my medical bills from three tries of in vitro, followed by a year of nonstop bleeding. As if infertility hadn't been bad enough, an emotional anvil had dropped on my head with my OB's declaration that I needed a hysterectomy. That surgery was three weeks ago, and now I couldn't get pregnant no matter what. Ethan wanted to apply for adoption, but I wasn't ready for that—didn't know if I ever would be. I had yet to grieve the loss of my dream to have a baby growing inside me, to give birth to my own flesh and blood.

For that matter, I needed to recover from the hysterectomy, and the recovery wasn't happening as quickly as I thought it should. I'd assumed that by now I'd have bounced back, my surgeon's prediction notwithstanding. I could hardly move for the pain, yet here I was, walking a huge event-hall floor. But this show was too important to miss. I'd been working on it for months, and the payoff would be big. No way could I trust it to another event manager, especially when that meant saying good-bye to a pretty obvious promotion. I'd rest next week when the wedding show was over.

Chuck's setup crew had just about finished putting up the booths; I was glad they weren't totally finished, because this new order would have annoyed them if they'd already put away the aluminum poles and stacks of drapes. As I headed past a worker on a ladder, he lost hold of an eight-foot aluminum pole, which fell to the ground. I yelped and scrambled out of the way, only to slam into a six-foot table in a booth and twist my ankle. The worst of the pain, though, was my still-healing abdomen; it felt like I'd pulled a stitch inside or something.

Ethan kept telling me to take it easy. "Remember, Ilana, you basically had someone go in and rip out your guts. Your body needs rest."

At the time, I'd laughed—he was a doctor, but he wasn't using medical speak. Right now in the exhibit hall, I hated the fact that he was right.

Ripping out my guts felt accurate about now. It was too late for me to attempt to get any rest today. I closed my eyes and breathed through my mouth, hoping the pain would recede.

The bottle says Vicodin lasts four to six hours. Liars. A glance at the clock at the back of the hall confirmed my fear: I had an hour before I could take another dose.

"Uh, sorry, ma'am," the man said—or rather, the boy. Now that he'd scrambled down the ladder and was standing at eye level, he didn't look old enough to shave. Which was pretty much the only reason I didn't lay into him.

I shouldn't have come in today. I should have passed this show on to Anthony like Ethan had begged me to do. But overestimating my strength turned out to be awfully easy when my body had no outward evidence of surgery—or gut rippage. I sat on the table with one hand on my ankle and the other holding my middle. The boy eyed me, eyebrows raised, waiting for a response. Only then did I realize I hadn't answered.

"It's okay," I said as I realized the table I was sitting on belonged to the Elegance Photography booth. I rotated my ankle to work out the twist and realized how weak I still was, like I'd been trampled by a rhinoceros. I probably looked like it too.

Worse, for the first time since my surgery, after weeks of lying around feeling like an ugly couch potato, I'd given in to vanity and put on a pair of killer hot boots with three-inch heels, which I'd bought yesterday as a little retail therapy.

I'd worn them because they were awesome and because heels made me look more professional and put together than, say, more comfortable but utterly hideous Crocks. From my spot on the table, I looked over the setup so far. The Long Beach Wedding Show had picked patriotic colors for the booth drapery. Maybe I could have understood if it were in honor of President's Day, but in January? I'd tried talking the owner into using plain black—a classy color that would match whatever vendors used in their displays, many of which would likely have a lot of ivory and pastel colors, but no. He'd insisted on paying tribute to our country and armed forces. In January.

Worse, he hadn't picked classic red, white, and blue; these colors were more of a cranberry red, a yellowish off-white, and an electric blue. The table skirts alternated red, white, and blue every three booths. It hadn't even looked good on paper; in real life, it was hideous. The vendors' products were sure to clash. Elegance Photography, if their reputation was any indication, would swath the booth in fabric, likely covering every inch of the patriotic drape. Maybe other vendors could camouflage their booths too. One could hope.

My headset crackled with a voice. "Hey, Ilana?" It was Chuck. "I've got the forklifts taking vendor loads to booths. That okay?"

I pushed a button on my earpiece to answer. "Do aisles one and two first," I told him. "The poles and drapery look pretty much done, but I've got an order for two more booths at the back of three that your guys will need to add. Oh, and go ahead and send the carpet in."

"Already on it."

Good. We were running behind, mostly because Chuck's men had shown up a full two hours late. Now I had vendors calling every two minutes, asking when they could start setting up, and others were already in the hall, waiting at the sides until they had the go-ahead. I'd worked with Chuck for many shows, so he was a friend, and I didn't feel the need to dance around the situation like I did with other companies. Besides, he'd already apologized several times for his guys' tardiness.

I heard a female voice in the background, followed by Chuck asking, "Oh, hey, which booth is Chrissy May Candies in?"

I double-checked the floor plan and pushed the button to answer. "One-oh-one and one-oh-two—the endcap between one and two. May as well bring theirs in first." I clicked off my headset and pulled out my cell to call Chrissy May. I hesitated for a second, suddenly remembering the call the other day from Ruby at book club, inviting me out to lunch. I'd promised to call back when I found a day that worked, but then I'd hung up and never given it another thought.

Ruby was our book-club mother. She was sweet and older than my own mother, and I had absolutely nothing in common with her. She was a mother and widower. She wore bright, flamboyant colors. She made her own pillows and jam. I preferred black business clothes and bought most of our apartment's accessories from IKEA. Besides, my work schedule had been difficult; it wasn't like I'd had time for lunch with anyone.

I sighed and found Chrissy May's number. One ring later, she answered, and I let her know that in a few minutes, she could set up her booth. As soon as I got the words out, I saw Chrissy May herself walking toward me from a side aisle.

She clicked her phone shut and said, "We're still up front, right?" She approached with a bulging neon-green purse over one shoulder. She probably weighed at least twice what I did, and she had two inches of gray roots at the base of a dingy brown dye job.

"Ilana?" she said, marching toward me. "Ilana, did you hear me? I want to be sure I get the endcap at the front like you promised." Her high-pitched voice grated on my nerves. Why was she asking me if I'd heard her when I'd confirmed her booth moments before? And why wasn't she talking to the show owner? He was the one who'd given me the final floor plan; I had nothing to do with those decisions.

Get a grip. Be kind. I'd skipped dinner, so my blood sugar was low; I was running on cappuccino and whatever remained of the Vicodin. Yet my stomach still ached, in more ways than one.

I'll never, ever have a baby now. The thought smacked me out of the blue again. How long would it do that? Would I ever go a day without that thought shooting through my very soul?

I nearly burst into tears—again—because I no longer carried the organ needed to make a baby. I took a deep breath and smiled in an attempt to fake a good mood for Chrissy May. She was a regular, high-paying client— she'd rented out an endcap for three shows already this year. I needed to be nice. She was sweet, if a bit of a handful.

"Hi," I said, certain my smile was tighter than Kenny Rogers's facelift. "You're right up front, next to the concessions, just like we talked about," I said. "Same spot as in the Christmas Gift Show in November. One of Chuck's guys is bringing your stuff around on a forklift any minute."

She put a pudgy hand to her chest and sighed dramatically. "Oh, I'm so relieved."

"Watch out for the forklift," I said, walking backward as a hint that I was leaving. "The operators don't always pay attention to the people around them."

"Oh, I hope they don't break the toffee," she said, looking around for the forklift as if it were a predator. As my distance from her increased, she spoke louder. "Oh, and the candy boxes—they could get crushed. And the ribbon . . ." She seemed ready to burst into tears.

"I'm sure your things will be fine," I called, although I wouldn't trust the forklift guys with a dog I hated. But Chrissy May always packed her things properly and then some—I was quite sure she'd packed everything in triple layers of bubble wrap. Even an idiot operator wouldn't be able to cause problems.

Chrissy May hurried off toward her booth to preside over the forklift once it arrived. As she left, I pictured her packaging—pink-and-purple polka dots with brown bows. Next to red-white-and-blue drapery? I shuddered. Poor Chrissy May.

I headed for Chuck's station at the back of the hall to finally give him that new booth information and to make sure what I'd marked on my clipboard matched the reality of which vendors had already checked in. I made a check mark next to Chrissy May's Candies in the delivered box. For trade shows with simple setups, like business conventions, where the displays—such as they were—consisted mostly of pamphlets, posters, and stand-up signs—setup happened the morning of the show because it took all of twenty minutes.

But this was a wedding show, which meant hours of elaborate preparations. My heels clicked on the floor as I consulted the floor plan on the second page of my clipboard. There was still so much to do tonight. Setting up the midway would be a nightmare—it would display dozens of wedding dresses on mannequins. Then there was the endcap of aisles three and four with a display of no fewer than five chocolate fountains and the back of the hall, which hosted the wedding cake competition—with twenty-eight cakes entered but not to be touched. Oh, and a grand piano, where a hopeful wedding musician would play, business cards perched on the edge of the piano. For his sake, I hoped his music would carry across the hall instead of being sucked up in the vast space, but I had my doubts. I considered getting him a mic and a stand and pumping his music into the PA system for ambiance, but that was a decision I'd leave for tomorrow morning—and for the pianist, as he'd have to fork over the cash for the mic and outlet.

My headset beeped again, and Chuck's voice came across with urgency. "Ilana, I've got someone from Rockefeller and Sons' Catering here."

I didn't remember a vendor on the list by that name, and Janette, the wedding-show owner, had not mentioned them to me when I got the final list. "I don't think we have a vendor by that name." I knew we didn't; I would have remembered a pretentious name like Rockefeller. No way would some dinky caterer I'd never heard of be related to the Rockefeller family. And I bet the "and sons" part was made up.

"Don't see them on the floor plan you gave me either," Chuck said. "Are they one of the two last-minute booths?"

"No, those are for an invitation printing company and a florist."

"He's pretty insistent he paid for a ten-by-ten, and he's ready to set up. You'd better come back to talk to him." His voice lowered. "He says he needs to report to the management how poorly he's been treated."

I tried to run a hand through my hair, but my fingers got tangled in the curls. "I'll be right there." I headed toward Chuck's station while navigating my cell phone to Janette's number. She could confirm whether this guy had a contract with her show. She was the one who'd hired Chuck as her display company, so why he didn't call her first, I didn't know.

Halfway to the back of the hall, I had my eyes on my phone, ears attuned to my headset, boots clicking away on the smooth concrete, when

Chrissy May's voice overpowered it all with a call from her booth. "Ih-laaaaah-naaaaah!"

Chuck's voice buzzed in my earpiece again. "So what do I—"

"Hold on just one second, Chuck," I said, turning around to Chrissy May. "Do you need something?" I called, walking backward, hoping that whatever it was could wait until after I'd dealt with the Mr. Rockefeller caterer dude. Everyone seemed to need me at the same time, all the time. Chrissy started talking fast about something I couldn't make out from fifty feet.

I was about to ask her to wait five minutes when a deep voice behind me yelled, "Comin' through!"

Something moving hard smacked my calves. I flailed, cell phone and clipboard flying, and the next thing I knew, I was facedown on the floor. I instinctively looked over to see what had knocked me off my feet—a big roll of bright red carpet, which came to a stop six feet away. Stars of pain burst into my vision, making me clutch my left arm.

Crud! My funny bone! The immediate shock of pain in my elbow was eclipsed shortly after by my abdomen feeling like fire had erupted inside me.

With the position I'd landed in, sprawled across the floor, I had the fleeting thought that I was glad I'd worn slacks today—no skirt to provide an extra view.

Chuck's carpet guy glanced my way. "Sorry," he mumbled as he kicked the carpet roll again, sending it thudding open three more times. With each thump, a blow of pain went through me.

I'd tripped on a stupid roll of carpet.

Get back to work, I commanded myself. The pain in my arm would pass. It would. I put my left arm out to help me stand, but the moment it bore any weight, I collapsed. I landed face-first on top of it, my cheekbone hitting the floor. A new wave of pain shot through me. I couldn't get up. This is more than a bump on my funny bone. Now what?

I sat there for a moment, waiting for the white-hot heat in my middle to subside. When it did, the sharp stabbing in my elbow took over. Feeling faint, I looked around for aid. Carpet Guy had kept going, but Chrissy May flew toward me. She hit a bump in the carpet and almost tripped too but regained her balance with two hops and kept running. She dropped to my side. "Are you okay?"

After weeks of being on the receiving end of Chrissy May's whining and worry leading up to the wedding show, I never thought I'd be so grateful to see her face. "I can't get up," I said, trying not to clench my teeth from the pain. "I can't use my left arm."

"Here, let me help you." She went behind me and pulled me up by the arm pits—not the most graceful way of rising to my feet but definitely effective, and it didn't hurt my arm. Much.

I stood there trying to get my bearings as my head swam.

Chrissy May eyed me. "You look faint."

I felt faint. Trying to think made me feel like my brain was swimming through smoke, and I didn't think it was because of the postsurgery pain meds. All I could think about was that Chuck needed me to talk to the angry caterer. "Where's my cell? And . . . my clipboard?"

Chrissy May grabbed a chair from a nearby booth and dragged it into the aisle. "You sit here. I'll find your things. Don't you worry one bit."

"Thank you," I said, sinking onto the chair with relief. Something was definitely wrong with my arm; I couldn't move it without sharp pain shooting through it. I hoped for a pulled muscle or a simple bruise.

"You should go see the doctor right away," Chrissy May said after gathering my stack of papers that had flown off the clipboard and reattaching them. After placing the clipboard on my lap, she held up my phone. Fortunately, the screen hadn't shattered. "Anyone you'd like me to call?"

"No," I said with a weak shake of my head—which I immediately regretted, as it made my vision swim and the pain intensify. I felt ready to pass out. And puke. I held my limp left arm with my right hand. "I'll make an appointment with my doctor later. I can't leave right now."

I held out my hand for the phone and tucked it into my pocket. I still had to deal with the surprise caterer plus all the other vendors and the setup with the cakes and dresses and getting the piano delivered and tuned. I also had to make sure the hall would stay cool enough for the cakes so the icing wouldn't droop—and then, somehow, smooth out the ruffled feathers of the chocolate fountain people, who would freak out if the room wasn't warm enough for the liquid chocolate to fall in pretty sheets. I had to keep my focus. If I could keep all of the balls in the air a little bit longer—and if the show's attendance was good and the vendors got lots of business—that promotion would be mine. And if that was going to happen, I absolutely couldn't leave.

Now my head ached along with my arm. How would I get through all of that? I wouldn't be out of here for another four or five hours.

"Can I get you anything, dear?" Chrissy May said again.

"Do you have any ibuprofen?" That wouldn't interact with the Vicodin. At least, I didn't think it would; ibuprofen didn't have Tylenol, which I knew was a no-no with Vicodin.

"Sure do." Chrissy May was about to scurry off, but then she stopped and turned back. "I really think a doctor needs to see that arm. You sure you're okay? I don't know that you're safe to drive."

She had a point about driving.

But I couldn't exactly be replaced right now, even if someone else took me to an ER. And I didn't want to worry Ethan at work; his night shift at the ER had already started. Plus, I didn't want to show up at my husband's workplace, only to have him worried over seeing me in this condition—and I'd get a lot of "I told you so."

"I'll see how I'm doing half an hour after I take the ibuprofen," I said.

And I would—I'd see how I felt. Not that feeling like crap would change my plans. But as Chrissy May handed me a water bottle and two oblong, brownish tablets, I sure hoped that an hour from now I'd be feeling a whole lot better.

About the Author

JULIE WRIGHT WAS BORN IN Salt Lake City, Utah. She's lived in LA, Boston, and the literal middle of nowhere (don't ask). She wrote her first book when she was fifteen and has since written sixteen novels—nine of which were traditionally published. Julie won the Whitney Award for Best Romance in 2010 with her novel *Cross My Heart*. She is agented by Sara Crowe at Harvey Klinger, Inc.

She has one husband, three kids, one dog, and a varying amount of fish, frogs, and salamanders (depending on attrition).

She loves writing, reading, traveling, speaking at schools, hiking, playing with her kids, and watching her husband make dinner.

She used to speak fluent Swedish but now speaks well enough only to cuss out her children in public settings.

She hates mayonnaise.